WHISKEY
ROAD

Also by Karen Siplin

**SUCH A GIRL**

**HIS INSIGNIFICANT OTHER**

# Whiskey Road

*A Love Story*

KAREN SIPLIN

WASHINGTON SQUARE PRESS
New York London Toronto Sydney

Washington Square Press
A Division of Simon & Schuster, Inc.
1230 Avenue of the Americas
New York, NY 10020

This book is a work of fiction. Names, characters, places, and incidents are products of the author's imagination or are used fictitiously. Any resemblance to actual events or locales or persons, living or dead, is entirely coincidental.



First Washington Square Press trade paperback edition May 2008



For information about special discounts for bulk purchases, please contact Simon & Schuster Special Sales at 1-800-456-6798 or business@simonandschuster.com.

Manufactured in the United States of America

10 9 8 7 6 5 4 3 2 1

Library of Congress Cataloging-in-Publication Data

Siplin, Karen.
Whiskey Road : a love story / Karen Siplin.
p. cm.
1. African American women—Fiction. 2. Women motorcyclists—Fiction.
3. Paparazzi—Fiction. 4. Victims of crime—Fiction. 5. Race relations—New York (State)—Fiction. I. Title.

PS3619.I65W48 2008
813'.6—dc22

2007043449

ISBN-13: 978-0-7432-9762-2

*For Robert and Helen Siplin*

*For Alice and Donald*

*For Harris*

*And for Jason and Matt Bick—*
*thanks for telling me about the real Whiskey Road*

# WHISKEY ROAD

"I found you," he says.

"I wasn't lost," she tells him.

"Where is it?"

In the motel hallway ice tumbles into a bucket. A voice curses as some lands on the floor.

"Listen," she starts.

He takes something from his pocket. A flash of metal. She hates guns. Really despises them. He holds it like he doesn't want her to see it. Then he hits her in the face.

"*I* didn't steal anything," she reminds him.

"Shut up," he says.

She rolls off the bed and lands on the floor with a thud. She can hear him heading for her. Before she can stand up he's on her, grabbing her by the back of her jeans and pulling her up. He pushes her against a wall, holds her there. A rough hand slips over her mouth, pulling her head back. She can feel her neck come *this close* to a crack.

"Come on," he rasps. "Don't make me hurt you."

She whimpers when he holds the gun to her temple. She rests her forehead against the wall and slackens.

"Okay," she surrenders. "Let me go and I'll get it."

# Darby

# One

Caleb's thinking about what he's going to do tonight. He's been keeping a low profile for the past four days. To avoid trouble. But it's Thursday, the beginning of his weekend, and he doesn't want to spend the evening alone.

Since his wife left six months ago, he's been suffering through a lot of lonely evenings. Weekends are the worst. He hates the way people look at him when he enters places alone. Lately, he's noticed an eerie silence blankets the rooms he walks into. This silence hounds him in Frenchman's Bend, where he lives, and it's the reason he comes one town over to Wheeler's Coffee Shop in Darby. At Wheeler's people understand a twenty-nine-year-old man makes mistakes and is bound to face heartache because of them.

For the past three weeks Caleb's been meeting a married woman at her house a little over a mile from the coffee shop. Emma is sixteen years older than he is. She's small and beautiful, paints pretty pictures and sells antiques for a living. When her husband's at work she helps Caleb get through a lot of lonely afternoons. Most evenings are spent listlessly in Frenchman's Bend. Channel surfing and chain-smoking. Drinking with his friends. Coasting. His life is about coasting these days. Just until another distraction comes along.

Outside, a black girl clad completely in black motorcycle leather gets out of a car and watches it drive away. She adjusts the knapsack on her shoulder, picks up a duffel bag and helmet from the ground and looks at the coffee shop. After a minute, she limps over. Caleb wonders idly where her motorcycle is.

She pulls the coffee shop's door open confidently, not at all deterred by the six white men sitting at the counter drinking their late-afternoon coffee. Including him. Everyone looks up to greet her. No one says a word when they see her. They just stare.

She has ebony hair that grazes her shoulders. Except a lock that hangs in front. Pink, defiant and alone. Caleb kind of smirks at that. A lone pink lock of hair probably has a story. Her right eye is bruised a dark purple and her bottom lip is busted. There's a gash across her forehead. She's a pretty girl, and watching her, Caleb wonders if she took a nasty spill on her missing motorcycle, or if someone did that to her.

Caleb's the type of man who can't help feeling vaguely protective of women he thinks are in trouble. Some people have a soft spot for stray cats or missing children. He's always felt the tug on his heart for women with bruises. They remind him of his mother. She had a history of being involved with men who hurt her.

The number of women he sees with bruises never surprises him. He just wonders why it's such a common occurrence. Something every man at this counter comes across, but never mentions. Occasionally Caleb notices the same woman with a new bruise and he wonders how her man knew she'd be the one who'd let him get away with it. He never asks. He doesn't think they'd be honest with him. A woman who'd let a man hit her more than once wouldn't be able to tell him why it happens.

"Can someone recommend a decent motel?" the girl asks in a voice soft enough to give everyone an excuse to ignore her. Caleb looks at the paper he's been pretending to read for the past twenty minutes, aware of the deafening silence. Seconds later, he looks at her again. He can't help it.

She's wearing the same leather uniform he's seen in print catalogues and on the Internet. It's tight, Italian and very expensive. But the duffel bag she's carrying is worn and scuffed. She has a death grip on it, like it's packed with her life—everything that's good and worth holding on to. Caleb has an unfamiliar desire to empty it and wash it for her, but he knows he'd never get his hands on it.

She sets the bag and her helmet on the stool at the end of the counter, rests a heavily booted foot on the stool's base. Jennifer, the owner of Wheeler's Coffee Shop, refills the coffees and all the men stare solemnly into their full cups.

"Can someone recommend a decent motel?" the girl repeats slower, a little louder. "Or directions to an actual town that would have a decent motel."

Everyone looks at her. She's rolling a lighter gently between her fingers, waiting patiently for someone to answer her question. Her nails are short, unpolished and clean. The skin around her knuckles is swollen and scabbed. When she sets the lighter on the counter, Caleb notices her hands are shaking. He thinks: *She fought back.*

"Are you gonna order something?" Jennifer asks the girl.

"Sure," the girl says, unfazed by Jennifer's rudeness. "Coffee. Black. No sugar. And a pack of Marlboros."

Jennifer turns her back to the counter and Caleb watches her fill a take-out cup with steaming coffee. She sets it in front of the girl and places a lid on top of it. The girl stares at the cup, not unaware of what this gesture means. Caleb thinks she's going to leave. He would. Instead, she looks at Jennifer with an arched eyebrow. She unzips her leather jacket, takes it off to expose a sleeveless undershirt and bruised arms and sits on the stool next to her stuff. Caleb smirks at that also.

"Thanks," the girl says with a smile.

Jennifer nods stiffly, glancing up for a second to wave goodbye to a man who has left exact change for his coffee. Then she pulls a pack of Marlboro cigarettes from the dispenser and tosses it carelessly on the counter. Caleb stares. Jennifer has never been anything but kind and smiling in his presence.

"No motels, then?" the girl says, tapping the pack of cigarettes on the counter's edge.

Jennifer sighs quietly, kind of rolls her eyes. "Nothing around here," she says.

Percy from the hardware store looks at Caleb, curious if Caleb will offer the girl a place to stay. There are cottages behind his house in Frenchman's Bend. One of them is still in decent condition. Years ago, his uncle opened them to tourists, but Caleb nipped that in the bud when he inherited the property. Caleb can see a joke formulating in Percy's eyes. Caleb doesn't like strangers. Percy knows this. So it'd give Percy a laugh to put Caleb in an awkward spot. But Caleb flashes him a look and Percy swallows hard, nods his apology, turns back to his coffee.

And Caleb looks at the girl. Her eyes are on him. Large, dark eyes. Wide and inquisitive. As if she knows what's just passed between him and the old man. He looks away.

He hasn't ever considered reopening the cottages. And definitely not for a girl as cute as this one. He glances at her again. She's no longer looking at him. He checks out her body and decides it's probably nice underneath all the leather. No one notices the once-over. He's quick.

Jennifer starts to refill everyone's cup again. Except the girl's. The girl doesn't seem to notice the slight, even though Caleb thinks her coffee's finished. Her head is lowered; her hair falls forward to cover her face. Caleb tries hard like everyone else to pretend she isn't there, but just like everyone else, he can't stop glancing at her every two seconds. She's different. Strange for this part of the world. She's brought with her an energy that has set this diner on edge. When he senses her eyes on him he looks up, feeling the jittery tinge he feels when he thinks someone's going to accuse him of something. But she still isn't looking at him.

He stands, a little disturbed by his discomfort. In the back of Wheeler's, Jennifer keeps a refrigerator stocked with six-packs. He grabs his usual pack of Budweiser.

"Try Main Street," he suggests when he returns to the counter. "It's about fifteen minutes away. In Frenchman's Bend."

He can feel every eye in the room on him, but *his* eyes remain only on the girl. Her expression is unreadable. He thinks she's going to ask him some impossible question he can't answer; he doesn't know why. Instead, she smiles.

"Thanks," she says.

She slides off the stool gingerly and sticks her hand inside her jacket. He can't help but watch as she pulls some cash from her pocket and drops it on the counter. She grabs her things and limps out of the coffee shop. She doesn't look back when Jennifer calls out for her to wait for her change.

# Two

Jimi Anne Hamilton has been on the road for sixteen days. She's twenty-nine years old, but she's starting to feel older. She wakes up in the morning and her back and shoulders ache. It's the weight of her backpack and the duffel bag, and the way she hunches over when she rides her motorcycle. Her anklc hurts, too. Sharp needles when she stands a certain way, otherwise a dull throbbing.

*Payback,* she thinks grumpily.

The pain is the sole reason she stopped inside Wheeler's Coffee Shop a few minutes ago, the only sign of life for miles. She thought a brief respite would alleviate the hurting and rejuvenate her. It's only made her weary.

The town, Darby, is dusty and ugly and neglected. She'd half expected the people inside the coffee shop to look the same way. She hadn't expected friendly and she didn't get it. She's stopped in enough small towns on her way here to know better. On the road, people regard her with suspicion. She's keenly aware of discomfort and defiance from small-town folks, but she's uncertain how much of it is reality, and how much is her own paranoia.

Riding her bike cross-country, West to East, heading "home"

after a year away, she's learned to feel unsafe in certain places. It's in the looks of many of the provincial white men she encounters. She thinks they may want to hurt her and maybe they think she wants to hurt them. She's unsure if their prolonged stares are licentious or hateful and she finds herself hoping every look is sexual. She can deal with men wanting to violate her body for pleasure more than she can deal with men wanting to violate her body to cause pain.

This morning, the man who'd attacked her in a cheap motel on the border between Pennsylvania and New York hadn't been looking for sex. He wanted Jimi's duffel bag and didn't care what he had to do to get it. In it she carries over ten thousand dollars.

Technically, the money belongs to him. She has no proof it's the cash he earned from selling the motorcycle he stole from her—a BMW K 1200, a gift to herself after taking her first $300,000 photo. Still, as payback for stealing her bike, she took what she knew he'd miss most. His money. Everyone regrets losing money.

How the hell did she know he'd track her down and find her?

She shakes her head. Only sixteen days on the road and not only has her bike been stolen and sold, she's already made a decision that nearly got her killed. She doesn't regret taking the money. She just wishes she'd pulled it off like a true rook.

Now she walks a half mile away from Wheeler's Coffee Shop before she sits on the ground to give her ankle another rest. She's decided not to dwell on the incident, on the way people look at her. She's decided not to care. But inside the coffee shop, she felt the eyes on her body and she heard the silence and she smelled the fear. *And she cared.* She knew asking the locals for the quickest route out of Darby was out of the question. And the waitress was a true bitch.

She pulls out a cigarette. She shouldn't smoke. It's a nasty addiction and it's hotter than hell out here. The air's dry. Too dry and hot for moving, let alone expending the energy to smoke. And she should have passed on the coffee. Her stomach's rumbling and she feels dehydrated. Her throat's clouded with road-dirt, too. Every time a car passes, the wheels kick up a new tornado of dust that shatters around her like rainfall. She's coated. Her scalp itches. And she's sweating. All she wants to do is take a shower and rest.

She sticks the cigarette in her mouth and slides her knapsack around to her lap to look for her lighter. A pickup truck drives by at a crawl. A burgundy Ford. Oldish. It pulls off the road ahead and Jimi recognizes a man from the coffee shop when he hops out of the truck. She stands, drops her unlit cigarette on the ground and watches him intently. She's cautious, scrutinizing every move men make when they come near her. She prefers her violence on her own terms. She's not wild about ugly surprises.

He walks slow, looking off to the side, then back at her. His cap is pushed down low on his head. He's wearing paint-stained clothing: jeans and a white T-shirt. She notes the way he smokes his cigarette, holding it between his thumb and pointer finger like he's holding a joint. He tosses it into the road just before he reaches her.

"Hello," he says, eyes squinting at her as though the sun's shining into them.

"Hi," she says, guarded, trying not to stare at the scar on his arm or his tattoo.

"You were at Wheeler's," he says.

She nods.

"Are you okay? Do you need help?"

Jimi thinks she can tell the ones who are trouble in a couple of seconds. She has a strong feeling this one is harmless. But the stained clothes, the tattoo and the scar make her skeptical and force her to decline his help. She wants him to go away.

"No," she says.

He nods and heads back to the truck. When he stops and turns around again, Jimi's stance becomes defensive. He raises his hand slightly, letting her know he isn't about to do something aggressive.

"No, you're not okay, or no, you don't need help?" he asks.

A car passes; the driver honks. The man ignores it, staring at her as he waits for her to clarify her original answer. He doesn't seem threatening. His face is solemn, serious. His eyes show concern. She decides he has the face of a man who wouldn't desert her even if it meant he might be hurt. She suspects every town in the universe has a man with a face like this one. It's probably why so many women go missing.

"I don't need help."

He nods. "Did you take a spill on your bike?"

"What bike?" she asks.

His smile is lopsided and mischievous. "I was just going to ask you that."

She doesn't say anything and his smile widens.

"You look hurt," he continues. "I can take you to a hospital. I know a nurse."

Jimi curbs the instinct to touch her lip, the other wound besides her ankle that's bothering her. She's a chronic lip-biter; the wounded lip isn't healing.

"You can go in alone," he adds off her silence. "If you tell her Caleb sent you, she won't ask you to fill out paperwork."

"You're Caleb?"

"Yeah," he says. "She'll help you. Just make sure she knows I didn't do that to your face."

"Why would she think you did?"

He holds up his hands. "I'm the last guy in the world who'd do that to a woman."

"Says you," she quips though she believes him.

He shrugs. "Got no reason to lie to you."

"I guess not."

"A guy did that?"

She turns her back to him, looks up the road and wishes an eighteen-wheeler would drive by to distract them.

"Why?" he asks without waiting for an answer.

Jimi stiffens, and after a pause turns around again, her expression bordering on irritation and disbelief. "It's a long fucking story and I don't know you that well."

Disarmed, he grins. He's amused by her. "Did I mention there's a motel in my hometown? Frenchman's Bend."

Her annoyance takes a new, curious direction. "On Main Street. I remember. Thanks."

He doesn't go away.

"Is it clean?" she asks.

"Clean? Yeah. Pretty much."

"Pretty much?"

"There isn't another place for at least fifty miles," he says. "Have you ever stayed in an immaculate motel?"

She hasn't.

"Thanks," she repeats abruptly. This is not a true thank-you. The tone of her voice indicates this is really a good-bye.

"If you don't mind me saying it, you're in no condition to walk."

"I don't mind you saying it," she says.

He's confounded, maybe even insulted. He returns to his pickup truck without another word, but he doesn't drive away. He waits, watching her in the rearview mirror. His persistence ignites even more curiosity in her. She appreciates his interest. She remembers he looked directly into her eyes while they were talking. No one looks into your eyes before they hurt you. She knows this from experience. She's been mugged a few times, roughed up by a couple of bodyguards. She knows when her life's in serious danger.

She starts to walk toward the pickup. She knows she's taking Another Big Risk by doing this. A Budweiser-drinking hillbilly in a pickup truck would not be her usual first choice to accept a ride from. But she isn't afraid. Even getting her ass kicked in rural Pennsylvania hasn't ruined her idea of the world being her oyster and people being basically kind. She can defend herself. Growing up in Brooklyn has spoiled her rotten on that account.

"Okay," she says when she reaches his window.

He leans over to open the passenger door and holds out his hand to help her up. She can barely stand on her ankle now, but she declines his aid.

Once she's inside he says, "Don't try to be brave."

She ignores him, noticing the large, silver cross dangling from the rearview mirror. It distracts her. She drops her knapsack on the floor by her feet, keeps the duffel bag and helmet by her side, wonders if he's some kind of religious fanatic. Then she rubs her ankle, turning her head to the window so he doesn't witness her grimace.

He continues, "I don't want to hurt you."

Finally, she looks at him. "Good. Because I don't want to hurt you, either."

He smirks, nods and then he pulls away.

# Frenchman's Bend

# Three

It isn't the fact that he's a stranger that makes Jimi uneasy—she didn't know the woman who picked her up at a gas station in Pennsylvania and dropped her off in front of Wheeler's Coffee Shop, either. It's the pickup truck, and the type of man she associates with owning one. Redneck, hillbilly, racist.

She glances out the passenger window at the countryside whizzing by, struck by how odd it is to be in a part of New York that looks like Kansas. She reminds herself not to judge a man by the vehicle he drives. Or by the town he chooses to eat breakfast in. She'd rather judge him by his actions.

His right hand maneuvers the steering wheel while his left arm rests lazily in the open driver's side window. He keeps glancing at her. The silence is the only hint that he shares her wariness. But she's sure she can trust him not to do anything violent.

And just as she thinks this stupid thought, he makes a sharp turn onto a narrow path. He must hear her sudden intake of breath because he looks at her. He doesn't say anything and she thinks about jumping out. *Your guard drops for a second and the next thing you know people are out looking for you.* Before she can take action he stops the truck in front of an old Victorian house shrouded by trees. A sign on the porch reads "Earl's" and another one propped on the ground advertises "Guns. Buy. Sell. Trade."

"Why are we stopping?" she asks, disgusted by how alarmed she sounds. Before the incident in Pennsylvania, this guy wouldn't have even sent a chill through her.

"You in a rush?" His tone is soft and he looks as if he wants to laugh. "It's on the way."

He gets out, leaving the keys in the ignition. She stares at them, dangling, enticing. But she doesn't reach for them. She respects that he trusts her not to use them. So she waits, maybe foolishly, tossing around the idea of getting out and walking. And then it's too late. He's exiting the house with a paper bag. Their eyes meet and he holds her gaze. When he reaches her, he drops the paper bag through her window, into her lap. She flinches.

"Nothing in there is going to hurt you," he tells her. He turns his back to her, pulling a cellular phone from the front pocket of his jeans, and makes a call.

Jimi opens the bag, pulls out a tube of Bacitracin and an ACE bandage and stares at them. This is one of the reasons why she loves what she does. There are no gray areas in her line of work. No room for ambiguity. A celebrity is a celebrity and a bodyguard is a bodyguard. And she's the enemy. They treat her exactly how she expects them to. Caleb's actions disrupt the order of things. The confusion she feels about him, what he's supposed to be and what he's turning out not to be, is what she likes to avoid. People have proven her wrong on this trip, but it's been the exception more than the rule. She flushes, embarrassed that she didn't believe her initial instinct about him. She knew he was harmless. But it's hard to tell the good ones from the bad when you're on the road alone.

She uses the rearview mirror to apply the ointment to her forehead. The cut looks worse than it is and probably won't leave a scar, but it stings when she touches it. She sits back in the passenger seat and looks out the window at Caleb. He's smoking now, watching her. He drops his cigarette and gets back into the truck, bringing a heavy scent of tobacco and something else, possibly clove, with him.

"Thank you," she says once he's settled.

"No problem." He starts the truck, glancing at her head, then back out the windshield. "It's for your knuckles, too."

Instinctively, she turns her palms up. She stares at the old Victorian as they pull away.

"How much do I owe you?" she asks after a minute.

"It didn't break me," he says, propping his left arm in the window, focusing his attention on the road.

They don't say anything else to each other, but the silence is no longer uncomfortable. Jimi feels better about accepting the ride from him. She fingers the bandage and the tube of medication, glancing at him, toying with things to say and not saying them. She knows they've reached Frenchman's Bend when the highway morphs into smooth paved road and trees open up to small buildings and shops. It's brighter and cleaner than Darby.

Caleb stops in front of a No Parking sign. She pushes some hair behind her ear and feels self-conscious. She wonders what he thinks of her, but when she looks at him he's messing around with something under his steering wheel. He isn't thinking about her at all; he's just waiting for her to get out.

"This is your stop," he says. He leans past her and opens her door.

She stares. In Los Angeles no one did a favor for her unless they wanted something. Everyone had an ulterior motive. Why did he give her a ride if he doesn't want money?

"Thank you."

He nods without looking at her. The cap is pushed lower on his head so she can't even look into his face. She leans forward to look out of the windshield at the motel he's brought her to. It's a narrow, three-story white building; flower boxes adorn every window. The elegant lettering across the top of the entryway reads THE INN AT FRENCHMAN'S BEND.

It's an inn, not a motel. Leave it to a man not to know the difference. Inns make Jimi uneasy. There exists a feeling that the people who operate them are always watching, listening, waiting for a guest to misbehave so they have a reason to invite her to leave. She looks at Caleb again.

"Are we near Willow Run?" she asks.

He glances at the inn. "This not good enough for you?"

"I'm curious."

He waits for her to elaborate, but she doesn't. He says, "I can get you to Willow Run in five minutes, but there's nothing there. Just houses and shops."

"It's that close?"

He smiles a little. "No."

Jimi smiles, too. She appreciates speed and arriving places sooner than she's expected to.

Caleb shifts, wipes his nose. "I have to get back to work. Do you want to stay or do you need me to take you someplace else?"

Again, she's struck by his willingness to help her.

"I'll stay," she says.

"Are you gonna be okay?" He indicates her face.

"It's not as bad as it looks," she says.

"It looks pretty bad."

She touches her lip involuntarily. "I'm okay."

Unsure how to end it—she thinks offering him ten dollars

will insult him—she says "Well" as she opens the truck's door wider and steps down. She lands on her bad ankle and nearly loses her balance. He pushes his cap up, but watches passively, bored.

"Thanks again," she says, "for the bandages and ointment. And the ride, of course."

Amusement flashes across his face, then fades. "You can stop thanking me."

"Okay," she says.

When she closes the door, he starts the engine and takes off.

The inn's lobby is designed to look like a cozy living room with plush sofas and armchairs, a stone fireplace, plants and a wide curving staircase leading up to the guest floors. The atmosphere could compete with some of the boutique hotels Jimi's stayed in on the West Coast. That's impressive for a small town in rural New York. Jimi never heard of Frenchman's Bend before today and she can't imagine the town as a huge tourist attraction.

A woman is sitting on one of the sofas, reading a book. She turns around to look at Jimi. "Hi," she says.

Jimi smiles. "Hi."

"What can I do for you?"

"I'd like a room."

The woman drops her book on a coffee table and makes her way to the front. She's young. Not a woman, but a girl. A teenager. Sprinklings of red and brown acne scar her forehead and chin. "Was that Caleb Atwood's truck you got out of?" she asks, eyes riveted on the computer sitting atop the front desk.

"Yes," says Jimi, though Caleb hadn't told her his last name.

"Yeah?" The girl grins, still staring at the screen. Her grin holds a hundred juicy secrets Jimi would love to know if she weren't so tired. "How do you know him?"

"Old friend."

"Yeah?" She chuckles, mostly to herself, as if she's remembering something not exactly funny, but affectionate. "Why aren't you staying out at the cottages, then?"

Caleb hadn't mentioned any cottages. "Decided to change it up a bit."

The girl looks at Jimi, smiling, and seems to notice her face for the first time. She stares at the cut on Jimi's head, and then the busted lip. The girl's eyes are round and very blue. Her expression is curious.

"How long do you want to stay?" she asks.

How long. Jimi doesn't know. How long does it take a sprained ankle to heal? A black eye to fade? Her brother, Troy, is expecting her, but she hasn't given him a definite arrival date. She'd like to unwind. She'd like a shower and a bed. A place to convalesce.

"Three nights," she says. "I'll pay cash."

"We require you to pay now if you don't use a credit card." The girl's tone is apologetic.

"Okay." Jimi pulls out some money.

"Do you have a preference?"

"Preference?"

"Like smoking or nonsmoking . . . well, all the rooms are nonsmoking rooms but I can give you the one with the big window facing the back so Mom won't know. Do you smoke?"

"I do."

"Me, too." The girl's smile is genuine and Jimi decides to like her. "I'm Lucy, by the way."

"Nice to meet you, Lucy. I'm Jimi."

Jimi refuses Lucy's help with her bags and follows her to the second floor to a room in the back of the building. Lucy unlocks the door and tells Jimi to check out the window and make sure everything is acceptable.

The room smells faintly of smoke and the flowery disinfectant housekeeping uses to mask it, but it's clean and pretty and the window, as Lucy promised, is huge. It makes her think about the last motel she stayed in. She'd trusted its cleanliness, brightly lit hallways and key cards. The window had been large enough for her to escape through.

"It's really great." Jimi tries to sound more sincere than exhausted.

"Good!" Lucy clasps her hands together, delighted, and Jimi thinks the teen's presence is nice. Jimi's wariness, for the first time in two weeks, dissipates. Lucy makes her want to thank Caleb again.

"Is Caleb coming back for you?" Lucy asks.

The question takes Jimi by surprise, but she can tell there's no other intent behind it except polite curiosity. Jimi told her Caleb was an old friend and Lucy took her word for it. Why wouldn't an old friend be coming back for her? "I don't think so."

"Okay. Well. That's cool. Mom doesn't like him. We serve a light dinner in the dining room between six and eight and it's complimentary. There's good Chinese up the block on Main Street. Well, it's the only Chinese restaurant in the Bend, but it's very good. And there's a vending machine on this floor at the other end of the hall. I noticed you're limping. There's an ice machine in the same place as the vending machine if you need some for your foot."

"Thank you."

"Caleb's always at Fifth Amendment after eight. Not always, but most of the time . . . if you get bored later and want to see him. We keep the front door unlocked until midnight during the summer months. Where are you from? You don't look familiar. How do you know Caleb?"

Lucy's speech is slow and deliberate, but Jimi isn't sure if she really wants answers to all of her questions. She decides to answer the easiest one. "I'm from New York . . . City. Brooklyn."

"I love the city."

"You do?"

"Yes." Lucy takes a tentative step inside the room. "I won't tell Mom you know Caleb."

Jimi doesn't know what to say. She's tempted to ask why Lucy's mother doesn't like Caleb. But asking could open a can of worms Jimi doesn't want opened right now—it might keep Lucy talking for another twenty minutes.

"I appreciate that" is all she says.

"Press zero if you need me. I'm off at nine, but I live here with Mom, so the calls come directly to our rooms downstairs." Lucy steps outside the room again and bows, comes up grinning. Jimi grins back. "We're very happy to have you with us."

After a shower, Jimi tries to nap. She lies on top of the bed's quilt and stares at the ceiling, thinks about all she's been through just to end up here—five minutes from her brother. She remembers the relief in Troy's voice when she called him two weeks ago to say she was heading back to New York for a vacation. He'd expressed a hope that her vacation would become permanent. He hated her job. "A job you will never be proud of," he called it. "A job that makes it hard to wake up with yourself every morning." She couldn't bring herself to admit she was quitting then.

When people ask her whether or not she does it for the money, Jimi always says yes. There's something less repugnant about admitting she's paparazzi because the cash is good than admitting she does it because it allows her to be brash and reckless. Drugs have nothing on the enormous adrenaline rush she gets from chasing celebrities through the streets of Las Vegas and Los Angeles. She can't explain in a way that would make sense to most people why it's exciting to her, why she lies under a Dumpster for two hours to be the first person to get a shot of an actor making out with a rock star. It's hard not to get caught up in the sheer excitement one feels when a tip about a certain hot actor being in a certain place turns out to be true. She admits, instead, that it's hard to feel guilty about taking a picture of the latest Double A–list celebrity when that picture sells for $500,000.

People understand doing things for money.

But not her brother. Troy hasn't been able to say the word *paparazzi* since Jimi moved to the West Coast. It's one of those shameful jobs no one talks about, like stripping and prostitution. Freelancing, however, isn't much better. There's no 401(k) plan, no healthcare benefits, no stability or protection.

And Troy would remind her how miserable she was as a freelance photojournalist—taking pictures of dreary apartments in bad neighborhoods for New York newspapers, listening to people share harrowing stories with writers because they hoped the attention would make a difference. Jimi often wondered what purpose any of it served. The stories were never *featured.* Nothing ever changed. And she hated being reminded that life has always been shit for some people and it never got better. That some people—*her*—were lucky to have dodged suffering. That luck was random. In L.A. she felt far removed from reality. In L.A. she was no longer invading the private lives of poor people for her own benefit. She didn't give her subjects false hope. She just pissed them off a little.

She massages her good ankle and admits to herself that she's too tired and too hot to actually sleep. She puts her leather pants back on and a clean T-shirt, and stores her duffel bag in the closet. She leaves her room to take a stroll down Main Street. The lobby is empty. She missed the complimentary dinner. The muted sounds of a television drift through the cracks of a closed door.

Frenchman's Bend has a bit of charm to it compared to Darby. Main Street isn't a dusty road, but a strip of small, bright shops that make this part of the town feel quaint and Mayberry-esque. Jimi isn't surprised to see so many people on the street, strolling. Some of them stare at her. She tries to walk without the limp.

The bar on the next block is open. The laughter inside feels contagious and Jimi stops to listen. After a minute, she notices the name on the window. Fifth Amendment. The bar Lucy said Caleb frequents.

A few men are playing pool, but the laughter is coming from a back room. Jimi decides to avoid it. The bartender, a woman in her fifties with blond hair, does a double take when Jimi takes a seat. She stands up from her stool and slaps a napkin and a glass of ice in front of her.

"You show me some ID and I'll make that whatever you want it to be. Otherwise it's seltzer or ginger ale."

"Ginger ale would be terrific," Jimi says. Something strong, like a shot of tequila, wouldn't hurt. But Jimi doesn't drink in towns she has no friends in and she doesn't show ID to people who aren't wearing uniforms.

The bartender stares at her face a little too long. Like Lucy, she's curious. It makes Jimi smile a little. Most people she encountered in the small white towns she passed through these past two weeks weren't curious about her. She'd walk into a diner and they pretended she wasn't there, or they glared at her until she was too uncomfortable to stick around. Jimi thought curiosity is inherent in all people. She's disappointed she's wrong about that.

The bartender pulls up the spray gun and shoots ginger ale into the glass. "One dollar," she says.

A white man walks in as Jimi pays for her drink and sits three seats away from her. The bartender doesn't look at him.

"Rose," he says after a minute, "give me a tequila."

Rose points a manicured nail at the man. "Just one."

The man grins, and when Rose doesn't move from her place he concedes with a nod. "Just one."

Rose takes out a shot glass and fills it to the brim. The man puts a five on the bar and picks up his shot without spilling any of the liquor. Before he drinks, he fixes Rose with an intense gaze.

"Is she here?" His voice is low and menacing and Jimi doesn't like the sound of it. She gives him a sidelong glance that says *back off,* but he isn't looking at her. His eyes are steady on Rose's face.

Rose nods slowly. "She's in back."

"I thought I heard her laughing." He drinks his shot. He twists around, sits with his back to them, waits. After a minute passes, he says, "Bitch."

Jimi stands up and walks over to the pay phone in the corner of the bar. She opens the Yellow Pages and searches for Willow Run on the map. Everything is a sign of something else. She isn't sure what kind of sign this man is, but she knows she doesn't want to stick around to find out.

Willow Run doesn't make an appearance in the Frenchman's Bend Yellow Pages. She'll have to ask how to get there.

And she doesn't feel like asking. For the best, probably. She doesn't need to be in Willow Run right now, fielding questions from her brother and his wife, who bought a summerhouse in the small town while Jimi was in California. As much as she wants to see them, be comforted by them, she doesn't want them to see her. Not like this. She wants her bruises to heal first. She wants to walk without a limp.

If Jimi calls Troy and Sienna now, Troy will get into his car and pick her up tonight and they'll start off the visit with her already being Troublesome. Jimi doesn't want that. She closes the telephone book.

When she turns around, the man at the bar is gone, but a familiar face has replaced him. Caleb. He isn't wearing his cap. His dark hair is cut short and growing back unevenly, so she thinks he once had a mohawk. He slouches against the bar with the kind of attitude reserved for hot actors, only unaffected, because he isn't assuming people are watching. He looks arrogant and dangerous. Too bad he isn't famous. He'd be excellent to shoot.

He doesn't notice her; he's messing with his cellular phone: pushing buttons, checking for a dial tone. Behind him, a blonde is wrapping a sheer light blue scarf around her neck. She looks older than he does, pretty. Nothing to call the tabloids about. She notices Jimi watching them. Caught, Jimi smiles. The blonde's smile is slight and tentative.

Caleb stops playing with his phone and hands some money over to the bartender. As Rose counts the bills, Caleb puts his arm around his companion's waist and they walk past Jimi, out the door, without looking up.

Jimi returns to the bar to finish the soda.

"Want another ginger ale?" Rose asks.

"I think I'll finish this one."

"Want something stronger?"

"No."

"You look like you could use something stronger."

"I probably can," Jimi says, almost laughing, "but I'll stick with this."

Rose starts to wipe the counter, dismissing Jimi with a wink and nod.

Outside, Jimi's surprised to see Caleb on the ground, blood-coated fists covering his nose. For a second she's back in Los Angeles where so many of her nights were like this. Usually it was a photographer friend knocked on his ass after being attacked by a celebrity bodyguard. Lately, she's been thinking about the violent scenes the world misses and never pieces together. Individual encounters with violence playing out every minute that never merit a spot on the evening news at six. She's witnessed some of that anonymous violence outside clubs and bars in L.A., but it's only now, now that she's physically experienced it, that it matters to her. Here, Caleb's alone. The same way she was alone on that dark road in Pennsylvania and in her motel room last night.

"Are you all right?" she calls out, but he doesn't seem to hear her. She walks over and reaches down. He pulls back sharply.

"I'm sorry," she says.

His voice is muffled through his hands when he responds.

"What?" she asks.

He stands up with some difficulty. "Why the fuck are you sorry?"

She's unfazed by his fury. It isn't personal. But now that he's asked, she doesn't really know why she's sorry. Probably because she'd realized when she saw Caleb with the blonde who that man at the bar was looking for. "For sneaking up on you, I guess."

"You didn't." His face softens. "And you don't have to be sorry for that."

She steps closer and pulls his hands away from his face like she owns him. She presses her fingers against his flesh to check if his nose is broken. He jerks away in pain, but he doesn't hit her. Good sign. Once she'd tried the same thing with a colleague seconds after a rock star clocked him. Her colleague howled in pain and punched her in the mouth.

"It isn't broken," she declares. "You'll have a nasty bruise in the morning though."

He shrugs. Mr. Cool. Not even a thank-you. She takes a handkerchief from her pocket and wipes his blood from her hands. She hadn't been thinking about protecting herself when she'd touched him; she'd been thinking about last night and the front desk clerk who'd recoiled when she asked for his help. She hands Caleb the handkerchief. He takes it and pushes it against his nose. His eyes hold hers.

"I thought I would never see you again." Jimi keeps her voice soft, nonthreatening.

He doesn't respond.

"I thought I would never see you again," she repeats, a little louder.

He continues to stare, handkerchief held tight against his nose. "I heard you," he says quietly.

Her eyes move to his tattoo: a thorny vine that stretches down his neck and is lost underneath his T-shirt. It reappears again and snakes down his right arm, intersecting the scar. She can really stare at it now that she knows he isn't out to harm her. Richard, her best friend in Brooklyn, would call it a prison tattoo, but Jimi's impressed by Caleb's decision to draw more attention to his scar with it. In fact, the audacity of that decision makes her catch her breath. She wishes she still had her camera. And then she flushes, embarrassed by her reaction. She's fascinated by flamboyant tattoos. She only has a small one of her motorcycle. It's hidden right above the crack of her ass. Her little tattoo hurt like hell. She can't imagine the pain Caleb endured when he had his done. She's impressed.

When she looks at his face again he's still watching her. He pulls the handkerchief away and says, "There isn't anyone in the Bend who'd have done what you just did."

Jimi thinks of Lucy's offer not to tell her mother they're "friends." And instead of feeling repelled, Jimi feels drawn to him. Why is he an outsider in his hometown?

"Do you need a ride somewhere?" she asks. "I don't have a car, but we could use yours and figure something out."

He chuckles, shakes his head, then holds up her handkerchief. "I'll get this back to you."

Jimi waves her hand so he knows the handkerchief doesn't matter. "Now we're even."

"Is that so?"

"Yes."

"Okay." He steps back, looks past her, but doesn't walk away.

Jimi wonders if he's waiting for her to say something else, possibly invite him for a drink. She *had* considered inviting him to sit with her a little while longer. She could use the company. The idea of being alone again is unappealing. She isn't ready for bed. And his presence is overwhelming in such a way that makes her want to feel overwhelmed. She thinks they may have a few things in common. Not just this needing someone to help them out of things, this resisting. He's an outsider. An outsider in the place he was born. He still smells of clove and tobacco and she's noticing he has a very handsome face. She bites her lip. He could get her into trouble.

"I should get going," she says and starts to walk away. She turns back once and he's still watching her. She smiles a little and he waves, but doesn't move, letting her know he's enjoying the view.

*Trouble,* she thinks.

# Four

He thinks about her on his way home, holding her handkerchief to his nose even though it stopped bleeding twenty minutes ago. She's been on his mind since he picked her up this afternoon in Darby. Earlier, he called Dale at the office to find out if a black girl with a lock of pink hair had dropped by the hospital to see Dale's wife, Leigh. She hadn't. Caleb figured she changed her mind about staying and hopped a ride with someone else. He meant to follow up with Lucy at the front desk, but forgot. Emma tends to cloud his memory and all his good intentions get lost. When Dale asked why he was worried about some black girl with pink hair, Caleb told him she was probably a figment of his imagination and changed the subject. And then she was there. At Fifth Amendment. Not a figment of his imagination at all.

He was disoriented when she came over to him, and he flinched when she reached out to offer a hand. And then she planted herself in front of him the same way his brother Morgan used to after he had a fight in school, letting the world know he could tend to Caleb better than anyone else could. Why had *she* chosen to tend to him? Few people are kind to him by choice. Few people think he matters that much.

His thoughts shift when he reaches his house on Whiskey Road. Always, the porch light startles him. As if his wife returned unexpectedly while he was out. She has the timer set to come on at eight in the evening. She'd never liked coming home to a dark porch. Dark porches don't bother Caleb, but there's a part of him that knows unplugging the light means accepting his wife's never coming home.

The first thing he does when he enters the house is take a beer from the refrigerator. He drinks it quickly without closing the refrigerator door. Then he looks around the kitchen as his eyes adjust to the darkness. He isn't looking for anything in particular. Just trying to avoid his thoughts. He hates coming back to this house at night. It feels loneliest when he turns the lights on.

When he finishes the beer, he takes another one. This time he washes his hands before he drinks it. He finally turns on the kitchen light near the sink and looks directly at the answering machine.

He hopes there's a call from Sally. His wife. Not because he's still carrying a torch for her. It was over between them long before she walked out six months ago. No matter how sentimental he gets about a timed light on the porch, he knows that. He wants her to call so he can ask for a divorce. That's easy. A simple want. A simple need. But it isn't. She hasn't been in touch with him since she left and she won't respond to his e-mails. He thinks she's in California. She always wanted to live in Hollywood.

There's a hang-up call, a message from Dale asking him to come to the office tomorrow even though tomorrow's his Friday off and finally a message from Emma. She apologizes for leaving him bleeding outside the bar. She had no choice, she tells the machine. Ray took her by surprise. She couldn't nurse Caleb right in front of him. There's an accusatory tone in her voice that annoys Caleb. He hasn't even had a chance to tell her how he feels and already she's accusing him of being unreasonable. He would have told her she was right to leave with her husband.

In reality, he'd felt like a fool when Emma left him on the ground like that. His brother came to mind then, too. In high school, Morgan was the bully who was left back twice, so he and Caleb were juniors together. Morgan was the one who ended up without a high school diploma. Morgan was doing time at Bonham in Texas. But Morgan had always warned him about sleeping with girls who had husbands. Funny, that. Morgan warning him against doing something stupid.

Caleb carries the second beer to the bathroom, sets it on the sink while he undresses and starts the shower. He has the girl's handkerchief with him. It's soiled with his blood. He'll have to wash it and return it to her when he sees her again. His chances are fifty-fifty, he thinks. The Bend is a small town. If she sticks around, he'll see her. He remembers she asked about Willow Run. Maybe she's headed there.

Actually, she has the look of a lot of the artists who have been moving to Willow Run these days. The hair, especially. He's seen blue and green and purple over the years. However, the year-round artists don't eat meat, let alone wear leather. And he can't picture the girl eating plates of seitan and spinach, drinking wheatgrass, talking about how much she loves Shakespeare. There's something hard there. Something the poets and painters and actors he's worked for in Willow Run lack. Something he wants to find out more about.

In the morning, the telephone rings before he's out of bed.

"Yeah?" he says.

He can hear Emma breathing, which means Ray is still

home. They live above Emma's antiques store in Darby. She usually opens for business at noon. He doesn't know what time Ray leaves for work.

"Yeah?" he repeats. He's supposed to start the conversation, tell her things he'd like to do to her later, but he doesn't feel like making it easy. In the background, he thinks he hears Ray call out.

"He just left," Emma says in a whisper.

"You have a clock over there?" Caleb asks.

"I'm sorry, baby," she says. "I know it's early."

"Then why . . ." he says slowly.

"I want to make sure you're not mad at me."

He doesn't want to do this with her this morning. He has a black eye, thanks to Ray. He's tired. If he wanted a girlfriend, he'd go out and find a girl without a husband. His brother said he stayed away from married women because knowing he'd never really have them would eventually tear him apart. It's knowing he will never have Emma that keeps Caleb interested. Why is she making it so hard?

"I have to go," he says.

"Are you going out tonight?"

"I haven't decided."

"It's Friday. I want to see you."

Caleb wants to see her, too. He can't lie about that. Some nights he thinks about her, wishes they could be together to keep each other company. He hates those nights, when he can't sleep and feels vulnerable and lonely and can't stop himself from thinking crazy thoughts. But he always wakes up in the morning and thanks God she's married and has someplace else to go.

"Caleb?" she urges. "Please come out tonight."

Something about the desperation in her voice turns him off.

Maybe it isn't Emma he wants to see. Maybe he just wants to see someone. His thoughts immediately turn to the girl he met yesterday. He wonders how she made out last night. She should be okay. She looked like she could take care of herself. He might be more worried about her if she'd stayed in Darby. Darby's run-down and menacing to outsiders. The Bend's mostly progressive and accepting.

"Caleb?"

"I told you I prefer simple," he says.

"I know, baby. Are you hurt?"

"My left eye's purple."

She sighs, loud. "I'm so sorry. Let me make it up to you."

"I have to work through the weekend," he tells her. "Why don't I call you?"

"Will you?" Her voice is hopeful.

He often wonders what it is about him that makes her risk her husband. He thinks she's into the bad-boy image he once projected. It still lingers a little. He likes her despite the fact that she's married. She's pretty and she has a hell of a body: all curves. She makes him *feel* good. Her hands are always on him when they're alone together; her words are always flattering. She never says no. But, mostly, he likes her because she's what Sally, his wife, will be in fifteen years. Mature, curvy, still beautiful. He knows he won't have Sally then. So, for now, he has Emma.

"I'll call you," he promises. "You know I will."

He's in town by nine thirty. He parks his truck on the corner of Polecat Road and walks toward the office. He's glad it's Friday. He's already looking forward to meeting Dale at Fifth Amendment Bar for a drink after dinner. Dale always buys him a sympathy drink when he comes in to work with a black eye. In fact, he can hear Dale now, reprimanding him for taking Emma to the bar on a weekday. Caleb's supposed to be keeping a low profile, staying out of trouble.

The girl he gave a ride to yesterday is sitting on the curb in front of the Daily Sip Café on Main Street with a coffee, a cigarette and a paper. Caleb is all of a sudden distracted. She's wearing sunglasses and a sleeveless pink T-shirt. She has good arms. Well defined, muscular . . . very bruised. He noticed the bruises yesterday, but it's tough to see them again today. She's still wearing her leather pants despite the heat. Her bags are on the ground next to her. She looks like she owns the sidewalk.

Sitting there, she reminds him of what he thinks he's been missing by living here his entire life: confidence, nonchalance and spontaneity. Bend locals aren't exactly rushing home after work, but the idea that all folks who don't live in the city are laid-back and unpretentious is just that. An idea. No Bender would sit on a curb on Main Street with her coffee and paper. Especially not a woman on her own.

Neither would a local woman walk over to him while he's sprawled out on the ground outside Fifth Amendment Bar and offer to help him. Caleb's had a reputation in this town since he was a teenager and local women don't approach him unless they're walking into his office. Because people in Frenchman's Bend like to appear proper. And since Moss Bluff has been besieged by strip malls and chain restaurants, and Willow Run has been besieged by transplants from the city, the folks in the Bend fashion themselves a cut above the rest. Better than the aggressive transplants. Better than the tackiness of Moss Bluff. Better than the down-and-out in Darby. But the city girls he's met don't seem to care about any of that. They don't fear public displays of kindness and emotion.

As a rule, he avoids the Daily Sip Café with its blue-haired college boy and its dreadlocked blonde working behind the counter. Not because he has something against blue-haired college boys or dreadlocked blondes. He hates the front door. It's plastered with political flyers touting marches and protests no one in this town would ever go to. He hates that cheesy rainbow bright awning that screams "Pretentious motherfuckers drink overpriced coffee here." But he's gravitating toward it now and he notices a slight movement of the girl's head as he gets closer. He swaggers, kind of grins at her. She has no reaction, shows no sign of recognizing him. This bugs him. He recognized her immediately.

He enters the Daily Sip to avoid an awkward moment. The two employees stop speaking to one another when they see him. The dreadlocked blonde starts to wipe the counter. She's a little nervous around him. He's leered at her on the street a couple of times in the past to make her uneasy. The blue-haired college boy steps up, stares at Caleb's black eye for a moment, then looks smug. Maybe Caleb has leered at him once or twice, too.

Caleb stares at the chalkboard on the wall behind the counter. Everything has a ridiculous name with little indication of what it actually is. When the blue-haired college boy starts to ask him about the kind of coffee he wants to order, Caleb hears impatience and orders a cup of Java Goodness to shut him up. The guy kind of rolls his eyes and turns to the blender. He pours milk and ice into the container, and Caleb asks what he's doing. The guy pauses, sighs, turns around to look at him.

"I'm making your Java Goodness," he says.

"I just want coffee," Caleb tells him, irritation mounting.

"Well, you ordered a Java Goodness."

"A what?"

The guy stares at Caleb openmouthed. "Ja. Va. Good. Ness. A frothy milkshakey thing."

"You don't have regular coffee?" Caleb asks. "No flavors, no froth?"

The guy looks at the dreadlocked blonde, then back at Caleb, unaware of how close he is to having Caleb's foot up his ass. "What would you like, sir? A Regular?"

Caleb looks at the chalkboard again and notices it. Regular. In three convenient sizes. He missed it earlier because it's written smaller than the other items on the board. That can't be his fault. He settles on a small in a take-out cup. One-fifty for a cup of coffee. He will never come back in here. He's sure of it.

Outside, he glances at the girl. She's looking up at him. He feels stupid carrying a coffee in a bright yellow take-out cup with a smiley face. God knows it will make him sweat if he actually drinks it. And can she take him seriously when he looks like one of the trendy fruitcakes who come in here every day? The smirk on her face indicates she can't. So now he feels exposed, like she knows he only came over because he saw her. For a minute he doesn't know who the hell he is.

"I know you," the girl says, holding her sunglasses up so he can see her eyes. Bruised and unrelenting.

"The girl with pink hair," he says.

She kind of smiles and drops her sunglasses back over her face. "I'm sorry. I didn't realize that was you before. Come here often?"

"All the time," he says.

She laughs as if she knows he's lying and after a second she motions for him to take a seat on the curb with her. He just stands there. He wants to know her name, but he isn't sure how to ask. He wants to find out what she's doing here and how long she plans to stay. This urge to ask her questions unsettles him. He feels angry again. At himself. At her. At the Daily Sip employees for treating him like some college kid who would actually drink a frothy milkshakey thing.

"How's your face?" she asks, lifting the glasses again and letting them rest on the top of her head.

"Better, thanks."

"Slight bruising." She touches her own eye and winces to indicate she's empathizing. "Looks like it hurts."

He shrugs. "How's your leg?"

They look at her covered legs.

"Fine, I think."

"You like the motel?"

"It's an inn."

"Okay. Inn. Do you like it?"

"Yes. Lucy is very nice." She looks like she wants to add something. He waits. She says, "Are you looking for a tenant?"

He stares at her for a long time. "What?"

"Lucy saw me get out of your truck yesterday and asked how we know each other."

*That's the thing about the Bend.*

"I said you're an old friend and she asked why I'm not staying with you, in your cottage."

"Did she."

The girl nods. "I think her mother would like to see me check out today."

"Why do you think that?"

"Intuition. I met her for five minutes this morning and she stared at me the entire time. Without blinking. Made me nervous."

Caleb chuckles. He's known Lucy and her mother, Ruth, for years. It wouldn't surprise him if Ruth *is* eager to see the girl check out. But to be fair, wouldn't most people be uncomfortable having a girl as banged up as this girl is staying in their inn? You have to figure the man who did it can't be far behind. He's sure the old-timers are already gathered at Dusty's for breakfast, discussing Ruth's choice to let the girl stay with her even one night.

"Ruth doesn't blink," he says. "Seriously. It used to scare the shit out of me, too. You have to ignore it. I bet she's happy to have you."

The girl looks unconvinced. "So you aren't looking."

"It's nothing against you."

"Oh, well," the girl says and looks down at her paper.

He waits for her to say something else. She doesn't. He shifts his weight from his left foot to his right. "I don't know your name."

"Jimi," she tells him.

"Well, Jimi," he says, and then he pauses. What's left to say? Lame excuses about why he didn't invite her to stay on Whiskey Road yesterday won't cut it. He won't admit that he'd thought about asking her to come back with him once they left Earl's and stopped himself because he wasn't one hundred percent clear on his motives for wanting to ask. She's attractive. An attractive girl in the cottage less than eight feet from his bedroom is too tempting. And they'd have to share a bathroom and a kitchen; he's just not ready for that. But he also has this urge to look out for her. Make sure she ends up where she's trying to go. Another absurd urge he can't make sense of.

"Don't lose sleep over it," Jimi says without looking at him. "I like the inn. It's just . . . I want to relax and cheer up a bit before I move on. Being stared at isn't conducive to that. And Lucy's a talker."

He smiles absently. "Yeah, she is."

A man behind the wheel of a mud-covered 4x4 honks his horn. Caleb and Jimi stare. Caleb recognizes the driver and his immediate reaction is to step in front of Jimi. He half expects Ray to drive the 4x4 into them and the last thing he wants is Jimi in the middle of a dangerous situation because of him. But all Ray does is flip his middle finger as he passes. He wouldn't be the first man to threaten to kill Caleb and let him off with a black eye and a bloody nose. Caleb's relieved. He looks at Jimi. She's back to reading her paper.

"I didn't thank you for helping me last night," Caleb says to her. "Thanks."

"Looks like you're not off the hook yet."

"You remember Ray from last night?" he asks.

"Who could forget Ray," she says lightly.

"He doesn't scare me."

"I'm relieved." She sounds amused. "And, strangely, kind of curious."

Curious. He can't tell her Ray's mad because he saw Caleb walk out of Fifth Amendment with his arm wrapped around Ray's wife's waist. What a way to make a third impression. He's usually excellent at discretion, but Emma forgot to mention Ray wasn't working last night. He changes the subject.

"Anyone ever tell you—?"

"That leather chafes in the summer?" She turns a page. "No. I had to figure it out on my own."

"Um, no," says Caleb. "Has anyone ever told you it isn't safe to go home with strangers?"

Finally, she looks up at him. Her eyes are glinting mischievously, but her face is serious. "I had to figure that one out on my own, too. But it's good to be reminded. Thanks for the tip."

"You might ask the wrong guy next time," he says, feeling inexplicably defensive.

She nods, somber now that she realizes he doesn't have a sense of humor. "You're right. Thanks."

"Do you have any idea how careless that is?"

"Are you kidding?" she says.

"No, I'm not kidding." He wishes he were kidding. Since when does he give a damn how careless someone else is? But he had to say something. One look at the gash on her forehead and the busted lip makes saying something necessary. The next guy she runs into won't be him. If he can make a difference with one woman, it would mean something. "You really could ask the wrong guy. From the look of you, I have to wonder if you already did."

"Listen," she says, closing her paper. "I'm an adult. And the one thing they teach you where I come from is to *know your enemies.* Know your enemies and everything will be okay."

"Did you know your enemy when he punched you in the face?"

She stares at him for a long time and he stares back. He thinks he sees what other men have seen in her in the past, men he'll never know about. She's very pretty. But there's more than that. Her face is both vulnerable and fierce. Is she truly a badass, or is she just scared? There's no settling on an answer. It's hard to look at that face and not wonder what she's really thinking, what she'd be like alone in a room after too much to drink.

"Point taken," she says softly. "And, yes. I did know him. I was unable to stop him."

"I'm sorry," he says. "Who was he?"

"Why do you want to know?" She's back to smiling at him. "Are you going to beat him up?"

"I just want to know why it happened."

"It was a misunderstanding."

"That had to be one hell of a misunderstanding."

Now she's silent, staring straight ahead.

"Okay," he says, "I don't tell my secrets to strangers, either." He looks inside the café and notices the college kid and the blonde are watching them. He turns away, annoyed, and looks up Main Street. He should leave, but he doesn't want to. He bought this coffee.

"Listen," he says, "I feel fucking stupid holding this coffee on the street like a pretentious yuppie."

She looks up. "Then why are you standing there?"

It's on the edge of his tongue to tell her that he wants to know more. That he wouldn't have to be standing here if she'd get up and take a walk with him, instead of sitting here on view for everyone in town. But he catches himself. She might find him insensitive, considering she has a bad leg. And he's not supposed to be the kind of guy who cares what people think.

And why would she take a walk with him anyway? She probably hates guys like him. White and restless. Nothing important to do on a Friday morning, except stand around drinking coffee, attempting uninspired conversation with girls sitting on curbs. He has another urge. This one to tell her that he's on his way to work. He has a job. He owns a business. He's not some loser cruising Main Street in the morning.

She's still staring at him, probably trying to guess what he's thinking about. Or, maybe, she's waiting for an answer to the question she just asked him.

"I don't know why I'm standing here," he says. He tosses the coffee in a nearby garbage can and takes off.

"Hey," she calls out once he reaches the corner.

He stops, turns around. She motions for him to come back. After a moment, he does.

"You're not a stranger," she says.

He frowns, uncomprehending.

"Three unscheduled meetings in two days," she explains. "Somebody's got a plan."

"My Uncle Pete used to say there are no coincidences. God has a plan."

"For the record," she says, "I knew you'd say no about the cottage."

"Yeah? Did I pass or fail some kind of test?"

"No test," she says.

"How'd you know I'd say no?" he asks.

"You look like the kind of guy who doesn't want company."

"Looks can be deceiving."

"Obviously not."

He smiles. "No hard feelings, then?"

"None."

"Then you should stop by Fifth Amendment again," he tells her unexpectedly. "Tonight. I'll buy you a drink."

She frowns as if he's asked a challenging question. He holds his hands up as if to say he's harmless.

"No strings," he promises.

"No strings?" she repeats.

He nods. "I leave work at six."

She smiles wider, and then she looks back down without another word. After a while he realizes he's just standing there staring at her, so he walks away. When he turns back to have one last look at her, she's watching him. Their eyes meet and they share something. It's brief. Hardly matters. Yet he holds on to it.

# Five

Dale's on the phone when Caleb walks into the office. He's speaking in that soft way of his that always makes Caleb lean in a little closer, shake his head and tell him to speak up. He swivels around when he hears the door and less than a minute later hangs up the phone.

"Ray?" he asks, half amused by the black eye, half disapproving.

"Yeah," Caleb says.

Dale rocks back in his chair the way fat men smoking fat cigars in black-and-white movies do. But Dale is the opposite of fat. Since graduating high school and giving up football, he's thinner than Caleb, lithe and muscular. "What the hell were you doing in Darby last night?"

Caleb and Dale have known each other for years. In high school, they were adversaries. Dale was a popular jock, a quarterback who'd parade through the halls garnering attention from all the girls worth getting attention from. Caleb was a hard-edged blue-collar who viewed Dale and his crew with disdain. These days, all their high school animosity is water under the bridge. Forgotten about after Dale came to Caleb's aid during a bar fight in Moss Bluff two years after they graduated. Dale's been hanging around and getting into trouble with Caleb and his crew ever since. They've co-owned Bend Contractors for three years.

"Wasn't in Darby," Caleb tells Dale now.

"Where were you?"

There's a pot of coffee on the burner, but even with the air on, the office is too hot for it. Caleb grabs a can of cola from the mini-refrigerator between their desks, pops the lid and drinks half of it in less than a minute. He doesn't want to talk about Emma or Ray or anything else, for that matter. He just wants to stand here and think about Jimi and how alluring she looked sitting on the curb in front of the Daily Sip Café.

"Fifth Amendment," Caleb finally says. "Ray followed her."

Dale shakes his head, then leans over and removes a fax from the machine next to his desk. "How long is this *thing* going to continue?"

"There's no thing."

Dale drops the fax on his desk and gives Caleb a look. *How long have we known each other?* High school, beer, poker, wives, Caleb's women. *Are we friends?* Caleb looks away, anxious to be doing something other than avoiding Dale's stare.

"I thought it was supposed to be a one-night stand," Dale says casually. "Like you always say, 'No strings attached.' That kind of thing."

For once, Caleb's grateful for the softness of Dale's voice. He pretends he can't hear him.

"Ray could come in here and wipe the floor with you, me, both of us," Dale continues.

Caleb laughs. "You don't really believe that."

Dale doesn't say anything because the truth is Ray wouldn't get past the front door if he showed up at their office. Neither Caleb nor Dale would let it happen. What Dale's really worried about is Caleb's history of settling disagreements—big or small—with his fists. An argument with Caleb is bound to turn into something else, and Dale thinks one more major fight will be the end of it. After that last incident with Sally and her boyfriend, the sheriff made it clear he can't look the other way anymore.

"I was caught off guard. That's the only reason Ray got the punch in."

Something in Dale's expression changes. Caleb doesn't like the look on his face.

"What?" says Caleb.

Dale stands up, walks over to the window behind him and looks out at the road.

"What."

"Sally called this morning."

"My wife called you?"

"She called Leigh."

Caleb feels a stab of discomfort. Sally hasn't contacted Leigh in months. Funny how you can be having a seminormal morning and then your best friend hits you with news about your disappeared wife making a comeback. It's hard for him to think about her because their marriage reminds him that he's a failure. At being a husband, at least. He wants to end that part of his life. But he can't do that as long as he's in Frenchman's Bend.

"What'd she say?"

"She wouldn't talk to me."

Figures. She can't only punish him for not being the husband she'd wanted. She also has to punish his friends.

"She had news about Morgan."

News about Morgan. The *very last* reason Caleb would have guessed for a phone call from Sally. Before Morgan went to jail,

Sally had stopped thinking of him as a human being, let alone her brother-in-law, when he turned up at the house unexpectedly and refused to explain why he'd left his job in Texas and needed a place to crash. During his six months living in one of the cottages, he'd nearly burned down the house twice because he had a habit of falling asleep on their sofa while smoking cigarettes. And he ran over Sally's dog, though he denied doing it. Not long after he left, Morgan was tracked down by Texas authorities and arrested for attacking and nearly killing two girls a year earlier outside a bar in Bonham. Morgan swore he was innocent.

"Why would Sally have news about my brother?"

"He's out," Dale says. "Sally ran into him in San Diego. I guess he went straight to California when he was released."

Caleb sits. He isn't sure he heard Dale correctly. "You're sure?"

"That's what she said."

Morgan's been released from prison and he didn't bother to call? It doesn't exactly *surprise* Caleb. Morgan hadn't kept in touch while he was in prison. But it's still a shock that he's out. Not only has the man been released, he bumped into Caleb's estranged wife in California. Is such a coincidence even possible?

"California," Caleb says.

"Yeah."

"I wouldn't have imagined him in California."

"Me neither."

"*She* always wanted to end up there."

"You'll hear from him now," Dale says. "Now that he knows Sally isn't here."

Caleb agrees. Morgan probably avoided coming to the Bend to avoid Sally.

"He was with a woman. Sally didn't have a chance to find out who she was."

Caleb chuckles humorlessly, still stuck on the idea of Morgan on the West Coast. And then, there's Sally. She made it to California. Not Hollywood, but close. "Did she say anything else?"

"No. You want to tell people about Morgan?"

By people, Dale means their friends Kennedy and Joseph. And yes, they should know Morgan's out, in case he does come back to the Bend and decides to pay them a visit. As much as Caleb would like to believe this isn't a big deal, two years in prison changes people. With Morgan, prison wouldn't have changed him for the better. He doesn't want Morgan to show up anywhere uninvited, but that's always been his modus operandi. He never calls before he comes. He never warns anyone before he starts trouble.

"Funny how there's no word from anyone," Caleb says, mostly to himself, "and then . . ."

"I know," Dale says. "Anything I can do?"

"Not unless you can tell me what Morgan's plans are."

Dale makes some calls while Caleb waits. For what, he doesn't know. For some lightning bolt to strike him, maybe, and miraculously point him in the right direction. But how does he know he isn't already heading in the right direction? All he has to do is glance at Dale. Instantly, Dale looks at him with encouragement. *Pick up the phone,* his look says. *Set up an appointment with one of the clients waiting for you to call.*

"It's after eleven," says Dale, "and Kennedy isn't here. He's supposed to start on the change order that came in yesterday. Did you call him?"

Caleb scratches his nose. Was *he* supposed to call Kennedy? "I was supposed to call him?"

"Yeah. We talked about it."

"I thought you were going to call him," Caleb says.

"No," Dale says real slow, "*you* were supposed to do it."

This isn't the first time Caleb has forgotten to call a subcontractor or a client about a job. Lately, he's been slacking. He takes long breaks, doesn't finish jobs, simply doesn't seem to care anymore. Why does he even bother coming in to the office if he doesn't want to work? Because he's *loyal,* that's why. To Dale and their business.

"If you want to talk, I'm here," Dale says. "Listening."

"Yeah?" Caleb says, distant.

"I don't want to see you piss your life away because you're bored or whatever. We both have a stake in this business. Let's not screw it up."

Caleb nods solemnly and a silence falls over the room. He wants Dale to ask. He's not the type to come out and say he drives to Darby for lunch to get away from what's familiar in Frenchman's Bend, even if it's just for ninety minutes. But Dale won't ask. He's been walking on eggshells since Sally left. Not that he'd rip Caleb's head off if Sally were still home, driving Caleb up a wall with all her demands, but he'd probably say something. He'd *ask* what's going on.

And what's going on is this: Caleb wants out. Out of New York. Out of this life. He wants to sell his half of the business and move as far away from the Bend as possible.

He sometimes wonders what things would be like if he hadn't started the business with Dale and hired their friends as subcontractors. If Morgan hadn't ended up in jail in Texas. If he had been able to control the love of fighting he's sure he picked up from the father he never met.

Despite what happened with Sally, and the occasional scuffle after too much to drink, he really doesn't fight as much as he used to. He works hard and minds his own business. Yet when he's in town with Dale, Kennedy or Joseph, people hesitate. Are they going to drink beer or break something? It doesn't matter that they're almost thirty, married, divorced and separated. They'll always be associated with Morgan, who stayed out raising hell long after they'd all gone home, looking for trouble, almost as if spending a night in jail was better than spending it in the same house with his little brother. Morgan and his fierce temper and his penchant for using tire irons to settle scores. Not much changes in a town like the Bend. Not the faces, at least. Not the memories. They'll always be remembered for what they once were. Four kids who looked up to a criminal. Four kids who mistook the criminal's rage for bravery. Sometimes, Caleb wished he were more like Morgan. Now he just wishes he knew him better when it mattered. Now he kind of wishes he could leave before Morgan makes it home.

The bad news is Caleb and Dale *need* the business. There are bills to pay, two loans and mortgages. They can't afford to lose clients. It's a hell of a time for Caleb to decide he wants to quit.

"Think you're up for taking a rush job that came in yesterday?" Dale asks him, hanging up the phone.

"How much of a rush?" Caleb asks.

"Five window replacements by Monday evening," Dale says.

"I'd have to work the weekend."

"Feel free to say no."

Caleb thinks about it. The only positive is that he'll be working the weekend after all and won't really be lying to Emma. "Yeah, okay," he says.

Dale nods. "I'll give you the address and you can head over after lunch."

Caleb leaves the office for Wheeler's Coffee Shop in Darby. He takes his time driving along Main Street, looking for someone he isn't sure he's looking for until he sees her. Lurking near the entrance of Fifth Amendment like a schoolgirl afraid to get caught sneaking into a bar. He stops and watches her.

When the John Lee Hooker CD he's listening to finishes, he switches to the radio. When he looks up, Jimi's no longer by the bar. She's walking toward the truck, moving slowly, trying to walk without the limp. He turns off the radio just as she stops at the passenger door. For some reason, a stupid one he's sure, he doesn't want her to know he listens to blues.

"Again," she says.

"It's a small town," he points out.

She looks up the street, then back at him, smiles. Each time he sees her, he's struck by how pretty she is. Especially when she smiles.

"Am I interrupting something?" she asks.

"No," he says, then adds, "Wanna join me?"

"Okay."

He's pleased she didn't say no and is willing to spend some time with him during his lunch break. He'd rather sit with her in his truck than go to Darby. He opens the passenger door and watches as she gets into his pickup carefully, her shirt rising up to expose her flat, muscular stomach. Just a flash of skin—*her* skin—and he's shifting, trying to be subtle about the need to adjust his jeans.

"Not wearing your leather pants," he says once she's settled.

"Jeans today," she responds. "I did laundry."

He gives her another quick once-over. She's casual. More like the local girls, but she still stands out. He prefers her in leather, but he likes her like this, too. He says, "I saw you lurking outside Fifth Amendment."

"I wasn't *lurking.*"

"Looking for someone?"

She shakes her head and he thinks she's embarrassed. And then he wonders if she has a reason to be. Maybe he caught her looking for him. He likes that idea.

"I was checking if Rose serves lunch," she says.

"You go to Dusty's for lunch," Caleb tells her. "Unless you mean a liquid lunch. Then you go to Rose."

"A bourbon is just what the doctor ordered," she says, and he can't tell if she means it.

"You like bourbon?"

"Not really," she admits, "but anything strong makes everything else a vague memory."

"Should I ask what you're trying to forget?"

She takes a pack of Marlboros from her back pocket and pulls out a cigarette. She lights up, takes a drag. "Depends."

"On what?"

"Well," she says, "it's . . ."

"A long fucking story?"

She looks over at him. She must hear the teasing in his voice, but her face is serious, so he can't tell if she remembers saying the same thing yesterday.

"Yes," she says, crumbling her Marlboro box, stuffing it in the front pocket of her jeans. He watches her lift her ass up from the seat to push the pack in further.

"I've got some time," he says, holding her gaze. She pretty much told him to fuck off when he asked her the same question yesterday. Now she seems to consider telling him what happened. This change of heart doesn't surprise him. Frenchman's Bend can be a lonely place for strangers, and loneliness is a death sentence for secrets.

"Why did you stop for me yesterday?" she asks, throwing him off a bit.

"Why did I stop?" he repeats.

"For me. Why'd you stop in Darby and give me a lift to Frenchman's Bend? Why'd you *help* me?"

He doesn't know how to answer her. When he passed her on the road outside Wheeler's he had the urge to stop. He knew no one would offer her a ride if they came up on her. Not Percy. Not a single one of them. Even without a bad ankle, a walk from Darby to the Bend is a bitch. He *felt* for her. But he can't bring himself to admit this.

"Because you needed a ride and I was going in that direction," he says.

"That simple?"

"Why can't it be?"

"Why are you different from everyone else?"

"Meaning?"

"You and I both know no one else would have offered me a ride."

"How did we get off the subject of you?"

"Why are we trying to get off the subject of *you*?" She raises one eyebrow, the right one. He's never known anyone who could do that. It makes him grin.

"Tell me," he says, "why did you stop for me last night? Why not leave me bleeding on the ground?"

"What comes around goes around," she says. "And who'd do that? Leave someone on the ground, bleeding?"

"I wasn't lying when I said no one here would've stopped for me."

They stare at each other for a minute.

"Okay," she says, "what did you want to know?"

Is this a trick question? All of a sudden he's blank. What *did* he want to know? He doesn't even remember what they were talking about before they got to this point.

"What happened to your bike?" he asks.

She doesn't blink. "It was stolen."

"By the guy who beat you up?"

"You're quick."

So, that's it. She was mugged. He'd wanted the tale of her bruises to be more dramatic. "That sucks," he says.

She shrugs, stares straight ahead, out the front window of his truck.

"You know bikes?" she asks after a minute.

"You can say that."

She looks at him blankly.

"I have a Harley," he tells her. Used. Very used. But he's proud of it, even though it's been collecting dust. He doesn't mention that to her. And he doesn't mention he's a part-time mechanic, either, that he spends every weekend messing with motorcycles. The city girls he meets think mechanics are losers. They think he's working on bikes until something better comes along. Jimi's different, but it's always better to hold a few things back until he's sure. "You?"

"A BMW K 1200?"

Dale and Kennedy would scoff. They only ride American. But Caleb wants a BMW. And no matter what Dale and Kennedy say, he knows they want one, too. They're sleek, impressive. Last year, Caleb promised himself a K 1200 for his thirtieth birthday. But thirty's just around the corner and he still can't afford a $20,000 motorcycle.

"No wonder you're so blue," he says.

"Maybe it was a mistake to ride it from Los Angeles," she muses.

Caleb pauses. "You rode a K 1200 from California alone?"

She nods.

"No offense, but of course it was stolen." He shakes his head. "A girl riding a K 1200 cross-country. Alone."

Jimi looks offended. "A *woman* should be able to travel in America without being attacked."

"I agree. But you could be the poster girl for why she can't."

She bites her lip. After some silence she says, "I don't regret the trip."

It's the perfect time to ask about that trip and why she ended up here, and where she's going. But Caleb's concentrating on the twinge of jealousy he feels. He's glad he didn't mention he's a mechanic, that he loves bikes and has been riding used ones since he was seventeen. Because she's a spoiled, rich girl. Only a spoiled, rich girl would believe she could ride an expensive bike like a BMW across this country, *any* country, alone. Her daddy probably gave her that bike. Her daddy made her believe she had every right to ride a K 1200 cross-country without someone taking it from her.

He shakes his head again. His uncle used to say that about city folk: they live in caves. They think they're worldly. They think they know everything about everyone in the universe. They think they're better than the rest of us. And the minute they leave the city, they're stupid and vulnerable like everyone else. Caleb knew there had to be something untrue about Jimi. She's seen more good than bad; had more days with money than without. He's got nothing against that. He just doesn't want to talk to her about what matters to him anymore. She's like the rest of the girls who come in from the city, carrying torches for boys on iron. The minute he sticks a hand down the front of their panties they go rigid. Because the boy on iron is real, not a silly, little-girl fantasy.

"I thought about buying a Harley," says Jimi. "Some of them are terrific looking." She stares at him like she expects a big reaction. He doesn't think she's said anything that merits one. She takes another drag from her cigarette. Long and slow.

She turns her head slightly to blow the smoke out the window. "I saved hard for that bike. I'd put money aside for my rent and my BMW. I went without everything else. You know how that is?"

It's not an assumption. It's an actual question. Caleb nods. "Sure, I know how that is."

"Then you know what it's like when you want something so bad and it feels like you'll never get it."

"More times than I can count," he says.

"That's how it was for me," says Jimi. "I thought I'd never be able to afford it. And then I had the money, and I owned it. And now it's gone." She tosses her cigarette out the window. "I shot Brad Pitt for that fucking motorcycle."

"What?"

She shakes her head. "Nothing. I feel kind of guilty, being so upset about it. People, every day, lose so much more. But I'm angry. It was mine. I worked for it. You know?"

"Oh, yeah. I know."

She seems to catch herself, glancing at Caleb with a self-conscious smile.

He had her all figured out a minute ago. He wasn't expecting this. To hear that she'd worked for the money to buy the K 1200. To hear that she'd saved for it, got it, and then lost it. He was wrong about her, and being wrong about her is a welcome surprise.

He says, "My brother crashed my first motorcycle."

"You're kidding."

He shakes his head. "I was crushed."

"How old were you?"

"Nineteen. He's older."

"Did he ever pay you back?"

"Morgan? No."

"Then he owes you."

"He owes me a hell of a lot more than a bike."

The bitterness in his voice is raw and he wishes he could take back the inadvertent confession as soon as it's out of his mouth. The look on Jimi's face tells him she wishes he could take it back, too. But she recovers quickly and looks as if she'd listen if he'd talk to her. He tries to appear relaxed, but his shoulders are tense and his neck is stiff. He shrugs like it's no big deal.

"I'm not trying to one-up you," he says.

"I didn't think you were." Her voice is quiet. She's back to looking like she wants to be anywhere but inside his pickup truck. He can't blame her. They sit in awkward silence for a while and the ridiculousness of the moment hits him. He wants to laugh. But *she* starts laughing. Not raucous laughter, intended to humiliate him. Her laughter is subdued, polite. She gives him a sidelong glance. He shakes his head and finally allows his own laughter to spill out.

"Was that funny?" she asks after a minute.

"No," he says.

They hold each other's gaze. It's been a long time since he's talked to a woman. Just talked. And her sitting here, next to him, he wonders what it would be like to seduce her. He shifts a little uncomfortably.

"You okay?" she asks.

He wants to have sex with her. Not at this very moment, but eventually. Sometime soon. Tonight. Tomorrow.

"Yeah," he says.

"Tired?"

"Not exactly tired."

"Bored?"

"Yeah," he says. "Bored, I guess."

He's wanted to sleep with her since he first saw her in Darby yesterday, but he hadn't known just how much until she started laughing. But something tells him Jimi isn't the type of girl to sleep with a guy she just met. Her clothes and her hair and her attitude scream *uninhibited,* but he's deciding her appearance has little to do with who she really is.

And how messed up is that? That he can tell. That he's even thinking about it. Caleb doesn't think about these things. Work them out in his head like some kind of math problem. When he wants a girl, he goes for her, and doesn't worry about what she'll think of him if he pushes too soon. He doesn't want to push Jimi. And the fact that he doesn't want to push her alarms him so much he thinks he probably shouldn't pursue her at all.

"I actually have to go in a minute," he says. He almost reaches over to push the lock of pink hair out of her eye, as if he's close to her. As if he has a right to. As if he hasn't just decided to leave her alone.

"Are we still on for tonight?" she asks.

He's wondering what she'll do if he kisses her. And then he realizes what she just asked. It's Friday night. He has a date with Dale at Fifth Amendment for a sympathy drink. "Tonight?"

"You invited me for a drink."

Did he? Yes. This morning. Outside the Daily Sip. That was before he knew he had to work all weekend. *That was before this.*

"Something came up," he says. "I have to make a run into another town for supplies. Leave now, return later, that kind of thing."

She tilts her head and looks amused. "You aren't afraid to be seen with me, are you?"

"I'm being seen with you right now," he points out.

"Yes, but—" She looks around. "This doesn't count. The streets are empty."

He shrugs. "Technicality. Anyway, you should be more worried about being seen with *me.*"

She turns in her seat and moves a little closer to him, as if he's said something she's been waiting to hear. "Why?"

He moves a little closer to her, too. "I have a bit of a reputation."

She nods and he blushes as her eyes move boldly over his face, his head, his tattoo. "I don't care about small-town gossip," she says. "I don't live here."

"But if you did live here, you would?"

"It's usually hearsay. Untrue."

"What if it isn't?"

She sighs. "So you and me not having a drink tonight is just about something coming up at the last minute?"

He can't tell her the truth. Because he doesn't want to explain why some people in the Bend don't like him. That the dislike goes way back to when he was a teen, selfish and dangerous. And how that dislike might be transferred to her. Guilt by association. Being acquainted with him could make the time she spends in the Bend unpleasant.

And he *won't* explain that he all of a sudden doesn't only want to fuck her. He wants to spend the night with her. He never spends the entire night with the girls he has sex with. He has no idea why Jimi's different. She just is. She's not like Sally or any other girl in the Bend. He likes talking to her. He likes her being near.

"So you'd still be interested in having a drink with me if you lived here?" he asks.

"Yes. Unless you tell me black women and white men having a drink at a bar together would be a problem. I wouldn't want to come home to a cross burning on my front lawn." She pauses. "I see. *You* live here."

No. She doesn't see. He doesn't fear what she thinks he does.

"We don't burn crosses in the Bend," he says. "It's not that kind of town."

"You can't know what people would do if they've never been tested," she challenges.

"I do," he says, stubbornly. "I know."

"Fine." She gives up. "Frenchman's Bend is not *that* kind of town. Something just came up."

She's back to looking amused, but he can tell by the tone of her voice that she doesn't believe him. And he hates that she thinks he won't have a drink with her because he's worried what people will do after a white man has a drink with a black woman in Fifth Amendment. *He hates that he hates what she's thinking.*

"People look at women harder when they're with me, that's all. I'm trying to save you some grief."

Jimi smirks. "Look at me now. You're a little too late for that."

"Hey."

Caleb and Jimi jump. Kennedy is standing by the passenger door, his icy blue eyes intent on Jimi. His hair, which he usually wears pulled back into a ponytail, is loose so his blond locks fall forward, nearly covering his face. Still, Caleb sees Kennedy take in Jimi's bruises before flashing Caleb an inquisitive look.

"This is Jimi," Caleb says, clearing his throat.

Kennedy and Jimi eye each other suspiciously. Jimi nods

first, smiles a little. Kennedy pushes some hair out of his face and holds up a hand for her to shake through the window.

"Kennedy," he says. They shake hands. "Firm grip."

Jimi stares at Kennedy. His voice is deep and Caleb knows she's trying to reconcile the voice with the person. Kennedy has always looked like a girl and sounded like a man. It doesn't cross her mind to be afraid of him. But how could she know there was a time when Kennedy would put a girl's head through a window if she stared at him too long? Even so, she should see something in his face, in his eyes, that tells her to look away from him, that something about Kennedy is a little bit off. Is she missing that instinct, or is she just fearless? He'd sensed fearlessness when he first saw her in Darby and it had impressed him. It still does.

"Kennedy's a good friend," Caleb tells Jimi.

"Why aren't you at work?" Kennedy asks.

"I'm on my lunch break," says Caleb.

Kennedy checks his watch, looks up to meet Jimi's gaze for a second, then frowns at Caleb. "What the fuck happened to your eye?" he asks slowly, then glances at Jimi again. "Excuse my language."

"Got into something last night," Caleb says.

Kennedy stares at Caleb for a minute. "Ray did that?"

"He caught me off guard." Caleb sounds defensive.

Kennedy looks at Jimi again, at the bruises on her face and arms. He remains expressionless as he turns his attention back to Caleb. "I'm heading over to the office. Are you going to be around tonight?"

"Why?"

"I want you to look at my bike. I rode her two days ago and everything was fine. I start her up today, pull the clutch, shift into first and she jerks and stalls. My truck's dead, too. I had to walk."

"I just got a rush job from Dale," Caleb says uncomfortably, aware that Jimi's watching him.

"You'll be at Joseph's tomorrow." Kennedy sounds impatient. "I'll bring the bike by after I get my truck looked at. All this shit's costing me a fortune."

"Let's talk about it later."

"When?"

*"Later."*

Kennedy hesitates. He's probably thinking about decking Caleb for snapping at him.

"Why don't you get us a table at Dusty's?" Caleb suggests, just to end the conversation. Kennedy doesn't wait inside restaurants or bars alone anymore. Caleb wouldn't ask him to go into Dusty's on his own unless he had to handle something. "I'll be five more minutes."

Kennedy stares at Caleb, asking whether or not Caleb's in trouble. Caleb shakes his head and Kennedy's eyes wander toward Jimi, curious.

"I'll catch you later," Kennedy says.

Once he's gone, Caleb expects Jimi to ask about him. She doesn't.

"My lunch break is officially over," he says.

She raises that one eyebrow. "Are you asking me to get out?"

He smiles. "Putting it delicately."

"Okay," she says. "Have fun picking up your supplies tonight."

"Listen." He sits up and they both know there isn't anything he wants her to listen to. He leans in for a kiss, but she pulls back. She says his name like a warning, like she thinks she can take him if she has to. Caleb's always been good at taking no for an answer, moving on, not thinking about being turned down. But that doesn't stop him from being embarrassed. He thought she wanted him as much as he wants her. If not, why did she keep hounding him about the drink?

He starts the truck's ignition out of habit.

"I'm not looking for a love interest," she says softly.

He turns the ignition off. Where's he going with her in the truck?

"I wasn't offering love," he tells her.

"Oh."

He glances at her to see if she looks disappointed. He can't tell. He'd have to look a little longer. But he doesn't want her to know he's curious. It's like high school right inside his pickup truck, a place he'd rather not revisit.

"You caught me off guard," she explains.

"You would have kissed me if you had a warning?"

She looks surprised by his question. He really wants an answer. But she opens the passenger door and drops out of the truck haphazardly. He stops himself from reaching out in a panic to prevent a fall. He doesn't want her to think he cares. Trying to kiss her was a mistake. A dumb macho instinct. There'd be no point to having her. She's just some girl he gave a ride to; she's planning to leave the Bend any minute. And he doesn't want her to become a habit. When he looks at her, she's still standing on the sidewalk, watching him.

"Maybe," she says. "If I'd had a warning. I don't like surprises."

Before he can think better of it, he smiles, slides over to the passenger seat and hangs out the window. "I should be back in town by eight."

"What happened to saving me some grief?"

Caleb shrugs. "We'll chance it."

Jimi nods, but doesn't say she'll meet him. She taps his truck lightly. "I knew this thing didn't suit you. You belong on a bike."

Caleb's smile widens and he slides back over to the wheel, starts the engine again and drives off. In his rearview mirror he watches her stand there until she's just a speck, until she's gone.

# Six

A week before she left Los Angeles, Jimi had everything. An exciting job, a Nikon with a 1500mm lens, a motorcycle and money. Jimi made a lot of money. She also had a company car. A black SUV with tinted windows, a police scanner and speakerphone. Her "informant fund" had been raised from Toole Lab's standard annual sum of $50,000 to $175,000 after only three months of work. But more important than all of that, Jimi rarely thought about New York City.

When she decided to leave Brooklyn a year earlier, she was seeking a refuge. She thought she'd like small-town life—the quiet and complacency. She applied for photography jobs at magazines and newspapers in Wyoming, Montana and the Dakotas. States she had romantic ideas about because she loves mountains, moose and blue sky—things that aren't readily accessible to a woman who only knows how to live in a city.

She received apologetic letters from most of the places she contacted, or no response at all. She stopped dreaming about a refuge. She just wanted to leave New York. Her friend Richard put her in touch with Russ at Toole Lab in California. Russ was looking for a new photographer, preferably someone who could drive a big car fast. He didn't ask about her experience.

He only cared that she was interested. He paid for her plane ticket to L.A. and met her at the airport.

Three months later Jimi could afford her own Nikon and motorcycle. Her BlackBerry was packed with enviable sources. No one at Toole Lab brought in as much income as Jimi. Because Jimi loved the *chase.* It was the chase that brought on the rush, the feeling that started in the pit of her stomach and rolled through her veins at warp speed. Jimi was an unsympathetic, reckless paparazza. She got the pictures that would make the most money because she was fast and relentless. And Russ sold them without remorse. Life had never been as carefree and careless. In the back of her mind, she knew there would be consequences.

The week before she left Los Angeles, she went after the ultimate photo. A shot of a Double A–list couple's nine-day-old son. Not one reputable or disreputable trade in the industry could score a picture and the couple wasn't offering anything. Rumor had it that a certain British tabloid would bid as high as one million dollars for a picture. And here was Jimi with an exclusive tip she'd paid twenty thousand dollars for.

People will do anything for money. Even sell the exact location of an in-law's newborn.

Being a paparazza was sometimes like being a private investigator. Finding the perfect informant and paying the right price. Piecing together what's true, and reading people well enough to know how heavily she could rely on them. This particular source had never disappointed her. The woman's sole demands were that Jimi never share her name with anyone, not even Russ, and all monetary transactions be made through a bank in Switzerland, to an account the woman's husband didn't know about.

And one evening, thanks to the informant, Jimi was in a tree on the grounds of a rehab center called Tiny Gardens, where rich drug addicts give birth to babies who need detox, snapping pictures of a famous young mother strolling in the garden, holding her newborn son. Every other photographer Jimi knew was either camped out in front of the A-list couple's mansion or stationed in front of the various hospitals the actress had reportedly given birth in. The misinformation had nearly been flawless.

Jimi had taken two rolls of film before a nurse spotted her. No guard came out to shake her from the tree; no police officer appeared to arrest her. The nurse whisked the startled actress and her son inside the hospital and Jimi was on her motorcycle by the time the black Lincoln Town Car came roaring out of the hospital garage. Ten minutes later, Jimi was crossing into oncoming traffic, racing through lights, pursuing a second Lincoln Town Car in a high-speed chase all the way to Sunset Boulevard.

On Sunset, the driver ran a red light to avoid Jimi's camera, expertly retrieved from a bag attached to the back of her bike. The driver slammed into a limousine, halting traffic, wreaking havoc, and Jimi hesitated for just a moment before taking off, making her way back to the office.

It was Russ's idea for Jimi to leave Los Angeles for a couple of weeks to avoid an arrest or a lawsuit. Not that anyone had seen her. She'd covered her license plate with black cloth and was wearing a helmet. Still, you can never be too careful. No one had been severely injured. In fact, after a full day of outraged coverage and the requisite vitriol toward paparazzi and calls for tougher laws, some reporters were starting to ask why the actress had been toting her infant around in a speeding car. Russ heard a tabloid was going to focus on a different angle altogether: the young star's rumored drug addiction. It would all die down to nothing in a few days and Russ would put Jimi's pictures on the market as exclusives, letting only Toole Lab's most trusted connections in on an auction. For Russ it was business as usual. But something in Jimi had changed. She didn't want to do it anymore. There was no question she was leaving Los Angeles, *this life,* for good.

Her colleague, Dan, suggested she take the northern route back to New York, avoiding major interstates to ride the "Blue Highways." Dan swore there was no other way to ride a motorcycle to the East Coast. Glacier National Park in Montana, Grand Teton National Park in Wyoming and Yellowstone had always been on Jimi's list of places to see in the world. She looked forward to riding through Idaho, Montana, Wyoming and the Dakotas. Through small towns her colleague called the "forgotten, idyllic, beautiful bits of America." Towns where no one locked their front door. He said the people he'd encountered when he rode his bike from Connecticut to Los Angeles six months earlier were either curious or indifferent to his presence, but always kind. He'd never felt unsafe. Jimi still idealized small-town life after a year in L.A. She hadn't abandoned her initial wish to settle somewhere quiet.

But the trip wasn't what she had expected.

The American landscape was beautiful. More glorious than she had ever imagined. The roads were wonderfully dangerous and curvy; the moose she spied were as majestic up close as they were in pictures. There was something special about these remote places so few people bothered to pass through. And when Jimi spent the night in some of these forgotten towns, she learned quickly that everyone couldn't settle in an idyllic, beautiful town in America because it wouldn't be an idyllic, beautiful town for everyone. She was reminded that leaving one's city in America is like leaving one's country. Things change: speed limits, gun laws, attitudes. People stared. And it wasn't the kind of staring small-town folks do when a woman in leather hops off a motorcycle and stops in the local diner for supper. The stares Jimi received were meant to send a message and she understood it. Never in her life had she felt as unprotected as she did when she was riding those roads. People made her feel like a foreigner in her own country.

She called Troy. Told him she was on vacation and wanted to visit him in the country. She didn't tell him she was *lost* and seeking him out because he's chosen to spend his summers in a small town. She wants to know if he understands something that she doesn't. He's the person who will clue her in without judging her ignorance.

But then there was the business in Pennsylvania, which she hasn't completely processed yet. She'd offered a woman at a gas station one hundred dollars for a ride. The woman agreed to take her as far as she could take her, which ended up being Darby once the pit bull in the backseat started getting cranky.

A few more days and she'll be walking like a normal person again; her bruises may even be gone. As much as she desires the kind of comfort an older brother can give, she can't go there yet. She isn't ready. Not to give up the freedom she worked so hard to attain again. Not yet. Just a few more days to let everything that happened these last three weeks settle around her. She can handle a few more days of being an outsider; a few more days of feeling alone, unsafe and unprotected; a few more cranky, disapproving faces glaring in her direction.

So Caleb's smiling face is a pleasure when he walks into Fifth Amendment Bar at eight-fifteen Friday evening. She's relieved to see him. The relief surprises her. She'd thought seriously about not coming out tonight. She felt strange about their almost-kiss this afternoon, not to mention blurting out that she wasn't looking for a love interest. She'd turned down something he wasn't trying to give her. And then she figured he wouldn't show up or that he'd show up with a group of rowdy friends. Or they wouldn't have anything to say to each other even if he did come alone.

But she'd started to miss human contact while she was lying on the bed in her room. And she'd started to feel sorry for herself. Every sound outside her door, every tiny noise, reminded her how vulnerable she is when she sleeps alone. She decided she'd rather sit at a bar with a boy than lie in a bed in a room in this small town in rural New York.

Rose, the bartender, stands up from her stool underneath the bar's mounted television as soon as she sees Caleb. "Gift from Ray?" she asks, indicating Caleb's black eye.

Caleb doesn't answer. His eyes are on Jimi as he walks toward her. She smiles; his smile widens. Rose sets a shot glass on the bar, a couple of seats away from where Jimi's sitting, and fills it with bourbon. Caleb stops in front of the shot, drinks it.

"Thanks," he says. "I'll have my usual. And get Jimi another of whatever she's having."

Rose pauses to watch Caleb take a seat next to Jimi.

"What is that?" Caleb asks, pointing at Jimi's drink. "Soda?"

"Yes," Jimi says.

"You want a beer? Let me buy you a beer."

Jimi hasn't had a drink with anyone who wasn't a colleague or an informant in over a year. Jimi pays. This is new. She thanks Caleb and assures him another ginger ale is what she prefers.

Rose delivers a pint of beer and another ginger ale, and

stares at them. "Were they giving away black eyes on special or something?"

Caleb cuts his eyes at her. It doesn't seem to bother Rose.

"I thought you were smarter than that," she continues.

"Why don't you take your seat, old woman." Caleb's tone is playful. "Last I heard, you food-and-beverage types work for tips."

Rose grins. "I own the place," she says, winking at Jimi. "Tip me or not, your money still goes in my pocket."

Jimi laughs. She guesses Caleb and Rose banter like this often. Their exchange doesn't sound rehearsed, but it does sound familiar. Rose pinches Caleb's chin then moves to the opposite end of the bar to perch on her stool. FOX News is on mute. They all stare at the screen. Caleb and Jimi drink in silence.

After a while, Jimi pulls out a pack of cigarettes, wondering about the things she has in common with this guy besides a black eye and, possibly, loneliness. And though he seems to get along with the bartender, she still gets a sense of *otherness* surrounding him. She takes a cigarette, lights it and smokes. Rose turns to look at her and Jimi remembers the no-smoking law in New York State. She looks up and down the bar for an ashtray. Rose brings her a plate.

"Where are you from?" Caleb asks, breaking the silence.

"Brooklyn," she says. "I was in Los Angeles for a while."

"That's where you're coming from."

She nods.

"That must have been some trip," he says, taking a drink.

"It was."

"I've always wanted to do a trip like that. Since I was about seventeen, I think."

"What stopped you?"

"I'm just a small-town boy, I guess."

Jimi smiles. "That's all?"

"Yeah. I'm not so complicated."

"I don't believe that."

"You don't have to."

Jimi flushes. It's true—sometimes a cigar is just a cigar. How many people have annoyed her by trying to analyze why she's added the pink strand to her hair? Why does it have to mean something? She just likes it. Oddly, she thinks of Caleb's friend Kennedy, and the way he'd looked at her face earlier and dismissed her. Maybe he *hadn't* dismissed her; maybe he'd just accepted what he saw. And thinking of Kennedy brings back something he said to Caleb before he left.

"Are you a mechanic?" she asks.

Caleb hesitates. "No."

"You work on bikes, though. Kennedy asked you to look at his."

"I work on them occasionally. Why?"

Jimi's surprised by how defensive he sounds. "No reason. I think it's fascinating. I love motorcycles, so I respect you for working on them. It must be a cool job."

His scowl disappears. "It's not my job. It's a side thing."

"What is your job?"

"I'm a contractor. I own a business with my friend Dale. Kennedy works for us."

"That explains why you had to pick up supplies tonight."

"It's just us," he says, "so we have to do a lot of stuff like that after hours."

"Do you like it?"

"I used to. I'm a hands-on kind of guy," he says with a smile. "Out of high school I wanted to work on bikes, but I can't make a living that way around here. So Dale and I decided we could do the next best thing and work on houses for a few years." He motions to Rose. When she comes over, he orders another beer. Jimi doesn't want anything. "See?" he says. "Not so complicated."

She nods.

"You?" he says.

It takes her a while to answer. She doesn't want to talk about her work. He'll think less of her. She'd started experiencing twinges of guilt a couple of months before the accident. With each new stakeout the feeling that she was doing something wrong worsened. She'd often wake up with a crushing feeling in her chest, a feeling akin to what she thinks a mild heart attack would feel like.

"Not much anymore," she says.

He lets that go. Rose brings over his beer.

"Brooklyn, huh?" he says.

She nods. "Born and raised."

He looks around the bar. It's still early on a Friday night. Hardly anyone around. He stands up, stretches, shirt rising so she can catch a glimpse of a beautifully cut belly. *Nice,* she thinks, and when she looks at him he's grinning as if he heard her.

"Come here," he says and heads over to the pool table. He gathers the balls, then takes a cue stick from the rack against the wall. "You playing?" he asks after a minute. "Thirty bucks a game."

She doesn't play any game for money and she sucks at pool, in particular. "No, thanks."

"I'll go easy on you," he insists.

"I don't know how."

He's surprised. This is an alien concept to him: someone who doesn't know how to play pool. "I'll show you."

She wants to decline again, but she thinks he'll keep insisting, drawing more attention to them. She slips off the stool, leaving her drink.

"You're a brave man," she says when she reaches him. He hands her his cue stick, and for twenty minutes he tries to teach her how to play pool. Once, an old boyfriend tried to teach her how to play golf. He yelled at her every time she held the golf club incorrectly. Caleb isn't impatient. He laughs when he realizes she's a terrible pool player, but he doesn't give up on her. He tells her the first rule of the game is to have fun.

"Well, that's the first rule of the game when you play with me," he clarifies.

Three people enter the bar. A man nods at her. A woman and another man frown at them. Without noticing, Caleb stands behind Jimi, the front of his body close to the back of hers. She tunes out the frowning couple and focuses on his arms encircling her. She knows this stance from movies. It's usually a man trying to find an excuse to get close to a woman, to touch her. Jimi takes a breath. He has strong arms; she has a sudden desire to hug him.

"Are you paying attention?" he asks, his mouth close to her ear.

"Trying," she says.

His laugh is a low rumble against her neck. This isn't exactly comfort, but she reacts, moving deeper into his embrace. Caleb takes the movement as an invitation and slides a hand over her waist, over her stomach; his fingers play at the edge of her shirt. "I'm warning you before I kiss you," he whispers.

She's going to let him, and then she remembers where she is and pushes away gently. "Not a good idea."

He stops stroking her stomach, but doesn't budge. "Why not?"

Away from him, but still feeling his breath on her neck, she braces against the pool table and looks around. Rose is watching from behind the bar; her face is unreadable. The couple that just walked in is looking at them as well.

"People are staring," she says.

"Of course they are. You're with me."

"So this is only about you."

"I told you people would look at you harder when you're with me," he says. "And you have pink hair."

The staring isn't about her hair. She's worn colored strands for years, knows the difference. People who think she worships Satan look frightened, threatened or amused. Never hostile or offended. And this staring, now, is not only about Caleb and his reputation.

Caleb presses against her before he moves away, letting her know he wants her. He leans on the pool table, takes the cue stick from her hand and stares at her. "I thought you don't care about small-town gossip."

"Usually I don't."

"So it's just us, in the Bend—" He looks directly at the couple at the bar as if he was aware of them all along. They look away. The man picks up his drink, motions for the woman to follow him to the back room. "We make you nervous."

"Rural America in general."

"You're prejudiced against rural America." He tsks. "We're not more dangerous than your big cities."

"Just scarier," Jimi says. "*Your* neighbor is more likely to bury people in his backyard than mine."

Caleb's face is grim. "You don't know shit about small towns."

"And you don't know shit about big cities."

"Okay." He holds up his hands. "You win. You aren't safe in Frenchman's Bend. Everyone looking at you is out to get you."

"Hey," she says, annoyed, "I don't give a damn what these people look at, talk about, whatever."

"You keep saying that, which leads me to believe you do give a damn."

In L.A., when she was out with Russ, people stared. She's black; Russ is white. Even in big cities some people hate to see that. But in the city, if someone harassed them, the police would be on their side. In Frenchman's Bend, how does she know whose side the small-town sheriff would be on? Who would he choose? An outsider or a local he's known since childhood?

"I'm not sure who's on my side here," she admits.

"I'm on your side," he says and walks away from her, back to the bar.

Jimi follows him. "Why?" she asks when she sits.

He shrugs, not looking at her. "I don't know. I just am. Just want to be. Why do you ask so many questions?"

"Because."

"Maybe that's your problem."

"I've always wondered what my problem is," she says sarcastically. "Maybe you're right."

She watches him finish his second beer faster than the first. He grabs on to the edge of the bar and pushes his stool backward.

"I'm gonna go," he says abruptly.

Jimi thinks he's joking, and then he stands up.

"You're really going?"

He nods and Jimi wishes she'd let him kiss her. Wishes she hadn't engaged him in a debate. She doesn't want to be alone again. She wants company. *His* company. She's used to nights that don't end until morning and being surrounded by people who think sleep is for pussies. Looking around she knows the bar will be full in an hour and she no longer cares if people stare. Caleb reminds her she should be *curious*, not wary. She's now curious about Friday night in a bar in Frenchman's Bend. Honestly, when she ignores her prejudices, she realizes she actually likes being in this bar, especially with a local. There's nothing like being someplace new with someone who lives there. And Caleb's relaxed, easy on the eyes, unaffected. He makes her feel interesting.

"Hey," she calls after him.

He stops at the door and turns around. He waits but she doesn't say anything, so he comes back, leans into her.

"Yeah?" His voice is gruff in her ear.

Jimi doesn't flinch, though she thinks he wants her to. He doesn't realize that more than menacing, he's tentative, as if she's a deer about to bolt, and this calls into question every dangerous vibe he's trying to project. She smirks.

"It's Friday," she says.

He chuckles, continues to lean into her.

"Are you sure you don't want to have another drink?" she asks. "I'm buying."

"Saturday mornings are busy."

"Okay," she says, and then he pushes away from her, smiling a little. She lifts her hand in a stiff wave, dismissing him, but he leaves without turning back. She feels dejected. Which is silly. He isn't even her type. Not that she ever really had a *type*. She knows she wouldn't look at him twice on her own territory. She prefers her men be a little less rugged.

When she turns back to the bar, Rose is staring at her.

"You aren't from around here," she says after a moment.

"Well . . . no," says Jimi, "I thought that was obvious."

"Now it is." Rose shakes her head and laughs. Jimi wants to ask her what she means by that: that shake of her head and that laugh. But Rose is already at the other end of the bar, eyes on the television set above her head.

Jimi sits a while longer, stirring the ice in her glass, watching it melt.

She can't sleep. Out of habit she purchased three tabloid newspapers and three entertainment magazines from the newsstand at the front desk. Picking out her colleagues' photos, as well as her own, usually helps take her mind off of the unpleasant things she tries not to remember. She's already picked out two of the last twenty-five photos she sold before she left Los Angeles. One of an actress shopping at Kitson's without wearing makeup; one of an actor having lunch with his girlfriend at the Ivy.

Her cellular phone rings. She checks the name on the phone's screen and isn't surprised to see "Unknown Caller." Russ. It's 1:30 AM in Los Angeles and he's working. Russ always had perfect timing.

"It's Jimi" she answers.

"Well, halle-fuckin'-lujah," Russ bellows. "It's about time you answered your phone. Where in the *hell* are you?"

"Hey, Russ," Jimi says. "I'm having a hard time getting a signal here."

"No kidding. I've been trying to reach you for *days.* When I get through, your voice mail's full. Where are you? Pacific? Mountain? Central? Eastern?"

She doesn't tell him.

"I want to see you," he says. He knows her well. He knows he can't trick her into telling him where she is if she doesn't want him to know. "So if you're in Vegas or . . . or fuckin' Frisco, would you get on your bike and come back? We have to talk."

Before she left L.A. she'd asked Dan not to tell Russ that she was heading to the East Coast. She didn't tell anyone she was quitting. They all think she's on vacation. "I don't want to talk right now."

"Where are you staying?" Russ asks. "Nice hotel?"

"An inn."

"You hate inns." There's a brief silence. "Are you okay?"

She imagines his pretty eyes twitching the way they always twitch when he's anxious. He's pacing. She can hear street traffic, so he's definitely on a stakeout, waiting for some superstar to finish drinking and dancing in the latest hot club.

"I can't see you right now," she tells him.

"Tell me where you are and I'll come to you. New York? They're filming a couple of hot movies in New York right now. I can put the trip on the expense account and get a couple of good pictures out of it."

Jimi has left this pushiness behind. Russ doesn't understand that he's no longer part of her life. Why should he? In L.A. they got along. They worked well together. They'd had sex once, assuming their mutual craziness on the streets would translate into thunder in the bedroom. It had not. Luckily, the misstep hadn't affected their working relationship. People often joked that they were like a husband and wife who'd had an amicable divorce. They've only known each other for a little over a year, but they get along like they've known each other forever. She likes Russ. Bad sex didn't make him less compatible. His energy was enticing. It fueled everyone at 2 AM. He knew how to keep his photographers going. Coffee and Russ. No problem. There were times she didn't get to bed until noon.

She takes a deep breath to calm herself.

"Russ." Her voice is gentle. "I really have to go. I promise I'll call you in a couple of days."

"*Fuck off, man!*" This is not directed at her. On the other end of the phone there's a commotion. Someone's probably trying to take Russ's camera before his target exits the club. Jimi can feel the excitement vibrating through the phone as she listens to the tussle. Russ is cursing, laughing, being jostled. Momentarily, she wants to be there. She misses the fighting, arguing, flashing lights and laughter. She misses the enormous adrenaline rush that came with every outing.

Jimi liked L.A. nightlife, though she'd never really been a part of it. She was always on the outside. With a camera. She liked the evening stakeouts outside nightclubs. Passersby would sometimes stop to ask her questions. She would always tell people what she was doing and most of the time they wished her luck.

There was no telling what a celebrity would do when they walked out of a club and she started shooting. Their drunken rage didn't scare her. She laughed at them. Their outrage fueled her. She feels that rush now, briefly. She wishes she had a place to store all the energy. She'd never thought leaving her work would be like going cold turkey.

She's about to press "End" and turn off her cellular phone, to get away from the feeling, when Russ says, "Don't hang up. Hold on a minute. Hold on."

"I really do have to go," she insists.

"I owe you money," he says, seriously.

"Put it in my account."

"Yeah, yeah." He's starting to sound annoyed. "That's not the point I'm making."

The thing is, Jimi couldn't tell Russ how much the job was eating away at her. Russ would write her feelings off. What other people think about what they do is irrelevant. It was an easy attitude to adopt in Los Angeles. In L.A. she'd become someone she wouldn't want to know in Manhattan. People weren't important to her unless they were famous or knew someone who was.

"What's your point, then?"

"I sold the pictures," he says. "Eighteen of them."

Jimi holds her breath and lets it go after a minute. "How much?" she finally asks.

It takes him a minute. "Three million."

"What?"

"Yeah," he says, "you heard me."

"Holy shit."

Russ whoops. "*Three fuckin' million.* You got the only shots."

Jimi looks around the room, afraid to scream or laugh or cry. She doesn't know what she feels. Three million dollars for eighteen pictures of a drug-addicted celebrity and her baby. She'd never imagined such a sum.

"What about . . . ?"

"No one gives a shit about the accident," he cuts her off. "It's a dead issue. They're focusing on the drug-addiction angle. I told you."

Jimi breathes deeply. "Isn't this just a little bit insane?"

"*Listen to me.*" Russ makes this sound urgent. "You *did not* do anything wrong. They crashed because her driver was speeding. You earned this. So come home and get your money. I'm not asking for something you can't give me."

But he *is* asking for something she can't give. He just doesn't know it. He doesn't know her. He can't fathom how guilty she feels.

"Russ," she says. "Don't. Just deposit the money in my account."

"I will, but you gotta call me," he says, and she doesn't say anything. "*Call me, Jimi.* Don't go hide under a rock somewhere. I want you back here in a week. You're my best photographer."

"Okay."

"And answer your fuckin' phone!"

She tosses the cellular phone on the bed, stares at it for a long time.

It's 5 AM. She goes outside and sits on the curb with her magazines and newspapers. The world is never more beautiful than at five in the morning. Quiet. Peaceful. Unharmed. She opens a magazine, but doesn't look at it.

Three million dollars. The amount is overwhelming. She can hardly get her mind around it.

A man in a suit walks out of the inn carrying his bag. He puts the bag in the trunk of the car Jimi's sitting next to. He smiles at her, then gets into the vehicle and starts to pull away slowly. As he goes, he rolls down his window and asks her if she needs a ride somewhere.

She thinks about it. How easy it'd be to get into the car with him and leave again. Disappear. Never look back. Forget everything. But she's shaking her head no, saying "Thank you" as she's thinking this. Where would she go? Even with all the money in the world, where could she possibly lose herself?

The car is gone before she can change her mind.

# Seven

Caleb's outside early Saturday morning checking his engine when Dale's SUV pulls up behind his truck. They were supposed to meet last night for a sympathy drink. But the drink and Dale had been forgotten. When Caleb left Fifth Amendment, Jimi was the only person on his mind.

This morning Caleb's leaning toward the instinct he had when she was in his pickup truck—before she admitted she might have let him kiss her. He's leaning toward avoiding her. That would make life easier. He wouldn't have to think about her so much. What's the point of getting to know a woman if she's just passing through?

Dale climbs down from his SUV, his handsome face grim under a baseball cap. "Everything okay?" He's carrying two mugs of coffee, probably lukewarm. Gifts from his wife, Leigh.

"Yeah," Caleb says, wiping oil on his jeans.

Dale hands him one of the mugs and leans against Caleb's truck. "What the hell happened to you last night?"

Caleb sips the coffee. Warm, but not yet disgusting. Leigh knows how Caleb likes it: scalding, so it burns his tongue and gives him a jump start in the morning. She sends him the coffee anyway, to remind him it's time for a visit. "Sorry about that," he says. "I got the times mixed up."

"I got there at ten, waited for an hour." Dale pushes his cap up so he can make eye contact with Caleb. Caleb doesn't apologize again. "How'd the job go yesterday?"

"Good. I got a decent start." Caleb likes to take his time when he works, no matter how easy a job is, no matter how fast he needs to finish it. But he'd rushed through yesterday's rush job. He was anxious to get back to town to meet Jimi. Dale would love to hear that. Caleb rushing a job to meet a girl. "I told them I'd be over early today. Probably finish tomorrow or Monday morning. Are you going to Joseph's later?"

"Can't. We have a lunch date with a couple of Leigh's friends at one-thirty." Dale drinks more coffee, shifts some weight to his left side. "Rose told me you were there last night. She said I'd just missed you."

"Oh, yeah?"

"She said you were with a black girl."

"Is Rose trying to get a job with the evening news or something?" There's an edge to Caleb's voice. He doesn't like the way Dale said *black girl.* And right now he's not interested in hearing anyone's opinion on the girls he should or shouldn't have a drink with. He's never sought approval from Dale regarding his women. He's never given anyone that much power over his choices. Dale's never wanted it.

"Were you?" says Dale.

The tone's still there; the one Caleb isn't wild about. It sounds mildly disapproving. It isn't Dale's style to disapprove of someone he hasn't met.

Caleb checks his watch, choosing to lighten the mood rather than point out Dale's attitude. "Do you know what time it is? You got here at eight in the morning to ask me if I was out with a black girl last night? You're worse than somebody's mother."

Dale stares at Caleb. "I made Leigh a promise a while ago, remember?"

Caleb scratches his nose. "I remember."

"Now, you take a good look at that eye of yours and keep remembering. I'm here to make sure somebody's husband didn't beat the shit out of you last night and leave you for dead in a ditch somewhere. That would really fuck up my weekend."

Caleb opens his arms to show Dale he's unharmed. Some coffee spills on the ground. "Still kicking," he says. "I didn't see Emma yesterday, so you don't have to worry about anybody else's husband."

"It's not just the husbands I'm worried about."

Dale and Leigh worry about Caleb, even though he's been taking care of himself for a very long time. Leigh reads books that suggest Caleb's depressed and his behavior is self-destructive. Caleb doesn't need a book to analyze his problems. He isn't depressed; he's unchallenged. He isn't self-destructive; he's always had a short temper. Born with it. Like his brother. But over the years, he can't deny, his temper hasn't only been short but unpredictable. Six months ago he nearly killed Sally's boyfriend when he found out about him, striking him so hard, so many times. That was the night Sally moved out. The kid survived, and now he's in California with Sally.

There has been plenty of fighting in his life, but that night had been out of control. Since then, Leigh has made Dale promise to keep an eye on Caleb. Dale tries. Caleb doesn't make it easy.

He dumps the rest of the coffee on the ground. "This coffee's shit," he says.

Dale stares. "You should've called."

"You're going to bust my balls about this all day?"

"Maybe."

"Well piss off until you get over it. I didn't put that ring on your finger."

Dale laughs, but the laugh is short and Caleb knows he's back to wondering about what Rose told him. And then Caleb remembers meeting Kennedy right before Kennedy went to the office. He doesn't think Kennedy would have mentioned Jimi to Dale. Kennedy isn't a big talker. He rarely asks for explanations; he waits for people to explain. Still, Caleb watches Dale for signs that he knows more about Jimi. That she was also sitting in his truck on Main Street when he was supposed to be in Darby eating lunch. But Dale finishes his coffee and looks at Caleb curiously. He isn't keeping anything from Caleb. He just knows Caleb's keeping something from him.

Caleb offers to wash out the mugs and Dale hands his over. Caleb sets them on the porch.

"I've been meaning to bring over Leigh's bike," Dale says. "There's something wrong with the cooling fan. It won't turn on unless it's hooked to the car battery, not even when the engine is about to overheat."

"Could be the thermal sensor," Caleb tells him. "Or a bad fan. Bring it over."

Dale nods. "She's been asking for you," he says after a minute.

"Maybe I'll come by and see her tomorrow." He'd like to see Leigh. She doesn't judge him. The first time she'd ever met Morgan she'd said, "It takes some of us a little longer to get our shit together." Caleb had always appreciated that.

"That'd probably be okay with her," says Dale. "She's going to church early because she's working the late shift. But I guarantee she'd like to see you come by. She keeps complaining about how you don't come by for your morning coffee anymore."

Leigh makes the best coffee in Frenchman's Bend: strong, smooth and competent. She started asking Caleb over to the house for breakfast a couple of weeks after Sally left. Caleb had refused to admit he was lonely, but Leigh knew better. Dale and Leigh don't have children and Leigh, being the type of person who can't stand silence for long stretches, prefers people in her house at all hours.

"Maybe Leigh could e-mail Sally and tell her I need to talk to her," Caleb says.

Dale looks interested. "You're going to try to contact Sally again?"

Caleb nods.

"You think that's a good idea?"

"It's a bad idea considering how things ended with her," Caleb admits, "but what am I supposed to do?"

Dale nods. He knows Caleb has a point. "She stopped answering Leigh's e-mails the last time Leigh passed a message from you."

"This message is different."

"In what way?"

"I want to ask for a divorce."

Dale hesitates. "What triggered this?"

"What *triggered* it?" Caleb repeats. "What the hell do you think triggered it?"

Dale colors. He knows Caleb's been considering divorce for weeks. *He* asked Caleb if he needed help finding a lawyer the day after Sally left.

"Sorry," Dale says. "It's just you've been resistant before."

"Not resistant," Caleb corrects. "Unsure."

"And you're sure now?"

"I guess I am."

Dale rubs a hand over his face. After a moment he says, "She's the girl you called me about. Black girl with pink hair. You told her to see Leigh."

Caleb nods.

"Well, she didn't see Leigh. Rose said she was pretty banged up."

"No, she didn't see Leigh."

"Where's she from?"

"Brooklyn."

"Who beat her up?"

"I haven't asked."

"Maybe you should?"

Caleb doesn't say anything. He doesn't want Jimi to be a secret, but he doesn't want the third degree, either.

"Okay," Dale says, "that's your call. But . . . some chick turns up out of the blue, you have a drink with her, and the next morning you're talking about asking Sally for a divorce. See where I'm going with this? It doesn't make sense."

The tone Caleb doesn't like has returned. Not only disapproving, but demanding.

"You fucking hypocrite," says Caleb. "Since when do you give a damn about Sally?"

"It's not Sally I give a damn about. It's you. And the things you've been doing since she left. Screwing up jobs, sleeping with Emma, running off to Darby every afternoon. Maybe you don't think you want Sally back—"

"I don't miss her," Caleb cuts in. "I *don't.* I miss something else. The way a woman looks at me when she isn't disappointed."

"And this girl looks at you like that?"

"No. Jesus. We just met."

"But you think she will look at you like that someday, is that it?"

"Fuck you."

Dale sighs, relents. "I didn't mean to sound like that."

"It was one drink," Caleb tells him. "She's around for another day or two, then she's gone."

"Good. You don't need the hassle."

Caleb hardly hears him. He's thinking of Jimi again, wondering what she's up to this morning, whether or not she's thinking about him.

"She's different. The opposite of Sally and everyone else I've gone with." He sees Dale looking at him, trying to appear objective, but only managing to look baffled. "We were sitting at the bar, Rose hovering over us the way she does when she's trying to overhear something, and I was having a good time. This girl, she didn't get me. She didn't automatically size me up and know my life story the way girls do here. I could say anything, be anyone, and she wouldn't know it all."

"Why would you want to do that?" Dale asks.

"Why wouldn't I want a chance to reinvent myself and pretend I can start over?"

Dale pushes his baseball cap back down so Caleb can no longer see his eyes. "I'll talk to Leigh about sending the e-mail."

Caleb backs up, hiding his annoyance. "Yeah."

Dale climbs into the SUV, leaning out the window as soon as he closes the door. "Don't get me wrong, buddy. I think it's admirable that you befriended this girl. It sounds like someone else gave her hell before she got here. She could probably use a friend. And I can't really say it surprises me that you'd give her the time of day. You've always been different from the rest of us territorial bastards." Dale sits back in his seat, staring out the windshield. "Just don't get involved in any crazy shit, okay?

Leigh would have my ass." He shakes his head. "You know what? Don't get *involved.* Have fun, fine, but cut it loose when she's ready to go. She could be trouble."

"I *am* trouble," Caleb reminds him.

"Yeah, well." Dale starts the engine as his cellular phone rings. He checks it. "I should take this," he says. "We'll see you tomorrow?"

"Sure," says Caleb.

Dale pulls away, phone to his ear, and Caleb thinks of Jimi asking why he'd stopped for her on Thursday. Asking why he's different from everyone else. Watching his friend's SUV disappear from view, he knows Dale wouldn't have stopped for her if he'd been the one in Darby that day. Not Joseph. Not Kennedy. Not even Leigh.

So maybe Caleb isn't like the average Bend local, who probably *would* prefer if black people didn't pass through Frenchman's Bend at all. It isn't malicious. It isn't racist. They'd just rather avoid getting involved with people they don't have a lot in common with. But he doesn't want to justify it. He doesn't know if that's really the case. Not for certain. The only things he knows for certain are that he doesn't care about Dale's concern and he wants to see Jimi again as soon as possible.

# Eight

The telephone rings and she sits up in bed with a start. She doesn't know where she is, and then she remembers. *The Inn at Frenchman's Bend.* After her conversation with Russ she couldn't fall asleep. She sat outside the inn for a while, then came back to the room, showered and watched television.

*Three million dollars.*

Toole Lab and the government will get the bulk of it. Jimi works on commission and pays taxes. She'll take home nearly six hundred grand. Not enough to retire, but enough to avoid freelancing for a few months. Not bad for eighteen hours' work.

She'd thought about the money in the duffel bag. She hadn't taken it because she needs it. And it feels stupid to continue wanting it, protecting it. She can afford to buy twenty BMW motorcycles now. But she wants that one. The one he took. That was her baby.

The telephone right now is still ringing and it seems wrong. It can't be Russ. Can't be her mother, father or brother. No one knows she's here. This is a rest stop between where she's been and where she's going. Shouldn't there be voice mail?

The bedside clock reads 11:57 A.M. She slept for four hours. Housekeeping probably wants to know whether or not she plans to leave her room so someone can come in to clean it. She answers, sounding cranky.

"Did I wake you up?" The voice on the line is unfamiliar.

"Who is this?"

"Caleb. Did I wake you?"

*Caleb?* She sits up straighter.

"Yes," she says. He doesn't apologize. "Why'd they let it keep ringing?"

"I told Lucy to let it ring until you picked up."

"Lucy does everything you tell her to?"

"Mostly."

"I guess that can come in handy."

"It did today. Can you be outside in ten minutes?"

Jimi's used to urgent phone calls drawing her from sleep at all hours. Russ, publicists, hotel bartenders, airline pilots, police officers. Nothing fazed her. But she'd never mastered the fine art of showering and getting dressed in under ten minutes, no matter who had just been spotted.

"No," she says.

"Why not? It's noon."

"Your point? I didn't get a lot of sleep."

"I want to show you something."

Jimi's curiosity is piqued. It's been a long time since a man awakened her by telephone, offering to show her something that isn't a famous actor sticking his tongue down another famous actor's throat.

"It better be something good," she accepts. She can actually hear him smile.

"I think you'll think it is."

"Make it forty-five."

"Thirty," he negotiates. "And bring your helmet."

He's waiting for her in front of the inn. Leaning on a black Harley-Davidson motorcycle. He looks good in the afternoon sunshine, dressed simply in black jeans, a white T-shirt and black boots. Her stomach tightens just a bit. Again she can't help but wish she had her camera. But he probably wouldn't let her take his picture. He doesn't seem the type to want that kind of attention.

Caleb grins. She's unsure if he's happy to see her or if he notices her attraction to him. She turns her attention to his bike. She isn't a Harley fan. They tend to be difficult for her to maneuver. But Caleb, leaning against the gleaming leather seat with his helmet casually resting on his thigh, makes the bike look inviting.

"Wow," she says. "This is a beauty." She walks around the bike once, stopping in front of it to touch the handlebars. Her eyes meet Caleb's.

"You like it?" he asks.

Jimi nods. She's impressed. It's an old bike, but Caleb has clearly taken care of it. She walks around the motorcycle one more time. When she looks at him again, his face is filled with compassion, as if he knows she's remembering what she's lost. She really misses her bike.

"When you asked about my connection to bikes last night, it took me by surprise. I'm not great at talking about myself, so I thought I'd show you."

"I'm glad you did. It's beautiful." She squints her eyes. "I thought you were busy."

"I cut out of work early."

"To show me your Harley?"

"No one should work on a Saturday this nice when he can show a girl his Harley instead."

Jimi smiles. "True."

"Get on," he commands, putting his helmet on and sitting forward, not giving her a chance to think about it. What's to think about anyway? The minute she saw the bike she wanted a ride.

She puts her helmet on and settles behind him. He goes rigid when she slides her arms around his waist, and then she feels him relax. He nods his head to indicate he's ready. Her arms tighten with anticipation. He starts the bike and takes off. Immediately, the tiny world around them disappears.

This is what she loves. *Speed.* The wind whipping at her as if in protest, then coursing through her body like new blood. Caleb goes fast; almost as fast as she does when she's riding. She can't stop herself from laughing out loud. Russ, the money and the accident are forgotten, replaced by memories of the good moments she had on her trip. *There were good moments.* When she was alone, navigating through curvy narrow roads on her motorcycle. She was free then. She was in control of where she was going and how fast she would get there. Now her bike is gone.

Caleb shouts something at her, but the wind is in her ears and she can't hear him. He shouts louder and she understands. He isn't saying anything to her. He's just shouting. That's how good it feels.

When they stop they're back on Main Street, a block away from the inn. Jimi climbs off the bike gingerly, careful not to damage her ankle any more than she has by taking the ride. She pulls off her helmet to see Caleb watching her.

"That was *amazing,*" she says. "Thank you."

"Is your leg okay?"

"Yeah."

"It's been a while since I've been on this thing," he says. "I thought I forgot how to ride."

"You never forget."

"No, I guess you never do." He rubs a hand over his head several times. "It's a part of you that never goes away, isn't it? And now it's back." He snaps his fingers. "Like that."

Jimi knows what he means. She felt it this morning when she was on the phone with Russ. "You can't forget how to do things that have shaped who you are," she says.

Caleb smiles. "You don't forget how to do things you love."

Jimi nods. "That, too."

"It was good to be on the road like that."

"I'm glad you invited me to share it with you."

"Yeah? Then I hope we'll do it again. Before you leave the Bend."

A sheriff's car pulls up behind them, coming dangerously close to giving Caleb's motorcycle a tap. They watch until it stops, then Caleb turns back to Jimi. "You know, I have this thing to go to later that I can't get out of. At my friend Joseph's place. Wanna come with me?"

Jimi looks away from the sheriff's car and tries to concentrate on Caleb. What she'd really like to do is go back to her room and stay there. At least until the sheriff goes away. "I think I'll stay in, get some more sleep. But thanks."

"Are you sure? I'm going home to pick up my truck. You can take a nap and I'll come for you in a couple hours."

Jimi shakes her head. "I'm afraid I wouldn't be good company."

The sheriff gets out of his car. He's a tall white man wearing a light-brown uniform, black sunglasses and a dark-brown

Stratton hat. If he weren't so tall, he might not appear so threatening, Jimi thinks. At the same time, there's something about the dark glasses and the Stratton hat that would make a small man equally intimidating. The sheriff nods at Caleb. Caleb nods back.

"Staying out of trouble, Atwood?" asks the sheriff.

"Sure, Herman," answers Caleb.

*Herman?*

"What happened to your eye?" The sheriff nods toward Caleb's black eye.

"I was working on a bike," Caleb answers smoothly. "Hit myself in the face removing a wheel."

"You gotta be careful." Herman pulls off his sunglasses with a flourish that reminds Jimi of a TV-movie sheriff pretending to be tough. He leans against his car, a hand resting lazily on his holster. His large blue eyes settle on Jimi. "Miss."

Jimi nods at his greeting. He isn't so scary now that she knows his name is Herman, but she feels herself stiffen as those eyes continue to look her over with a mixture of suspicion and concern. She knows this look. He's trying to determine if he should ask about her bruises or let it go.

Jimi keeps her eyes focused on the ground, darting glances at him through the curtain of her hair. The last thing she needs is a curious sheriff sniffing around her, acting concerned. Curiosity and concern can lead to a few days behind bars for something that never happened. The sheriff turns away.

"Caleb," he says, "I haven't seen you on that bike in a long time."

"Yeah," says Caleb. "I decided to take it out for a ride."

"Good day for it."

Jimi keeps her head lowered. She learned how to be invisible from Russ. All she has to do is remain silent. Most people don't want to listen to what other people have to say. They want to tell things. They want to share their own stories, not learn about someone else. Herman doesn't really want to know the story behind Jimi's bruised face. She isn't one of his. As long as she stays out of trouble, he can ignore her.

Caleb and Herman continue to make conversation and from this she gathers they've known each other for a long time. They went to grade school together. For years Herman's been bringing his motorcycle over to Caleb's place whenever he has trouble. He wants to bring it over next weekend if Caleb has time. It amazes her that someone like Caleb, who for all intents and purposes seems not to be a friend of the law, is making arrangements for the sheriff to bring his motorcycle over to his house. In Brooklyn, the police officers Jimi had come into contact with weren't from her neighborhood, not even her borough. In L.A. there were a few officers she did business with, but they were still authority figures with eyes like this sheriff's: penetrating, suspicious, cold.

Jimi listens to the conversation, happy to learn little bits of information about Caleb. Like the fact that he'd never bothered to pursue a family on welfare in Darby, who'd hired him to renovate their kitchen and bathroom and stopped payment on his check once the work was done. And the fact that Ray, the man from the bar, is Caleb's sworn enemy and Herman's worried the two men will eventually have a major clash that Herman will have to clean up.

And she's wondering at what exact moment she made the choice that brought her here. To one of a million Main Streets in America, listening to these two men talk about fights and motorcycles. One answer would be the moment she took a turn too fast on a lonely, dark road in Pennsylvania and skidded. A man in a beat-up caravan had stopped to help her; he took her bike and left her for dead. But the reason she's here, right here on Main Street in Frenchman's Bend, is something more fundamental. Caleb. He called her this morning and she accepted his invitation. Because she wanted to.

The thought is disquieting. He is, in his appearance, the epitome of what made her feel unsafe when she was riding across the country. Small town, rough around the edges, provincial.

"I think your friend is bored with our conversation," Herman says. "Or she doesn't like me."

Jimi looks up. Herman's staring at her.

"I took that turn on Upper Axle Road too fast and made us both a little nauseous," Caleb tells him. "We should probably take off."

Herman looks surprised, as if it hadn't occurred to him that Jimi had been on the bike with Caleb. Now she's more interesting to him. "You look a little banged up there," he says. "Also from that wheel Caleb was telling me about?"

"Different wheel," says Caleb, placing his hand on Jimi's back. "It was good to see you, Herman."

The sheriff smiles at Jimi, steps closer. "I heard there was a new girl in town," he says, then adds, "Small town. You have some ID?"

"Not on me," Jimi tells him.

"ID, Herman?" says Caleb. "Go hang yourself. She's with me. Not bothering anybody."

The sheriff pauses, considering his next move.

"Bring that bike by when you get a chance," Caleb says. "I'll have a look at it. No charge."

"Okay," says the sheriff, but the look on his face says it's not okay. One wrong move and this sheriff, Herman, will be on her ass without a single question. He puts his sunglasses back on. "Don't let me keep you," he says, and waves them away.

Jimi follows Caleb, concentrating on walking without the limp and not turning back. She knows the sheriff's watching them.

"Thanks for trying to maneuver his scent away from my trail," she says when they reach the inn.

"He's harmless."

"That's what they all say. But give a guy a badge . . ."

"Yeah, I see your point. But Herman's no one to worry about." He opens the front door and the bell tinkles. Lucy comes out of the office and waves.

"I hope you had fun riding," she says. "It was a nice day for it."

Both Jimi and Caleb tell her they had a wonderful ride. Lucy nods and looks happy for them, but Jimi spots envy in that look as well. A crush. She almost teases Caleb about it, but the words don't reach her mouth. She isn't in the mood for teasing. Sheriff Herman unnerved her. She can't put her finger on exactly why; he hadn't done anything particularly threatening. But there was something. It was in his voice and in his eyes.

Caleb closes the door to her room as she checks the closet where she stowed her knapsack and duffel bag. Housekeeping has made their rounds, but the closet has been left untouched. She leans against a wall and Caleb sits down in a chair by the window. She's still feeling on edge, but she's glad Caleb's with her.

"Thank you," she says again, setting her helmet down on the dresser. "For the ride *and* walking back with me."

"Thanks for coming," says Caleb, watching her intently.

"Would you mind . . ." she begins, grabbing the ice bucket, carrying it into the bathroom, washing it out in the sink, and then holding it out to Caleb, "filling this up with ice for me?"

Caleb stands and takes the bucket. "You okay? Listen, don't

let Herman get to you. I've known him since he was a kid. He's not going to talk to you again."

"I have to take a shower." She looks around the room, points to the key card on the television. "Take that."

"How many showers does a girl need in one day?" Caleb's smirking, trying for a light mood since Jimi has suddenly turned so serious.

"There's a film covering me," she explains. "Dirt. Grit. I can't get rid of it. Not because of our ride. It's been this way since I arrived here."

"Growing up, people called me crazy when I complained about it."

Jimi smiles. "We aren't crazy."

"No," he says, "we aren't."

"I won't be long," she promises.

Out of the shower and already she feels the thin layer of dust coating her skin. He's listening to her cry. She can hear him outside the bathroom door. She'd started almost as soon as she turned the water off. Loud, embarrassing *sobs.* But she can't stop. She promised herself she wouldn't start crying once the events of the past few days crashed down and hit her. And it hit her here, sitting on a towel on the bathroom floor in The Inn at Frenchman's Bend.

So he gets to listen.

She finds her cigarettes in the pocket of her knapsack, which she has brought into the bathroom with her. She lights one, smokes and then the knock on the door comes. She's been in here for a long time though she promised she'd be quick. He's going to ask questions. This crying jag has given him an opening.

"Just a sec." She stands up, mashes the cigarette in the sink, and washes away the ashes. She slips on jeans, a T-shirt and her black boots, leaving her dirty clothes hanging on the hook behind the door.

Caleb's by the window, watching her emerge. "Are you okay?"

"Yes," she says. "Thanks . . . for waiting."

He walks over to the ice bucket by the television. "Here. Why don't you have this? It'll make you feel better."

Caleb has brought three cans of ginger ale with the bucket of ice. It's a little thing, the ginger ale, but Jimi appreciates it. And it starts her wondering if she'd be attracted to him if he were sitting in her favorite bar in Brooklyn or on the F train during rush hour heading into Manhattan. His appeal has a great deal to do with this place, she thinks. Being alone, feeling shitty and alienated. He's a nice distraction. But she's sure she'd be attracted to him somewhere other than here. Because as she's wondering this, he's pouring some of the soda into a cup with ice and handing it to her. She takes the cup and drinks.

"Feel better?"

"Yes," she says.

"Good." He takes the cup, sets it down on the dresser behind him. When he looks at her again, his face is serious.

"Is Jimi your real name?" he asks.

"Yes."

"You have a last name, or is it just Jimi?"

"It's Jimi," she tells him.

"Are people looking for you, Jimi?"

"Maybe."

"People from New York?"

"No."

He lowers his head.

"It's not what you think," she says.

"How do you know what I think?"

"It's not a husband. Not cops."

"Why'd you get nervous around Herman?"

"Doesn't everyone get nervous around cops?"

"Maybe." He shrugs. "Who did that to your face?"

"I didn't lie to you," she says. "A guy stole my bike and attacked me."

"There's more to it." He watches her, determined.

"Yes."

"This guy who did that to you, is he the one looking for you?"

She closes her eyes, frustrated by the interrogation. "*If* someone's looking for me, it's him. I have no reason to believe he is, but I haven't ruled it out yet. I'm trying to put it behind me. You're not helping."

"Why'd you trust me with your key card?" He points to the card, back in its place on top of the television. "Why do you trust me?"

"Instinct," she says. "I have a lot of experience being in sticky situations . . ." Her voice trails off and he waits. "You're different. I believe you're as much an outsider here as I *feel* I am. I suspect."

Caleb shakes his head and his eyes darken. When he makes his way over to her, she doesn't move. A stinging pain grips her when he kisses her. The wound on her lip stretches and threatens to split open. She doesn't stop him, but he draws back a little, as if he can tell something's wrong.

"Am I hurting you?" he asks.

"It's okay," she tells him.

He presses his tongue against her wound; he licks her lips as though he's trying to heal them. She lets him taste her. She lets him kiss her for a long time. And then he stops, tells her she's gentle and he likes her boots. He asks if most guys just fall in love with her because she touches them when they make out.

"Not usually," she says. She hadn't been aware of the touching. She hadn't been aware of him noticing her boots.

He's an excellent kisser. For a brief, dizzying moment she thinks she can kiss him for hours. Sometimes, kissing for Jimi is more satisfying than sex. And then she has an alarming thought. Would *he* be with *her* if they were anywhere else? Would she appeal to him elsewhere? The thought humbles her, but she quickly decides it doesn't matter if he'd be attracted to her in Manhattan, Brooklyn or L.A.

He's here.

The kissing slows and Caleb steps away from her, glancing at her chest. Her nipples are hard and he's staring at them. He swallows, scratches his head, glances at the clock on the nightstand. It's 2 P.M.

"If I don't leave now, I won't make it to Joseph's."

She flushes. She hasn't been in a relationship in over four years. She doesn't want a boyfriend. She does, however, want to be held. And if being held involves casual sex, she'll take it. But she nods, regretful.

He also looks sorry. He moves to kiss her good-bye, then stops. A good-bye kiss would probably lead to more. In the doorway he stops and turns around, leans against the frame. "You know, last night, when I said I'm on your side?"

She nods.

"I don't know why, but I meant that." He shakes his head as if he's baffling himself, then looks at her again. "My number's on the nightstand by your bed. Call me. I won't look for you unless I know you want me to."

And with that, he's gone, and Jimi's left standing in the

room alone, hand on the door, feeling a combination of worry and affection. What has she gotten herself into?

She returns to the bathroom, undresses and stares at herself in the full-length mirror. She's scrubbed fresh and clean, but she couldn't scrub her bruises away. Not the bruises on her face, on her legs, or her arms and hips. For a moment she wonders who she is. Would her friends recognize her if she passed them on the street? Will her brother, Troy, recognize her? Would Caleb recognize the woman behind the bruises, the woman she was before she made this trip? Would he want *that* one?

Five minutes later, Jimi's sitting on her bed, staring at the inn's telephone, thinking about Caleb, Herman and her motorcycle. She thought a good shower and a long cry would put some things into perspective. But any good the shower did walked out the door with Caleb. She's alone again. Herman, with all his curiosity and concern, is probably standing outside, waiting for Caleb's departure. Probably already knows tonight is her last night at the inn. He'll keep a tail on her to see if she changes her plans. She doesn't need this. This was just supposed to be a rest stop. Just until the bruises and the ankle healed.

She dials her brother's number. He answers on the third ring.

"It's Jimi."

"She calls," he says quietly, after a minute.

"Troy," she begins, and pauses.

"I'm here." Troy doesn't push her. He's patient.

"I had an accident."

"Are you okay?" he asks and she hears the dread in his voice.

"Some bruises."

"Where are you?"

"I'm in a town called Frenchman's Bend. I've booked a room for the night. Do you think you can come get me tomorrow?"

"You're in New York." He sounds relieved.

"Yes."

"I can come tonight. You aren't far."

She has a strong urge to cry again, but represses it. "No. I've already paid cash for the room. I could use the rest. Come in the morning."

"Are you sure?"

"Come early."

"How badly are you hurt?"

She thinks of her black eye, her sprained ankle, her missing motorcycle and marathon kissing with Caleb. She thinks of the bumper stickers on the back of every fucking pickup truck she passed from Trego to Darby. They said things like "*I Love My Country*" and "*God Bless America*" and they shouldn't have filled her with dark, ominous feelings when she saw them. She thinks there's no point sticking around Frenchman's Bend, running into Caleb for a few more days, feeling this new desire to go to bed with him ratchet up a couple more notches, confusing her; confusing her beliefs about men who look like him. No point in dodging the sheriff. She thinks of the money she earned for sitting in a tree and taking pictures of a drug addict's baby, famous because his mother gets paid to cry on cue. That money can take her anywhere in the world, but she doesn't know where to go. And she thinks about Troy on the other end of the line, relieved she's back in New York where she belongs. Her life has changed completely and it has completely stayed the same. She's hurt pretty badly, she thinks.

"You'll see," she says.

# Willow Run

# Nine

Troy pulls up in a blue Dodge Dakota, rolls down the window and stares for a minute.

"Jimi?" he says.

Jimi stares, too. At her brother's ostentatious pickup truck, its shine blinding in the morning sun. She walks over to it and leans into the passenger window to get a better look at the man behind the wheel. They haven't seen each other in over a year.

She says, "Troy, what are you driving?"

Troy looks affronted. "We need this here."

"You need a pickup?"

"Four-wheel drive."

"In *June*?"

He scowls. "Is that the only thing you have to say to me after all this time?"

"Hey, big brother," she says, grinning. "I've missed you."

"Hey, kiddo." Troy grins, too.

Relief and happiness replace Jimi's annoyance about the pickup truck because it's so good to see her brother smiling. She forgets herself and pushes her sunglasses up on her forehead. Troy freezes.

"Shit," he says.

She drops her sunglasses back down so they cover her eyes and the cut on her forehead again. She didn't want to look like this when he saw her. She meant to keep her face covered, at least until the greetings were over. "Yeah," she says.

Troy takes off his sunglasses and blinks as if he's coming out of a daze, then jerks his door open. Jimi straightens as he walks around the front of the car to reach her. He's gained weight. His T-shirt clings to a nicely shaped, muscular body. He now looks normal, no longer gaunt and anorexic, which was good for TV, but alarming in person. He's kept his movie-star good looks, which were required when he was reporting the news on cable. He's always been terribly handsome. There's gray in his sideburns—a definite sign that he's growing comfortable with his off-screen persona. He would never be gray if he were still on television.

"What the hell happened to you?" he says.

"I told you I was in an accident."

"Yeah, but you didn't tell me that you look like *this.*" He grabs her shoulders and stares at her bruises.

"It looks worse than it is." She tries to sound light to quell some of his concern.

He grimaces. His face is filled with worry.

"I'm okay," she assures him. "I fought back."

"Fought back? Against what? You said you were in an accident."

"After the accident. My bike was stolen."

"*Jesus.*"

"Please don't freak out."

"You're being way too nonchalant about this."

"What am I supposed to do? I've cried already."

He pulls her into a tight embrace. She welcomes the hug and almost finds it overwhelming. Hugs between Jimi and Troy are rare. He's ten years older than she is. He'd already moved out of their parents' apartment when she was old enough to realize she needed him. She closes her eyes, buries her face in a chest that is warm and smells faintly of cigarette smoke and Grey Flannel. The smoke smell is wrong. Sienna made him give up cigarettes years ago. The Grey Flannel, though, is perfect. They pull apart.

"In the car," he says.

"Pickup truck," she corrects.

"Whatever." He opens the passenger door of the Dodge, picks up her bags and puts them inside the truck. He walks around the front again and slides in as Jimi tosses her helmet on the seat between them.

"What happened?" he asks once she's settled.

She knows by the set of his jaw that he isn't going anywhere until he gets the full story. Troy's always been incredibly protective of her. He taught her how to fight after she was mugged on a subway when she was seventeen. He was almost fanatical about teaching her how to defend herself, traveling from his studio apartment in Queens to their parents' apartment in Brooklyn every weekend. But in Brooklyn she'd never had to use the skills he taught her.

"Jim," Troy says sternly. "What happened?"

"Can I tell you about it while you drive?"

"No."

That's too bad. She doesn't want anyone to see her in this vehicle. Not only because it's a splashy embarrassment; she doesn't want it getting back to Caleb that she checked out of the inn and was seen with a man in a Dodge Dakota. She wants to keep him, and Frenchman's Bend, separate.

She looks in the side-view mirror, grateful the streets are empty. According to the young man at the front desk, everyone attends church on Sunday morning and Frenchman's Bend is a ghost town until afternoon. Jimi wondered if Caleb was part of the "everyone."

"*Jim,*" Troy pushes. "What happened? Out with it. *All of it.*"

She stares at him. When she arrived in Frenchman's Bend, she didn't want to contact him because she didn't want to start off her visit being Troublesome. And she didn't want to feel like she was losing the freedom and independence she worked so hard to reestablish in L.A. by being interrogated, babied, coddled. Then last night she'd felt overwhelmed and all she wanted was her brother. He's overbearing, sometimes, but not mean about it. His biggest crime is treating his baby sister like a baby when she gets herself into trouble.

So she tells him she took a turn in the rain on a dark road in Pennsylvania too fast, skidded and hit a tree. She suffered a sprained ankle; her bike barely had a scratch. She tells him how she lost the motorcycle to a man in a pickup truck—he'd stopped at the side of the road and offered to help her. How she nearly died trying to get her motorcycle back. "I was tired and I was riding too fast. My bike wouldn't start properly after the crash and I thought I'd have to spend the night on the side of the road. It was raining. A man and woman stopped for me. They looked like they'd just stepped out of a church. When they offered me and my bike a ride to town I accepted. If there hadn't been a woman in the truck, I probably would have been more careful. I don't know. I was a little freaked out from the crash and she was there and I didn't even think twice. I haven't done a lot of hitchhiking in my life, but it's hard to turn down a ride when the weather's against you and you're stuck in the middle of nowhere. So the man checked my bike and loaded it onto the back of the pickup and drove away. It had to be the simplest mugging ever."

Troy stares at her, his eyes taking in her bruised face, realizing there's more to the story than a simple mugging. He drops his head back on the driver's seat. "You went after them."

It isn't a question. He already knows the answer. He knows she didn't let the bike go without a fight. Couldn't. Their mother always called her brazen. Their father always told her she took action before she thought.

She hesitates, doesn't want to go any further. She had been dumb and proud and angry. She'd acted solely on instinct. "Yes."

"You tracked them."

"That's what I do. I track people. I can memorize a license plate number in less than ten seconds, and then I move. I track. I can't help it."

"Fuck, Jimi," Troy groans. "*Why?*"

"It was my bike," she tells him.

"You could get another one."

"I wanted that one. I worked hard for that one." She knows she sounds like a child, but if she can't sound like a child with her older brother . . .

"But you almost got yourself killed. Look at you."

"I couldn't stop myself."

"What is it with you? Why do you always go one step further than everyone else?"

Jimi thinks of the duffel bag under their seats. She keeps it even though she just earned more money than she's ever earned in her life. Carrying it is an act of defiance that she doesn't expect anyone to understand. It's all she has left of her motorcycle.

Troy pulls away from the curb, jaw moving methodically so she knows he's grinding his teeth. "Why didn't you call the police?"

"He laughed when I said I'd call the cops. And it dawned on me that he was probably right. No cop in backwoods Pennsylvania would take my side over his. Cops didn't even take my side in L.A."

"Do cops usually take the paparazzi's side in L.A.?"

"That's not the point. This guy had my registration, my camera equipment, my clothes, everything. I had nothing. And right then, I felt vulnerable."

"What'd you expect?" Troy sounds frustrated. The car slows, swerves a little. "You accepted a ride from a stranger."

The comment conjures up Caleb. Another stranger in a pickup truck she accepted help from. She'd trusted him, at first, because she'd had no choice. And then he was kind and she trusted him because he could be trusted. She thinks about sitting in his pickup on Main Street, having a drink with him at Fifth Amendment and sharing a kiss in her room, not wanting it to end.

Troy says, "You should have called the police. They wouldn't have taken his side. They're the law."

"The law is very different in these places."

"We're talking about Pennsylvania."

"*Rural* Pennsylvania. You know better than I do how fucking scary rural *anything* is. You're the reporter."

"That's a very narrow way to look at things."

"Well, *yeah.* I think it's time I had a chance to be narrow. Why do I always have to be the one who's open-minded?"

"It's not like that everywhere," Troy says. "With police. There's good and bad in everyone."

"I didn't feel like taking any chances."

She stares out the window. The road is narrow and winding. Occasionally they pass a farmhouse, horses and cows. Things she's already seen all across Middle America. The last time she was on this path she was on Caleb's Harley. It looks so different from a truck. Not as terrific. When she's on a bike, it's funny; she wants to take pictures of everything and she wants to be on the road indefinitely. Her life and her future are full of potential. In the truck, she just wants to get to where they're going.

"How'd you get to Frenchman's Bend?" Troy asks.

"I paid a woman on her way here."

"Another ride with a stranger."

"And I'm here. Otherwise I'd be walking." After a few minutes, she tries to change the subject. "How's Sienna?" Asking about his wife should distract him. After three years of marriage the spark is still there. And . . . yes, his eyes still light up at the mention of her name.

"Sienna's great," he says. "Excited to see you. But don't change the subject."

"The bike's gone," says Jimi. "I've made my peace with it."

Troy glances at her. "Have you?"

She doesn't answer and they continue the drive in silence.

Ten minutes later he turns off the main road onto a dirt road sandwiched between dense shrubs and trees. They ride for nearly a mile before the trees open up to massive flatlands dotted with houses of all shapes and sizes. They pass trailers raised high from the ground by cement blocks, ranch-style houses under construction and Adirondack-style cabins settled contentedly on acres of green grass. Jimi looks out for the house she thinks belongs to her brother. And then they enter yet another path surrounded by forest; this one is narrower than the first; the ride is briefer and within seconds they've turned into a clearing and Troy stops the truck in front of a midsize house with a gambrel roof and silo tower.

"It's a *barn*?" Jimi blurts and Troy looks at her sharply. She hadn't realized she was expecting something else.

"It is not a barn," he says. "It's a farmhouse."

They stare at it. Jimi looks at him again. "Are you sure?"

"It's meant to look like—" He sighs. "It's a custom-built *barn-style* farmhouse."

"You had this custom-built?"

Sienna comes to the front door, waves and points to the telephone against her ear. She holds up one finger to indicate it'll be another minute, then disappears back inside the house.

"Yes, we had it custom-built," Troy says and gets out of the car. He grabs Jimi's bags and she follows him at a very deliberate pace, unable to hide the limp completely. Troy stops and turns around to watch her. Jimi stops, too, a distance behind him. Their eyes meet.

"Are you limping?"

"A little."

He looks like his head is going to explode then starts toward the house again.

"You're sleeping in the den," he tells her, opening the front door built into the silo. "You'll have more privacy there than the second bedroom upstairs."

"In other words, you won't be able to have sex with your wife if you know your little sister's sleeping in the room next door."

"That, too," he says.

The instant Jimi enters the house she's hit with a strong sense of *being here before.* The silo serves as the house's foyer, with hooks for coats, a small table to drop keys and a bench. The foyer leads to living and dining room areas. Sliding glass doors in the dining room look out onto a deck and a large backyard. It's all very lovely. And rural. But the furniture is very Troy and Sienna and is part of what creates the sense of familiarity. All dark browns, light blues and whites, just like their color scheme in Manhattan. The same Basquiat prints hanging on the walls of their apartment in the city are hanging on these walls. The huge picture of the New York City skyline behind the sofa is new, but the view from the window in their Manhattan living room is the same as the one in the photo. And the air smells of sandalwood. It's a smell that has always reminded her of Troy.

"I haven't been here in a long time," she says, mostly to herself.

"You've never been here," says Troy.

She looks at him. "You know what I mean. With you."

He nods. "Yeah, I know."

She suddenly misses him very much and can't stand the idea that she disappoints him. Keeps disappointing him over and over with her choices. This feeling is why she didn't want to see him just yet.

When she hugs him, he hugs back without saying a word and lets her stay in his arms. His presence in this place, the smells, the colors and the furniture make her homesick for New York City. The New York City *before* the 2001 terrorist attacks. The New York City with clubkids and whores and lost souls who meant no harm to anyone except, maybe, themselves. The New York City that was fast-paced and crazy and easy to disappear in. The New York City that was unapologetic about being all of those things and more. There was no feeling then that life could be cut short any minute. No reason to question the future, the present or her purpose. She misses that city. Misses Troy.

"Oh, my God." Sienna's standing behind Troy, her intensely dark eyes taking in Jimi's condition. "What happened to you?"

"I took a turn a little recklessly," says Jimi.

"There's more to it than that," says Troy.

Sienna makes eye contact with her husband as she pulls Jimi into a gentle hug. "Troy told me about the accident after you called yesterday. What happened? It was more than an accident?"

"You could say that," says Troy.

Sienna pulls back and stares into Jimi's eyes. "This wasn't one of those crazy, I don't know, *run-ins* with somebody's nutcase bodyguard?" Sienna asks, alarmed.

"I was in a minor motorcycle accident," Jimi says, eyeing Troy with dismay for tattling on her to Sienna. "In Pennsylvania, not L.A. And then my bike was stolen. Hence the bruises, the sprained ankle and disenchantment. But I don't want to talk about it anymore." She sounds petulant so she adds, "Maybe later."

Sienna's face is filled with concern, much like Troy's.

Jimi adds, "Over a drink."

"Why don't you let Troy show you to your room," Sienna suggests. "I'll make tea."

The den, located in the back of the house, underneath the staircase, is spacious. There's a television, a telephone and a bathroom with a toilet and sink. The sofa has already been opened and the bed has been made.

"When did you leave L.A.?" Troy asks. He's leaning against a wall, watching her.

"Two weeks ago?"

"You haven't called Mom in two weeks?"

"I couldn't get a signal."

"For two weeks you couldn't get a signal?"

Jimi bites her lip. "I was in the mountains."

"Want to call her now?"

"Not this very minute."

"Okay. You can call her when you're ready."

"Thanks." She grabs her knapsack and begins to unpack the toiletries she's accumulated from the various hotels and motels she's stayed in during her trip. "Do you mind if I unpack on my own now?"

"Of course," he says. "Do you need anything?"

Jimi shakes her head.

"Okay." Troy heads for the door.

"I'm going to take a nap," she says. "I'll have tea later."

"I'm glad you're here," he says as he closes the door.

"So am I."

When you have an unpopular job, and you're doing it in a city that isn't yours, you forget there are people out there who know the real you and love the real you. Jimi's glad she's here, but now she feels the pressure to make sure Troy never regrets being glad, too.

Surprisingly, she sleeps. Since she left Los Angeles, she's had trouble. She's used to sleeping to the rhythm of daytime hours: wailing ambulances and fire trucks, crying babies, the jobless hanging out on the stoop in front of her building, her phone ringing until the call goes to the machine. At night, in Brooklyn and L.A., she doesn't have to turn on a light to find the door. She's used to seeing everything. Night is no different from day in the world she's used to.

In the tiny bathroom in the den, she splashes her face with cold water several times. The air is grimy and hot. The bright bathroom lights can't disguise the absolute darkness shrouding the house. It's like a tarp has been dropped over them. Is it midnight? She turns on the lamp by her sofa bed. The clock on the wall reads 9:00 PM.

She opens the door and steps out into the hallway, follows

the sound of Sienna's voice to the kitchen. She stops at the sight of her sister-in-law struggling to open a bottle of white wine with the refrigerator door still wide open, telephone to her ear.

"You slept," Sienna says without turning around. "Hungry?"

"I can make something."

Sienna lets the refrigerator door close, tells the person on the other end of the line she'll call back tomorrow and motions to the dining room with the bottle of wine. She's already set out a vegetable platter, a bowl of hummus, crackers and cheese.

"Sit down," she says as she fills two wineglasses. "Eat."

Jimi sits, starts to eat, and Sienna picks up one of the three newspapers spread haphazardly on the table. Troy and Sienna have always received the *New York Times*, the *Washington Post* and *USA Today* every morning. Jimi used to marvel at their commitment to the news, and then she realized they each had a section of the papers they skimmed and only if something was of particular interest did they recommend the other read it.

"Your mother called," Sienna says, not looking up from the paper as she sips her wine. "She'll try again tomorrow."

"Okay."

"How are you holding up, Jimi?"

When Jimi looks up from her plate, she's faced with Sienna's fiercely serious eyes. "How am I—? I'm fine, Sienna, really."

"Troy told me what happened with your motorcycle. I'm so sorry. I thought it would be such an amazing trip for you."

"It was amazing. It just ended badly."

"Yeah?" Sienna widens her eyes a little as a way of saying she doesn't believe it.

Jimi shrugs. "Maybe you can tell me why you've chosen to move to a small town."

"We haven't *moved,*" Troy says behind them. He takes a seat next to Sienna, puts his arm around her shoulder. "We bought a summerhouse."

"Okay," says Jimi, "but you chose here, not the Hamptons. When you told me about it, I understood. Now I don't. Small-town folks are *so weird.* This trip really fucked with my idea of America."

"Did you have a problem last night?" he asks.

"No. It was everywhere else. I liked Frenchman's Bend."

"Really?"

"It was a little different from the other towns I stopped in. Some of the people were really nice to me. You know, I made this particular trip because my colleague said it would be wonderful. And it *was* wonderful. Pretty. Exhilarating. But I'd also taken his word about how safe he felt riding the Blue Highways because I believed all those stereotypes about back-road Americans were exaggerated. Instead of suspicious, gun-toting, insular racists, I thought I might encounter curious, friendly countrymen."

"And you didn't," Troy says.

"Every night I put my bags up against my motel room door in case someone decided to rally the troops and pay me a visit while I slept." Ironically, she doesn't tell them, someone had. On the border between New York and Pennsylvania. She hadn't pushed her bags against the door that night. She was close to home. On the edge of New York. She doesn't think the bags against her door that night would have made a difference anyway. "My fears weren't unfounded. People stared at me. I'd just leave my motel room for something to eat and locals would openly stare. With hostility. Don't stare at strangers is, like, the most basic lesson we learn when we're taught manners as children."

"Didn't you once say *everyone* watches you when you put those colored extensions in your hair?" Troy asks. "People in small black towns would have stared, too. Pink hair, leather."

"It's a different kind of stare. Not anger. More like amusement. Or confusion. I didn't just feel like a foreigner on this trip, I felt unsafe. And feeling safe where I am is enormously important to me right now."

"I know," Troy says. "But I bet a lot of those stares were curiosity. Most of the white people you encountered in these places probably never come into contact with black people."

"I know what kind of stares Jimi's talking about," says Sienna. "There *is* a difference. And I think, for us, it's such a shock because we've been raised in diverse neighborhoods where whites and blacks interact on a regular basis. In cities where people aren't staring at you, or the guy wearing a turban, or the gay couple kissing, or the man with a dozen lip rings. And, for the most part, people in Manhattan see you as an American. So it hits you hard when you take your first trip through rural America. Maybe Troy hasn't had the same experiences when he leaves the city."

"I stopped in Mansfield, Pennsylvania, with my crew once," Troy says. "Small college town. We went for lunch at a restaurant on the main strip near the university. There were three of us. Two white guys and me. We sat at a table in the nonsmoking section. A white guy walked in with his wife and children, took one look at me and announced to the hostess he wanted to be seated in the smoking section. His daughter reminded him he wasn't a smoker and he told her, loudly, that he'd just started. The little girl said, 'But you've never smoked at all, Daddy,' and he said, 'I just started *today.*' And I knew he said it because I was sitting there and he wanted to make it clear I didn't belong in his town. And I became very aware, afterward, that every patron in the restaurant also requested to be seated in the smoking section. The three of us were sitting in the non-smoking section alone until another black couple walked in and was seated at the table next to ours. I know what it's like to step into a town in America and be made to feel as if you've just stepped on someone's private property. The feelings you get in these towns, well, it dispels the notion of a free society. But you can't let it hold you back."

"I thought people would be nicer to me. Especially after 9/11. You know, we're all in this together? But they weren't even curious about me."

"Yeah, but why would they be?" Troy asks. "Are we curious?"

"Of course we are." Sienna sounds appalled.

Troy shrugs. "We're paid to be."

"I'd be curious anyway," Sienna says

"Well, you know what I mean. As a whole, we aren't a curious society."

"So why did you choose to live in a small town?" Jimi asks.

"You don't think about it," says Troy. "You go about your business, enjoy the scenery and the cows and lock your doors at night."

Jimi stares at her brother. "Cows, Troy?"

He shrugs. "I like cows. Unfriendly locals are a small price to pay for this peace and quiet."

"So you just ignore the locals?" Jimi asks.

Troy nods. "Pretty much."

She was hoping he'd have some insight as to why, after her weeks riding across the country, she realizes she feels more protected by the anonymity of a big city and more vulnerable in a small community. The total opposite of what she'd expected when she left Brooklyn. Disappointed, she starts to clear the table, but Sienna stops her, motions for her to sit again.

"Troy and I had a conversation while you were sleeping, and we think you should consider staying with us for the entire summer."

Jimi looks at her brother. "The entire summer?"

"Yes. We won't grill you about the accident as long as you agree to stay and chill out for the next couple of months and think about what you want to do with the rest of your life."

"You're giving me an ultimatum?"

"No," Troy cuts in. "It's a suggestion. *I* think it's a good one."

"So this is about my future."

"We know you have some money stashed away and can afford not to work for a couple months . . ." Sienna says.

Even before she sold her latest photos, which Troy and Sienna don't know about yet, Jimi had enough money to buy a small house in Willow Run on an acre of land. Enough to live comfortably for a while without working. She can't deny that. But she's glad she hasn't admitted she doesn't want to return to her job in L.A. Then she wouldn't have an excuse to leave Willow Run if she decides she can't deal with it for an entire summer.

"Why don't we see how it goes?" Jimi says. "If I love it here, I'll call my boss and extend my vacation."

Troy and Sienna exchange glances, looking hopeful.

"You'll find something to love here," Sienna says. "I know it."

# Ten

He should be thinking about something else. Emma, for example. But Emma's nipping at his shoulders, making it hard for him to concentrate on her. The nipping annoys him. He imagines a dog, a poodle, biting at him, leaving marks. So instead of Emma, he's thinking about Jimi.

She hasn't called.

He almost rang the inn this morning, almost stopped in before work to ask Lucy what Jimi's been up to. But he'd told her, and promised himself, she'd have to make the next move. *She'd* have to call. That's just the way this thing is going to have to work. He's not going to pursue a woman unless he's sure she wants to be pursued.

He did stop by Fifth Amendment on his way home from Joseph's Saturday night, though. And again Sunday evening. Dropping by the bar isn't the same as calling. He'd had a couple of shots of bourbon. Rose told him Jimi hadn't been around at all.

Maybe she really has left. Checked out. Moved on to wherever it was she was going. He won't stop by the inn to find out. Doesn't want to know. Doesn't want to chase a woman.

But he'll give her until tomorrow before he gives up.

Since he's thinking about Jimi, he also starts to think about Saturday night at Joseph's place. The evening had been about the same as any other evening with his friends. He worked on Kennedy's motorcycle, ate too much of Joseph's chili, drank too much Bud and flirted innocently with Joseph's wife, Shannon. Dale and Leigh stopped by after dinner. They sat around Joseph's backyard and Shannon told them the house down the road from Connie, her sister, had been sold.

Joseph poked Caleb in the ribs. "Sold it to a bunch of fucking Arabs," he said and Connie said, "At least they didn't sell to ni—"

"Shut the fuck up, Connie," Dale snapped, cutting her off before she could actually say it.

Still, Caleb cringed and kept his eyes lowered once he realized Dale and Kennedy were watching him. He drank from his beer, shamefully relieved Jimi had declined his offer to be there.

"What?" Connie had squawked. "You're a member of the Anti-Defamation League all of a sudden?"

Kennedy turned his eyes on her. "Just shut up," he advised and she did.

Caleb felt like he'd stepped into a world where his friends said things they didn't say around him. No one seemed fazed by Connie's comment; they'd just silenced her, as if they didn't care if she said it as long as she didn't say it around Caleb. And he can't stop thinking he should have said something. But how could he? Out of the blue, he can't turn into a guy who tells people how to think or what to say at parties. He wonders how Jimi would feel about that.

"Babe," he says softly to Emma, but she doesn't stop nipping. He pulls away from her. "Quit it."

She stares at him, bottom lip poked out like a child. She's

invited him to dinner. He's already said no twice. He shouldn't even be here now. In the back room of the antiques shop.

"What's on your mind?" Emma asks, rubbing her hand against him, pulling him back down on the antique sofa. They've been messing around for ten minutes, but he still isn't in the mood to have sex with her. It would be a guilt fuck, anyway. He forgot to call her Friday and she's more than a little annoyed with him. The last thing he needs is Emma acting like a woman scorned. He's here to throw a little water on the fire.

"Take it slow," he suggests.

"I am." She sounds insulted, then she kisses him. He's always liked kissing Emma. Usually, he can't kiss Emma for more than five minutes before he's ready to jump in the sack with her. But after that kiss with Jimi Saturday afternoon, he isn't sure he'll ever feel the same enthusiasm when he kisses Emma. Just thinking about Jimi makes him hard, which Emma interprets as her doing. She moans and deepens their kiss. The bell above the front door tinkles.

"You have customers," Caleb says lazily.

"Yeah," Emma drawls, letting him go, pulling her shirt on, buttoning the buttons sloppily.

Caleb comes out a few minutes after Emma because the back room is sweltering. Percy from the hardware store winks at him from the other side of the counter.

"Another hot day," Percy comments.

Emma's riffling through some receipts. She looks up, distracted. "What?"

"Another hot day," Percy repeats.

"Sure is," she says.

"I don't have air-conditioning in the store."

"Well, you need to get some," Emma tells him.

"Home Depot has some decent models on sale," Caleb recommends. Emma stiffens at the sound of his voice behind her, then goes back to searching through the receipts. "Run over to Moss Bluff and pick one up. I'll put it in for you. No charge."

Percy waves a hand at Caleb. "Why should I spend my hard-earned cash on an air conditioner from Home Depot? You want me to give my money to the bastards trying to put me out of business? We used to have a place in town that sold air conditioners. Home Depot put him out of business."

"Yeah, yeah, I know," Caleb says. "But I bet you'll lose more business without air in the store."

Emma finds the receipt she's looking for. She tells Percy he owes ten dollars on the lamp he purchased for his wife three weeks ago. Percy pulls out his wallet and counts out ten singles.

"How's Ray?" he asks as Emma puts the money in the cash register. Caleb catches Percy's eyes on him for a second.

"Ray's fine," Emma says. "How's Mary?"

"Mary's good. She wants to have you over to the house before Labor Day."

"I'll give her a call."

Percy nods, winks at Caleb again.

"Let me know about that air conditioner," Caleb calls after him.

The bell tinkles, the door closes and Emma turns around to glare. "Why'd you show yourself like that?"

"It was too hot back there." He motions to the door with his chin. "Don't worry about him. He'll call me tomorrow morning, tell me he picked up an air conditioner from Home Depot and bust my balls until I install it for him. Free air conditioner installation is code word for keep your fucking mouth shut."

Emma relaxes. "What time's lunch over?"

Caleb checks his watch. "Now," he tells her.

"Remember this couple in Willow Run?" Dale hands Caleb a piece of paper the minute he walks into the office.

Caleb grabs a can of soda, then takes the paper reluctantly. He sits at his desk while he reads the message. "No."

"Neither do I. Apparently you did a shitload of work for them when they bought the place last September. Butcher-block countertops, cabinets, a pantry, a deck in the backyard, some kind of storage thingy in the laundry room."

"A storage *thingy*?"

"That's what she called it, a storage thingy."

Caleb tries to remember who they might be, but gives up after only a few seconds. "We built so many decks and installed so many cabinets last year . . . how many do you remember?"

"Well, they loved your work. And this is going to be their first summer in the place. They have a new project. They asked for you specifically."

"What's the project?"

"There's a homestead cottage in the back of their house," Dale says. "They want it renovated and converted into a guest-house without destroying the original framework. And they want one of the sheds they use for wood storage converted into an office."

Caleb nods, considering the job. He can do it. It's not hard. Just long and boring. And that's the key for him lately. Boredom. It's the reason he says no to a lot of things these days.

"I've converted way too many cottages this year."

"I said I'd call them back to set up an appointment. We shouldn't say no to this, but it's up to you."

"Okay," Caleb says, knowing it really isn't up to him. He's

obligated to take this job. They double their price when they accept jobs with weekenders and transplants. It's easy money, lucrative. "Set up an appointment for Thursday evening."

Dale writes something down on a Post-it, sticks the note on his telephone and turns back to his computer. He hasn't mentioned Jimi. Caleb had expected more questions. At first, he'd been thankful. He wasn't sure what he'd say to Dale, especially after the Connie incident. And then he was disappointed. He'd wanted to be able to tell someone: *Here's this girl from the city, keeps popping up wherever I am.* He'd wanted to tell someone about the ride on his Harley, about going back to her room and kissing her. About waiting for her to call.

Kennedy walks into the office with a pie.

Dale looks up. "Pie for lunch?"

Kennedy drops the pie on Dale's desk. "From the MacKenzies on J Street."

"Clients give you pies?" Caleb asks.

"All the time," Kennedy says, loosening his ponytail and combing his fingers through his hair.

"Clients never give me anything." Caleb sounds wounded.

"Not even a thank-you fuck?" Kennedy asks.

"I get those occasionally. But there's so much more effort put into a pie." They laugh. He looks at Dale. "You ever get pies from clients?"

"No." Dale leans forward and takes a closer look at it. "And it's not from someone you're sleeping with?"

Kennedy shakes his head, then pulls his hair into a ponytail again. "That elderly couple."

"Maybe they think you're a girl," Dale tells Kennedy.

Kennedy stares at Dale intently, waiting for him to admit he's joking. When he doesn't, Kennedy glances at Caleb for backup, then back at Dale. "Don't say shit like that, man," Kennedy warns darkly.

Dale grins and sits back.

Caleb picks up the pie. "Mind if I take it?"

"Have at it," says Kennedy, grabbing a soda from the refrigerator. "You going to another job?"

"Yeah," says Caleb.

"I'll walk out with you."

Kennedy and Caleb walk together to their vehicles.

"What'd you think about Connie Saturday night?" Kennedy asks.

Surprised, Caleb looks at his friend. Kennedy's eyeing him. The look on his face is straightforward, honest and curious. Caleb has never been a Connie fan, so what really disturbed him about Saturday night was Joseph's and Shannon's silence.

He says, "I've never been wild about Connie."

"I can't stand her," Kennedy says.

"I think—and you can tell me if I'm just talking out of my ass here—but I think the most boring people in the world are the ones who only want to be surrounded by people exactly like them."

Kennedy hesitates. "Yeah," he says slowly, "but where does that leave us? We're still here."

"You got out for a while."

Kennedy nods, but doesn't say anything. Years ago, he moved to Philadelphia to be with his wife while she studied at the University of Pennsylvania. It didn't work out. Kennedy moved back to their house in Frenchman's Bend and his wife still rents an apartment in a suburb of Philadelphia.

They reach Caleb's pickup truck first. Caleb opens the passenger door and sets the pie on the seat, and then walks around to the driver's side. Kennedy follows him.

"You miss Philadelphia?" he asks.

"I miss my wife." Kennedy looks up the street to make sure a car isn't coming. He looks at Caleb again. "Well, shit, yeah, I miss the noise sometimes. Like the guys standing around outside, laughing in the middle of the night. I used to want to be out there with them because they sounded like they didn't have a care in the world. If you mean, like, the different types of people, I kind of miss that. But I prefer it here. I can be myself because everybody's used to me." He loosens his ponytail, then tightens it. "How's your friend? The black girl."

"I haven't heard from her in a few days," says Caleb. "She's staying at Ruth's place. Was. Maybe she left by now."

"Why don't you call and find out?"

Caleb shrugs.

"You fuck her?"

"No."

Kennedy nods. "She was pretty."

He doesn't need anyone to confirm what he already knows, but it's odd hearing it come from Kennedy. Kennedy was married right out of high school and hardly ever looked at other women. Hardly looks at them now. He hasn't dated anyone since he returned from Philadelphia. For a while Caleb even started to wonder if Kennedy found women attractive anymore. "Yeah," he says, "she is."

Ray's 4x4 turns the corner so fast Caleb and Kennedy barely have time to move out of its way. The driver honks as he nearly grazes Kennedy's arm.

"What the hell?" Kennedy says.

"Ray."

Kennedy glares at the path the 4x4 took for a long time. "He'll get his."

Caleb gets into his truck, leans out the window. "Not from me."

Kennedy continues to stare at the empty street ahead. "Are you up for a drink tomorrow night?"

"Why not," Caleb says.

Kennedy looks at Caleb. "Better than sitting at home like some sad person, eating pie by yourself."

"That how you see me?"

Kennedy has to think about it just long enough to make Caleb uncomfortable. "No, man. It's how I see both of us."

Once Kennedy's in his truck and out of sight, Caleb tosses the pie out of his window. It lands squarely in a corner garbage can and Caleb hopes some down-on-his-luck hungry person walks by and sees it.

# Eleven

Tuesday evening, Jimi asks Sienna if she can borrow her car, a white Subaru Outback, subtle and unassuming and nothing like Troy's glaringly obvious Dodge. She tells them she's going to drive around the area, possibly catch a movie in Moss Bluff. Troy asks if she wants company. Jimi politely turns him down.

She's going to see Caleb. She's been craving his company since she left Frenchman's Bend Sunday morning. He doesn't look at her the way most people look at her: as if she's going to take something from him. As if her mere presence in his life will create strife or cause trouble.

She also misses Frenchman's Bend a little. It isn't as pretty as Willow Run, but the quaint shops in Frenchman's Bend aren't just for show. Locals still shop in them; prices are affordable. When Sienna took Jimi shopping on Monday, Jimi actually wondered what use anyone would have for the cute trinkets being sold on Main Street. Willow Run reminded her of the gentrified neighborhoods in Brooklyn. She told Sienna she thought it was funny how people escape to a place to have time away from home only to turn those places into everything that's familiar to them. Sienna laughed and said Troy had thought the same thing.

Jimi parks the Outback on a side street and walks along Main Street, taking her time, enjoying the night air. Faces pass her and they're familiar. Some people say "Good evening" or nod. When she walks inside Fifth Amendment Rose acknowledges her with a slight smile. Before Jimi sits down, Rose sets a glass on the bar and fills it with ginger ale. She says, "I thought we lost you."

Jimi doesn't know what to tell her, so she doesn't tell her anything. She thanks her for the soda and Rose comments on Jimi's black eye fading, then returns to her place under the television.

An hour later Jimi's sitting on a stool by the pool table, drinking seltzer, concentrating on the current game. She's been sticking to soda. Rose charges her for the ginger ale, but makes every other drink a free seltzer. Jimi isn't sure how much more of it she can drink. She's sure Caleb isn't going to turn up. She's sure she's given him a chance to forget her. She thinks about calling it an evening.

And then he walks in with his friend Kennedy around nine. Jimi sits up a little bit straighter. They stand by the bar and wait for Rose to acknowledge them. Caleb's wearing a Chicago Bears cap, jeans and a white T-shirt. She notices how lean he is, how muscular his arms are. He appears younger and livelier than everyone else in the bar. Kennedy also appears vital and fit. He wears tight clothes: black jeans and a thin leather jacket. He stands ramrod straight, pushing at his hair, which is in a ponytail this evening. With his delicate skin and long hair, Kennedy looks like Caleb's girlfriend. And then he rolls his shoulders back, looks directly at Jimi as if he senses her eyes on him and stares. He looks strong and masculine all of a sudden, like he could wipe the floor with her and everyone else in here. He is, without a doubt, unsettling. So unsettling that people in the bar have actually moved away from them. The fact that she knows them excites her.

Caleb hands Kennedy a beer. Kennedy says something and Caleb glances in Jimi's direction. She thinks he smiles, but she isn't sure. He doesn't come over, which disappoints her. A bald-headed man with a red beard asks her if she'd like to play a game of pool against him. She declines the invitation. When she looks at Caleb again he walks over.

Heads turn. He's definitely worth looking at. And there's something absolutely predatory about the way he moves. His eyes on her face make her feel a little warm.

"Hi," he says, looking at her from under the bill of his cap. He sits down on the stool next to her, pushing the cap up so he can see her better. She moves away so they don't touch, but he reaches over to push some hair from her face, fingers lingering to touch the skin around her eyelid. His touch sends a thrill through her.

"Eye's healing," he says.

"Yours, too," she says.

"How's that leg?"

"Better."

He leans in a little closer. "I thought you went back to Brooklyn. Without saying good-bye."

She shakes her head. "I just needed a couple of days to myself. I'm sorry I didn't call you."

"Everybody needs a little time to themselves," he says. "I thought about calling you, but figured it was something like that. Or that you didn't want to see me again. I didn't want to call if that was the reason."

"No, not that."

"Good."

They sit in easy silence for a bit and Jimi's glad he's not the type to grill her. But she's also ashamed that she can't bring herself to tell him she has already checked out of the inn and is staying with her brother in Willow Run. There are two reasons why she doesn't. For one thing, Troy and Sienna would strongly disapprove of Jimi seeking comfort and safety from a man like Caleb. A blue-collar *local.* His whiteness having nothing to do with it. *Not really.* It's the kind of white man he is that wouldn't sit well with them. If he were more like them, an intellectual, they'd feel differently.

But second, and most important to her, she doesn't want her Frenchman's Bend world to collide with her real one. Since she left L.A. she's felt like a failure. Here, her past doesn't matter. If she merges Caleb with Troy, it will. For now, Caleb's solely hers.

She smiles at the thought.

"You have a nice smile," Caleb says.

She stops smiling, embarrassed by what she was thinking. It's been so long since a man sparked her interest. She isn't sure what it's like to be smitten. She doesn't want to be too obvious. Doesn't want to walk into anything blind.

"What about your warning?" she says. "Shouldn't I be worried about being seen with you right now?"

"Forget what I said. No one's going to say a word to you while I'm here. I promise."

"Your friend isn't afraid of you," she says.

"Kennedy?"

"No. The one who punched you."

Caleb chuckles. "That particular friend, no. He isn't afraid of me."

"Did you resolve that?"

"It doesn't need to be resolved."

"It doesn't?"

He shakes his head. "Can I buy you a drink?"

"No. Thanks."

His eyes move to her mouth. He checks out her arms, her breasts and her stomach. She knows he wants to touch her again. He glances at the bar. Kennedy's still watching them closely. Different from the way everyone else is watching them. Not disapproving, but protective. Jimi bets Caleb would have more to say if Kennedy wasn't standing there, overseeing things. After a minute of awkward silence she asks if his friend has a problem with her or if he just has a problem. Caleb looks surprised.

"Actually," he says, "Kennedy likes you. He doesn't like many people."

She looks at Kennedy again. He nods, but nothing in his face gives away what he's thinking. He heads over.

"Kennedy," he says, holding his hand out to her.

Jimi shakes it. "Jimi. We've met."

"I know," Kennedy says. "How are you?"

"Fine. Thank you. You?"

Kennedy shrugs. "Hanging in there."

Jimi nods, her mind working furiously to come up with something to ask him that will require more than a three-word answer. But a man and woman walk past them and bump into Caleb, and then Kennedy. They don't apologize. Caleb and Kennedy watch the couple. There's something feral in the way they look at those two people that intrigues her. It's only when Caleb realizes she's studying his face that he catches himself, blinks. He touches Kennedy's arm. Kennedy looks directly at Jimi.

"What happened to your eye?" Kennedy asks.

Jimi's a little surprised by the question, but answers honestly. "My motorcycle was stolen and I didn't let it go without a fight."

"No shit," says Kennedy. "Not around here."

"In Pennsylvania."

"I used to live in Pennsylvania. Philadelphia."

"Really?"

"Yeah. Caleb tells me you rode cross-country alone."

"I did."

There's something softer in his face now. A hint of a smile. "I think that's admirable," he says. "Not many people give a shit enough to want to see the country anymore. It's all airplanes and cars and trains." He shakes his head, then turns away, the smile lost as he starts watching another couple.

Caleb stares at his friend as if he's seeing him for the first time. And then he stands.

"Already?" Jimi says.

"Already," says Caleb.

He pats Kennedy on the back and they walk away without saying good night or good-bye. Kennedy turns back to look at her as they reach the exit. He genuinely smiles this time. Jimi smiles back, waves. She finishes her seltzer and tries to decide whether or not to stay. She feels wired. She doesn't want to go back to Willow Run yet. She catches Rose staring at her from behind the bar and starts to feel self-conscious. She returns her empty glass and smiles stiffly.

"Watch yourself," Rose tells her, another one of those nearly imperceptible smiles gracing her face. "And don't be a stranger."

"I won't be." Jimi feels something close to affection for the old bartender. Her smile comforts Jimi. Her version of an invitation to come back to Fifth Amendment makes Jimi feel really good. She hadn't realized how much Rose could grow on her in just a few days. It's that realization that makes her hesitate. "Is there something you think I should know about him?"

Rose pauses. Her eyes are hard. "Our boys are good boys until they have a reason not to be," she says.

"What does that mean?"

"Not much if you have to ask." Her face softens. "You take care, that's all."

Jimi waits for more, but Rose is already heading off to take an order. "Thanks," Jimi says, but Rose doesn't hear her.

A block away, Caleb's leaning against his pickup truck, smoking a cigarette.

"I thought you left," Jimi says, looking around for Kennedy. He's nowhere.

"I did leave."

"I thought you were going home."

He drops his cigarette and steps on it. "Couldn't."

"Why not?"

His smile is lazy. "You didn't call."

"That really bruised your ego, huh?"

"Not really." He reconsiders. "Maybe a little."

Jimi laughs. "If it's any consolation, I've missed your pickup," she admits.

"Yeah?"

"Being inside it," she says.

He swallows hard. "Yeah?"

"I don't like many pickups."

He grins.

She leans against the truck, close to him. He smells good and familiar. She hooks her pointer finger in his front pocket and they stare at it there. She looks up first.

"I recognize people," she tells him. "Not just you and Rose. People on the sidewalks, in the shops. Some of them say hello. I could go to the same diner in L.A. three days in a row and not see the same person twice."

He looks up now. "Is that good or bad?" he asks.

"I don't know."

They hold each other's gaze for a full minute. He says, "I think it's good. It means you're aware of us. I can't see living in a place where no one's familiar. Running into strangers every day."

She feels a distant disappointment. "Sometimes I prefer strangers," she says.

"Yeah?" He shifts, seems distracted. "You don't know how bad I want to kiss you right now, do you?"

Jimi drops her finger from his pocket as he moves away from the pickup truck. He leans into her, his left hand against the truck's roof for support, and kisses her. She's surprised by how good his lips feel against hers. Her bruised lip has healed considerably since the last time she saw him, but he's gentle anyway. And in a matter of minutes they're both breathing hard, sweating, ready for something else. She stops him from going further.

"I think we should go to your room," he says.

She agrees, but she doesn't want to explain there's no room to go to. "We can't," she says.

He pauses, his open mouth grows still over hers. He drops his head so their foreheads rest against each other. His hand lingers at her zipper for a few charged minutes. If they were anywhere else, she'd let him in there. But they're here. And a responsible adult would head back to Troy and Sienna before she ended up submitting to something premature.

Caleb reaches behind her and opens the passenger door. "Get in," he tells her.

She gets in. The same big cross she noticed the first day they met dangles from the rearview mirror and she reaches out to touch it. When he gets into the truck, she jumps.

"I can tell that makes you uneasy," he says. "Are you an atheist?"

"No. Are you a religious fanatic?"

Caleb snorts. "How do you get fanatic from a cross?"

"How do you get atheist from uneasy?"

He stares at her for a minute, and then a big grin graces his face. "It's just there," he tells her. "I'd take it down, but it works for me. If I get into a fight, all the old ladies are on my side as soon as they see it."

"So it's a deceptive device."

He grins again, then leans forward and kisses her as he starts the truck.

"Be careful," she manages to tell him as he pulls away from the curb, still kissing her, one hand on the steering wheel. She pulls back, but he stops her.

"I know these roads," he says.

She starts laughing. She's tried a lot of things on her motorcycle and in Russ's company cars. She has points on her license for reckless endangerment. But she's never tried driving while kissing. It's a new and exciting experience. "Where are we going?"

"My house," he says. Off her silence he adds, "It's okay. No strings."

She hasn't had a one-night stand in a long time. And definitely not with someone she's attracted to. Her one-night stands in Brooklyn were about being drunk. Russ was the only person she slept with in Los Angeles. "Where's your place?"

"Here. Right here." He stops kissing her to pay closer attention to his driving. It's pitch-dark. The headlights flash on scampering critters. She can't believe how easy it would be to drive right off the side of the narrow, winding road. She thinks this must be a wonderful road to ride a motorcycle on.

He stops the truck, turns the ignition off. She doesn't see anything ahead of them, around them. She reaches up and turns on the truck's interior light and he looks at her. All of her. He takes his time. Her breathing slows. When his eyes meet hers, he's also having trouble. He says, "I want to get to know you."

She bites her lip. "What happened to 'no strings'?"

"No strings." His eyes focus on her lips. "Just dinner, sometimes. Maybe lunch. Drinks . . . while you're here." He moves forward, starts kissing her again, then slides out of the truck, pulling her with him.

Outside, he swats mosquitoes away from them as they walk the short distance to the house. "Smells like rain," he says. He opens the front door—it isn't locked—and holds it for her. "Do you want to see where I live?" he asks.

# Twelve

His house is the only house on Whiskey Road. Tucked away on ten acres of untamed woodlands, just a mile off Main Street, it's easy to mistake the graveled entrance for a trail to something beautiful. There is no scenic route though. At the end of the long, winding road is just home.

There hasn't been a woman here since Sally left.

Feeling almost shy, he doesn't turn the lights on. She could take one look at him, at this place, and change her mind. He doesn't want her to. Just as he pulls her into an embrace, the porch light comes on. She jumps and he rushes to turn it off. But he hesitates. Unplugging the porch light, this last reminder of Sally, is like taking another step forward. Moving on. Saying good-bye to her for good.

"What's wrong?" she asks, startling him back to the here and now.

"Nothing," he says and unplugs the light.

It's the first time he's had sex in this bed with someone other than Sally. It's a milestone he doesn't feel like celebrating. But he pushes aside the touch of discomfort he's feeling and tightens his arms around her.

"I don't want you to regret this," he whispers.

"Sex should be regrettable," she says.

He laughs; he can't help it.

"You offered something. I took it. I don't regret it. Do you?"

"No." In the past, he would have been happy if a woman said something like this to him. She's relieving him of any responsibility.

"What time is it?"

Caleb looks at the bedside clock on the dresser behind him. "It's 12:23 AM."

"Shit," she says, pulling away from him.

Feeling possessive, he says, "Got somewhere else to be?"

She stops fidgeting.

"You can stay here," he says.

"I can't."

He has an urge to turn on a light, to see her naked. What stops him is his desire to remain invisible a little longer. He's never tried to hide his scars from women. He knows they don't make him beautiful. But it never mattered before. This is different. He wants it to make sense to Jimi before giving her a reason to decide it doesn't.

"Not yet," he tells her. "Where do you need to be now?"

He feels her relax. "Okay." Her voice, like his, has dropped to a whisper, as if she also understands what they're doing can, at any minute, be shattered. After a while she says, "Do you get bored seeing the same people every day?"

"Yes." It's easy to answer honestly in the dark. "It gets boring." He's always bored, always wishing he could leave the Bend and be someone new. "I've wanted to ride out of here since I was in high school. I still think about taking off sometimes. But things come up. Life happens." He remembers what

Kennedy told him the other day. "And I can be myself here. Everybody's used to me."

"Where would you go if you left here?"

"Scotland," he says without hesitation. "I've got some Scottish blood in me. I think I'd like it there."

"Have you ever been overseas?"

"Never been on a plane. You?"

"Yes. To other places. Not Scotland."

"Where?"

"Switzerland, Italy, Holland, Belgium. I was a kid. Eighteen. I couldn't appreciate it. I just wanted to get laid and eat lots of gelato."

"Did you?"

"Eat lots of gelato? Yes. Tons."

"Get laid."

"Twice. In Holland."

He chuckles.

"I bet Scotland would be an awesome trip to do by motorcycle," she says. "I think I'll go with you."

"To get laid or eat gelato?"

"I don't think we'd find gelato in Scotland, so it'd be to get laid. And ride in the Highlands."

"I'm going to hold you to that."

She laughs into his chest as if she thinks he's joking, and then he's aware, again, that they're both naked. He likes the way they feel together, warm and still wet from lovemaking. He likes the way she smells—a combination of peppermint and a scent he can't pinpoint, a scent that reminds him of the lotion Emma uses.

"Tell me something I don't already know about you," he says.

"You don't know a lot."

"Tell me what you do for a living."

She pulls back, out of his arms. "Why do you want to know?"

"I want to know about you."

"I take pictures of celebrities," she offers carefully.

"Portraits?"

"Candids."

"You make money from that?"

"Well, yeah." There's something in her voice that makes her sound like the people he works for. They always manage to make him feel like he should be following some news ticker that updates their lives. As if what's important to them should be important to him. And then she adds, "I was a paparazza."

He remembers a show Dale and Leigh were watching a few months ago about a bunch of guys chasing pop singers and celebrities. "Oh," he says.

"Sometimes I think my bike being stolen is payback for my sins."

He doesn't know what to say to that. He doesn't believe in retribution, especially for something as trivial as taking pictures. "Why did you get started?"

She pulls back again. "You really want to know about this?"

"I wouldn't ask if I didn't want to know the answer."

"I'm used to talking to people who don't give a shit about anything I'm saying until I mention money."

"I'm not them."

She's quiet for a long time, and then she turns onto her back. He places his hand on her stomach beneath the sheets. She covers his hand with her own and he smiles at her, even though he knows she can't see it. She says, "It made me feel invincible."

"So you liked it?"

"A lot. I liked the hunt. The chase. The competition. Every minute of my life held the potential to make money as long as I had my camera ready. And there were things I hated. Bodyguards feeling important for a minute, flashing lights in my face just as I was set to take a picture. Arguments, fist-fights, accidents." She takes a breath. "In the beginning I didn't care about anyone else's pain. I wasn't afraid to take the tough pictures."

"What were the tough pictures?" he asks.

She hesitates. "They were the ones I knew would hurt my subject most."

"I bet they were worth the most, too," he says.

She turns over again, his hand sliding onto her waist. "It's appropriate that I'm telling this to you in the dark. So I can't see your face."

"I thought you don't care what people think. Or maybe you care what I think."

"I wouldn't mind knowing."

What *does* he think? He rarely goes to the movies. Everything he knows about Hollywood he's heard from Sally or Leigh. These days, when he's over at Dale's watching television, Leigh's always cutting in with some gossip about the people on the screen. He barely pays attention. All he knows is they earn a lot more money than he ever will. "I think I can see the allure in it," he says. "But that kind of lifestyle has to take a toll."

"Which one? Mine or theirs?"

"Both."

She touches his face, tickling his nose and mouth with light fingertips. "It does."

"Why'd you quit?"

She laughs. "There are some things I will never tell you."

"Well, don't beat yourself up over this," he says. "It's not like the world's going to spin off its axis because you took a bunch of pictures."

"When you put it that way . . ."

He kisses her shoulder, decides to change the subject. "When are you leaving the Bend?"

"I don't know," she says. "I'm not ready to return to the city."

He's never understood how anyone can live in New York City. He'd visited with Sally once. She'd loved it. The cacophony of jackhammers, car horns and foreign voices, the flashing lights, the crowded bodies. People were a blur. He remembers there was a different stench at every corner. No public bathroom or bench was clean. They were there for four days and he fell asleep each night with an excruciating headache.

"I can't figure out why people choose to live in Manhattan," he says. "With so many other options. If I could afford to leave my life, I'd pick someplace safe. With mountains and gorgeous sky."

She sits up, allowing the sheet to fall away from her. "It's not so easy to relocate. Even if you can afford to."

"Why not?" he asks.

"It just isn't," she says softly.

He touches her, worries this is the end of their evening. This is new for him. This wanting a woman to stay and share his bed with him until morning.

"It's raining," he says.

She listens. "I really do need to get going."

He considers fighting her on this, but he hears the finality in her voice. He doesn't want to give her a reason not to come back. He gets out of bed, grabs his shirt from the floor and puts it on, then struggles into his boxers, and then his jeans. She dresses, too, then turns on the light on the nightstand. When he looks at her again she's watching him. Her smile is divine. Her skin is lovely. He loved fucking her last night. He isn't sure this can be a one-night stand.

"Can I use your bathroom?" she asks.

He shows her to the bathroom, leaning against the wall next to it, watching her.

"Are you going to stand there while I use it?" she asks, sounding amused.

"Let's go out tomorrow night."

She leans against the opposite wall. "Is this still 'no strings'?"

"I'm not sure," he says, words almost catching in his throat. "You're the one going back to Brooklyn."

Her eyes search his face, settle on his mouth. His lips are slightly parted, waiting.

"Okay," she says.

# Thirteen

In the bathroom, alone, Jimi tries to sort through all the feelings she isn't used to having. She's nervous. And excited. And a little concerned. It's the same thing she goes through when she's waiting for an A-list celebrity to walk out of a nightclub. But this time a big-shot actor isn't causing the knots in her stomach.

Caleb had been a gentle lover, afraid to hurt her though she assured him several times that he couldn't. He held on to her afterward, not wanting to let her go. *Not yet,* he'd said. So many times she'd wanted to turn on the light, to *see* him, but worried the bruises on her body would make him even more tentative.

She had determined, before she even walked through his front door, this would only happen once. A one-night stand. So why has she just agreed to see him tomorrow? Why is she now trying to think of a reason to borrow Sienna's car again?

A crack of thunder makes her jump. She listens to the rain beating against the roof for a few minutes. She hopes Troy and Sienna are sleeping. Troy isn't the type to wait up for her, but circumstances are different these days. He's worried. Keeping a close eye on her. How would he react if he knew she'd borrowed his wife's car to drive to Frenchman's Bend to see Caleb? That she knew, in the back of her mind, the kiss they shared Saturday afternoon would lead to this?

Her eyes adjust to the dark again when she comes out of the bathroom. She walks down the hall to the living room as lightning courses through the house, taking her breath away. She opens the front door to step out onto the porch and see the storm up close. A man is standing there, fist poised to knock. He pushes her so hard she stumbles, falls and hits her head against a wall. She feels her lip split open, tastes the blood. *Just when it was beginning to heal.* Panic overtakes her. She's stunned by how easily she was knocked off her feet. She moves when she hears footsteps. She stands, bracing herself for a fight. Preparing herself to bite, kick and gouge. But the living room light comes on and Caleb shoves the intruder, shouting, "What the fuck are you doing?" as if he knows him, then makes his way over to Jimi.

"What the fuck are *you* doing?" the man shouts back, but Caleb ignores him.

"You're bleeding." Caleb uses his thumb to wipe at Jimi's lip. She flinches, pulls back, glares at the man who is now on the other side of the room.

"Hey," he grunts, "I didn't do that shit to her face."

Breathing hard, her hands clenched into fists, all she wants to do is clobber him. Her buttons have been pushed. Caleb's breathing hard, too, but manages to use a gentle touch when he turns her face to him.

"I'm sorry," Caleb says. "That's my brother. Morgan."

Jimi looks at the man again. Caleb's brother? Short and wiry, hair cut close to his head like a marine. His clothes are drenched from the storm—khakis that are too long and ripped at the bottom; a black shirt, its sleeves rolled up to his shoulders. Tattoos on both arms. And his eyes, fastened on Jimi's face, are empty. She wants to look away, but they hold her.

"I didn't mean to hurt you," he says, "but it looks like someone else got there first."

"Fuck you," says Jimi and at the same time Caleb says, "Shut *up*."

Morgan looks amused. "I thought she was trespassing."

"*Trespassing?*" Caleb balks.

"How was I supposed—" Morgan stops speaking and looks as if he's changing his mind. "Whatever I say, right?" He shakes his head. "It won't matter," he finishes with a sneer in Jimi's direction.

Jimi decides it's time to leave.

She goes back to Caleb's bedroom and puts on her shoes. She doesn't want to run away like this, but she doesn't want to fight, either. She'd rather calm down, put something on her lip to stop the ache. Anything but let Caleb's brother get to her. And then she remembers she left Sienna's car in town. So much for leaving through the back door.

She returns to the living room, meeting Caleb just as he's about to come after her. She wants him alone. She wants this other man to disappear so she won't have to ask Caleb for a ride back to town in front of him. If it weren't raining so hard, she'd walk.

"Hey, I'm sorry again," Morgan says.

Jimi looks at him involuntarily. He doesn't look sorry. His face is mildly amused, like someone just whispered a joke in his ear. She looks at his tattoos. One of an alligator ripping off a baby's head transfixes her, making her wonder what on earth he was thinking when he chose it. And then he notices her noticing the spiderweb tattoo on his right elbow as he rubs his hands over his head. He grins.

"Roll down your sleeves," says Caleb.

Morgan glances at Caleb, then back at Jimi. "You don't like tattoos?" he asks.

She feels like cowering and hates herself for it. Ever since she watched a piece on television about neo-Nazi soldiers at Fort Bragg with spiderweb tattoos on their elbows, Jimi has found herself looking at the elbows of all white men with shaved heads who cross her path. She'd checked out Caleb's elbows that first day they met as he walked back to his pickup truck. She's seen the tattoos three other times, in California. Seeing them jarred her each time. Not causing her to fear the men, but causing her to feel sad and disappointed.

Morgan's grin irks her. It lets her know he's the type of person who feeds off of another person's discomfort. She wants to turn the tables on him. She's so tired of people making her feel uncomfortable.

"I love tattoos," she answers. She reaches out and touches the spiderweb on his elbow, closing the distance between them, forcing him to acknowledge her in a way he wasn't expecting to. He tenses and moves his arm a little, staring at her intently with what she thinks is a mixture of confusion and hatred. "Yours must have hurt."

He swallows and glances at his brother, who looks on the verge of intervening. "Bourbon."

Jimi nods. "Tequila."

"You have a tattoo?"

"I cried despite the alcohol."

He *almost* smiles. "Where is it?"

She steps back. "My back. Just above my ass."

He pauses. "Of?"

"My motorcycle."

"I'd like to see that."

"Not in this lifetime," Caleb says.

Caleb's voice brings Morgan back to his cocky self and he moves farther away from Jimi, looks slightly disturbed by what just happened. And then he grins. "Do you know what a web means?"

She nods.

"Somehow I don't think you do, darlin'."

"Then why don't you tell us." Caleb sounds disgusted.

"It doesn't mean I killed someone black." Morgan's words come out slow, as if he thinks she won't understand otherwise. "Nowadays it just means I did time."

*Prison,* Jimi thinks. Figures. Her luck's been shit since she left California. It's only suitable that she'd sleep with a guy just before his recently-released-from-prison brother decides to pay a visit. Caleb had told her a little bit about him, but he'd failed to mention that. *Tell me something I don't already know about you,* he'd said. It seems he should have been the one doing the telling.

"Seriously, sweetheart," Morgan continues, "I know what you're thinking and I gotta tell you you're wrong. Just ignore it." He shrugs at her lack of reaction and walks around the living room, checking out things. Caleb had failed to give her the tour. Now she doesn't bother to look around. She keeps her eyes on Morgan.

He says, "Hasn't changed much since the last time I was here." He rolls down his sleeves to cover his tattoos, then turns around and catches Jimi's eyes again.

The front door opens. Caleb and Jimi jump. A young woman storms into the room, soaked. Her dark hair is plastered to her head and her mascara is smeared all over her eyes and face.

"*Why didn't you wake me up?*" she thunders. She looks at Caleb, then Jimi. She stares. "Hey," she says after a minute.

"Hi," Jimi and Caleb say in unison.

She walks over and puts her arms around Caleb. Caleb accepts the hug stiffly. "I'm Tara."

"Hi, Tara," Caleb croaks, pulling away from her.

She steps back. "I've never had a brother before," she says.

Caleb looks over at Morgan, nonplussed.

"Oh, yeah." Morgan sounds embarrassed. "This is my wife."

"Your wife," Caleb says.

Morgan laughs. "My fucking wife."

Tara catches Jimi staring and smiles.

"Tara," she says.

"Jimi," Jimi says.

"It's nice to finally meet you."

"Finally?"

Tara looks at Morgan and when he doesn't say anything, she looks at Jimi again. "I'd love to stand around and chat, but I'm cold and I'm wet. Where's the bathroom?" She directs the question at Jimi, but Caleb tells her where the bathroom is. She walks off to find it.

"How old is she?" Caleb asks.

"I'm eighteen," she calls out just before she slams the bathroom door shut.

Caleb looks stunned, and then his face becomes unreadable. He reaches out and touches Morgan's head, rubs his hand back and forth to feel the stubble and says, "You're married." Morgan pulls out of Caleb's reach, glancing at Jimi. He twitches his mouth in a strange way and Jimi isn't sure if he's smiling or sneering.

Then Caleb looks at her. "I need to drive you back to town," he says.

"Where are you from?" Morgan asks.

"Brooklyn," Jimi tells him.

Morgan makes a noise with his teeth. "I don't get out to the city much. I don't like to get shot just driving in my car."

"Because there's no way you can get shot here, in deer country," Jimi retorts.

Morgan laughs. "I take it you don't like it here."

"I do. I just find I always have to be prepared."

Morgan snorts. "Prepared for what?"

"Anything," Jimi answers.

He shrugs, raps his knuckles on the wall and says he's going to check on Tara.

Abruptly, Caleb goes outside. An orange light flares in the window and startles Jimi. Light from a match. He's leaning against the porch railing, smoking a cigarette. The screen door squeaks when she opens it. Caleb turns around.

"I'm sorry," he says.

"I have to go," she tells him.

"I know."

They don't move.

"How's your lip?" he asks.

"It'll heal again." She stares at the rain coming down hard.

"I wasn't expecting him." He takes a last drag on his cigarette, then tosses it into the rain. He steps off the porch without looking at her again. She follows, suddenly aware of Morgan watching from the doorway.

"See you," he calls out.

Jimi turns back, but she doesn't say anything.

They ride to Main Street in silence. Caleb feels distant. She's sure she feels the same way to him. When they stop in front of the inn, he turns off the truck's ignition and looks at her. She meets his eyes.

"What did he do?" she asks. She doesn't have a right to ask him, but she wants to know what Morgan's capable of. She's just had sex with his brother.

"He attacked a couple of girls in Texas."

Jimi nods. She'd hoped it hadn't been something like that. "Did he kill them?"

"No. He beat them up, put them in the hospital. He says he didn't do it."

Jimi nods again.

"I'll be honest with you," Caleb says quietly. "I don't know what the truth is. There weren't any witnesses."

No witnesses. What a surprise. The side of her that wants no part of Caleb's family secrets wants to know the details. The side of her that considers Caleb a part of her Frenchman's Bend life doesn't want to know anything. Not even the things Caleb just told her.

"Thank you for being honest with me," she says and it sounds colder than she meant it to.

He nods, looks hurt. "I won't ask if we're still on for tomorrow."

She opens the door, feels the rain pelt her arm. She gets out and runs toward the inn. He doesn't drive away until she opens the front door. She waits for the truck to disappear around a corner before she makes her way back to Sienna's car.

# Fourteen

Morgan's home.

Not *home,* really, but here. In Caleb's house. It hasn't been Morgan's place since he sold his half to Caleb and moved to Texas. He can't just appear at the door in the middle of the night and uproot Caleb's life whenever he pleases. Caleb has to figure out how to remind him of that without raising hell. But not tonight.

When Caleb walks into the house, soaked to his skin after dropping Jimi off at the inn, Morgan's slouched on the sofa. The television's blaring. Two beer cans are on Sally's antique trunk next to a package of rolling paper and tobacco.

"You think you know someone . . ." Morgan looks up from the television.

Caleb runs his hands over his head, kicks off his shoes and pulls off his shirt, dropping it by the door. "What?"

"You," says Morgan, "shacking up with a black chick."

"Not exactly."

Morgan checks a nonexistent watch on his bare wrist, then looks at Caleb with a smirk.

"She's a friend," says Caleb.

"Right." Morgan chuckles. "Friends. I didn't think you'd do that."

"What, make a friend?"

"Shack up with a black chick. I thought you were into . . . other things."

"I like nice girls."

"Since when?"

"Maybe you don't know me as well as you think you do."

They stare at each other. It's not that Caleb never liked nice girls. He just never gave a damn one way or the other. And staring at Morgan now, he knows he does want a nice girl. And he doesn't want to be that man who lets someone go because people think his attraction to her is wrong. He *is* different from people. From Morgan.

"I'm sorry I roughed her up," Morgan says.

The ride back to the inn had been awkward, to say the least. The incident with his brother was the last thing in the world Jimi needed. She's just starting to get over the ordeal with her motorcycle. And she was beginning to trust him. He could tell by the way she smiled after she turned on the light in his bedroom. She was going to see him again tomorrow night. And then he noticed her staring at Morgan's tattoo and he could feel it slipping away. He felt ashamed and impatient. How does Morgan always manage to show up at the most inopportune moments?

In his pickup, Jimi's silence was relentless. She only spoke to ask why Morgan had been in jail. She had looked so cold. He knew he'd be setting himself up for rejection if he repeated his desire to see her.

"Why'd you jump all over her like that?" he asks Morgan.

Morgan looks at him as if he isn't sure Caleb's asking a serious question. "I come home to find some stranger in my house. How'd you think I'd react?"

"*My* house?" Caleb says.

Morgan stares and Caleb notices his brother is still a handsome bastard, much better looking than Caleb. It's why women have always put up with his antics. They put up with Caleb's antics, too, but Morgan's meaner and his women always outlasted Caleb's. Morgan waves his hand. "Your house; my house. We're going to argue about stupid shit? I just got here. What kind of hello is this for your big brother?"

Morgan's right. Caleb doesn't want to argue. He has a lot to take in right now. *Morgan's back. Morgan's married.*

"Speaking of *nice girls,*" Morgan says, "I ran into Sally when I was in California."

"I know."

Morgan looks surprised. "She called you."

"She called Leigh."

"Not you?"

Caleb shakes his head.

Morgan nods, taking in this turn of events. "So that ship has sailed, huh? I wondered what she was doing in California without you."

Caleb says nothing.

"She looked real good. Had one of them short haircuts that made her look like a little man. It suits her."

Caleb tries to imagine Sally with short hair. Can't. "Why didn't you call when you got out?"

Morgan shrugs. "I thought about it."

"And you decided not to because . . . ?"

"I didn't think I'd be high on your list of people to see and I didn't want to make any trouble for you and Sally. Little did I know . . ."

"I wrote to you."

"Yeah." Morgan is suddenly distracted by the television. "You divorced?"

"No."

Morgan laughs, then stops when he sees the look on Caleb's face. "Me and Tara will be staying for a while," he says.

"How long is 'a while'?"

Morgan stares at the television, hypnotized by the image of a girl in a bikini. He looks at Caleb once the girl leaves the screen. "What?"

"How long is 'a while'?"

"Hmm." Morgan considers, then frowns. "Hey! You're dripping all over the carpet."

Caleb grabs a hand towel from the kitchen and walks back into the living room while he dries himself off. He stares at his brother, smoking, staring at the television, acting like he's home after a short vacation. What the hell is Caleb going to do with him? So far, he doesn't seem changed. He was born difficult. Smoking cigarettes and dope by twelve; fucking high school girls at thirteen; breaking into houses when he was seventeen. He'll always be the same.

"Where's your wife?" Caleb asks.

"Probably taking a shower," says Morgan, reaching for the tobacco and paper, rolling a cigarette without even looking away from the television. He's been rolling his own cigarettes since he was fifteen. "She takes a shower every ten minutes, that one. Hey, where do you want us, man?"

Caleb rests the towel on his shoulder and shrugs. "You can sleep wherever you want to. The cottage has to be aired out . . ."

Morgan's nodding. "It'll be like a fucking palace compared to some of the places we've been staying. We'll get settled as soon as she gets out of the bathroom. Sheets for the bed still in the hall closet?"

Caleb nods. He still can't believe Morgan's here. He'd expected him to return to the Bend, but not this quickly. "Tara."

Morgan looks up. He blows smoke out of the side of his mouth. "What about her?"

"She's a child."

Morgan lowers his eyes as he puts out his cigarette in the ashtray on the trunk. He stands up, raises his arms above his head and yawns. Caleb notices he's thin, thinner than a man just out of prison should be. One thing Morgan would have done while incarcerated was weight lifting. Tara had also looked very thin.

He clears his throat and looks Caleb squarely in the eye. "I did something stupid," he says.

Morgan's "something stupid" has always meant something irreparable: from taking some high school sophomore's virginity when he and Caleb were in junior high to killing Sally's new dog when he lived with them.

"Couple of guys," Morgan continues, "looking for Tara and me."

"What guys?"

Morgan shrugs. "Those girls, you know. The ones I went to jail for hitting? Their brothers paid me a visit before I got out, said they'd be waiting for me."

Caleb stands absolutely still, hands tight at his sides, actually holding his breath.

"Thought I'd head up to Canada somewhere," Morgan says. "If you have a couple thousand to hold me over until I can work some things out. I'll get the money back to you as soon as I can."

"I don't have a couple thousand dollars to hand over to you just like that."

"I wouldn't ask if I didn't need it."

"I don't have it."

Morgan narrows his eyes. His jaw tenses. "This is the wrong crowd to tangle with."

"Then why'd you tangle with them?"

Morgan sits down again and starts to roll another cigarette. "I hear ya."

"What aren't you telling me?"

Morgan shrugs again. "You don't need to know everything."

Caleb feels rage building up in him. Before he can stop himself, he shoves Morgan so hard the tobacco in Morgan's hand scatters across the table and onto the floor. Morgan looks alarmed, angry and then amused, all in a matter of seconds. He starts to laugh. "I guess that means you do," he says.

Morgan brings out the worst in Caleb. The slightest provocation sets Caleb off and he feels his blood pumping, pressure rising. Morgan hasn't been here two hours and he's already doing it, making Caleb wonder why he ever thought he was anyone other than the man the world already thinks he is.

"You just got out of jail," Caleb says.

"And that is precisely why these guys are on my ass," says Morgan, sounding glib.

"Maybe you should think about getting a job."

"A *job*?" Morgan looks incredulous. "I need that money now. I needed that money yesterday. I can think about getting a job when I get to Canada."

"I can't help you."

Morgan stands up again, walks around the table and leans into Caleb, his mouth close to Caleb's ear. "I'm in big fucking trouble, brother," he whispers hoarsely. "I need you to come through for me."

Caleb closes his eyes, exhales. "Why'd you bring it here?"

There's a silence, but Morgan doesn't move. He leans in a little closer, and Caleb feels the weight of him. "I had nowhere else to go."

"Morgan."

Morgan and Caleb separate. Behind them, Tara's leaning against the wall, looking bored. She wears an oversized T-shirt that says "California" across the front of it. Morgan walks over to her, strokes her hair until it's flat on her head and starts whispering in her ear.

"We're going to get some sleep." Morgan and Tara are staring at him. "You going to be around tomorrow?"

"I have to go to the office." And he has to call Dale, Kennedy and Joseph to let them know Morgan's back. He suspects the first thing Morgan will do once he's had some sleep is stroll down Main Street and pay a few social calls.

"We'll try to catch you before you leave," says Morgan, ushering Tara down the hall toward the back door that leads to the cottage. "I'll call you at work if I miss you."

Caleb nods, dazed. When he hears the back door close he opens the front door and looks out. It's still raining, but not as hard as it was earlier. He heads directly for Morgan's Dodge 4x4. It's new, black and imposing with a band of orange lights across the roof and a lip over its windshield. The windows are dark and hard to see through even with his face pressed against them. The license plate on the rear of the Dodge is from New Mexico and on close inspection Caleb can tell someone has used light-yellow and white paint to turn the eight into a zero in an attempt to match the paint with the license plate's colors.

*Stolen.*

Caleb leans against the truck as rain runs over him. What has his brother brought to him? And just as he's starting to believe he can reinvent himself.

# Fifteen

Maybe it's wrong to punish a man for not telling her about his brother. *Punish* probably isn't the right word. Not driving to Frenchman's Bend for a drink at Fifth Amendment and, possibly, some heavy kissing in his pickup truck isn't punishment. It's a reaction to meeting Morgan. A man she doesn't want to see again, but knows she will see if she visits Caleb. Morgan is a jolting reminder that no matter what you share with a man, he's still a stranger until you meet his family. And even then you don't know everything.

It's true that first impressions are important. Being shoved by Morgan left Jimi with the impression that he's someone she doesn't want to be around. He's an ask-questions-later kind of guy. That can be handy if he's on her team, but she can't think of a reason why he'd ever have to be.

Of course it isn't Caleb's fault his brother's an ex-con with a web tattoo, sinister mouth and blank stare. But when she took off yesterday, she wanted so much to be taking off for good. And here it is, Thursday. And already she's trying to come up with an excuse to leave Troy and Sienna's dinner party so she can track Caleb down.

*No.* Not track Caleb down. She isn't going back to Frenchman's Bend to see him.

She has no excuse to leave the dinner anyway. It's in her honor. With six journalists from Manhattan Troy and Sienna used to work with. Jimi finds these intimate gatherings daunting. There's never a private moment for someone, *her,* to regroup in a quiet corner and gear up for the next round of invasive questions about her job, her love life and her political convictions. Everyone is required to be "on" every second of the evening. Jimi likes to be able to fade away, daydream and tune people out. It's the only way she can deal with them for long stretches.

Right now she's sitting on the rim of the bathtub in the second-floor bathroom, smoking, even though Sienna has asked her twice not to smoke in the house. When she hears the last guest leave at 8:30, she drops her cigarette in the toilet, flushes and escapes the bathroom for the kitchen. She pours two glasses of wine, grabs the stick Sienna gave her as protection against coyotes and bears, steps through the open screen door and follows the scent of tobacco to her brother. As soon as he notices her, he drops the cigarette on the ground and steps on it. Jimi hands him one of the wineglasses.

"Hey, kiddo," he says.

"Hey yourself." She doesn't tease him about the cigarette. The last thing she wants to do at the moment is bring up the secrets he keeps from Sienna. "Let's walk."

He sips the wine, hesitates. "You have the stick?"

Jimi hands Troy the stick. She wonders what Caleb would say about it.

"You were distant tonight," she says.

"I'm sorry," he says, grinding the cigarette deep into the grass with his foot, no longer caring whether or not she sees it. They start walking toward the front of the house. "I was listening to you talk to my friends tonight about your job," he says, "and you were being very careful. Making it not sound like what it really is."

"Which is?"

"Stalking."

"I think 'stalk' is a little harsh."

"You're better than that job."

She chuckles. "Maybe."

"It *diminishes* you."

"I've been trying to think of a reason why I do it and part of it is that I'm not pretty enough or glamorous enough to be a celebrity. Being part of the paparazzi allows me to live out the Hollywood fantasies I didn't know I had. But it's also . . . the excitement. I like being in control of the danger I'm in."

Troy thinks about it for a minute. Maybe a glimmer of understanding passes across his face. She isn't sure.

"I still can't believe you do it."

"Why?"

He stops walking and looks her squarely in the face. "Because paparazzi photographers are *assholes.*"

"Have you met any? Besides me."

"No. But that's my point. I don't think you're an asshole."

"The question has never been whether or not we're assholes," Jimi says, "but whether or not we have a right to be."

"But what about people who say you're violating someone's privacy?" Troy asks.

"They're usually the same people who buy the magazines my pictures are in. They're hypocrites." They walk back to the deck. "Listen, Troy, it's danger on my terms. I control it."

"No one controls danger."

Sienna slides the screen door open. "Why don't you two come in and help me finish this bottle of wine?"

Troy looks at the glass he's holding. Nearly empty. He goes up the stairs to the deck and inside the house. Jimi follows him. In the dining room, Sienna sets the open bottle of wine in the middle of the table as Jimi and Troy sit. Sienna kisses the corner of Troy's mouth, then narrows her voracious eyes at Jimi. "Tell us all the gory details."

Troy groans. "Sienna."

"Honey, you know you want to know."

Troy doesn't deny it, but Jimi feigns ignorance. "About what?"

"Your brother turns on the television every weeknight at seven sharp," Sienna tattles. "And we watch *The Insider* and *Entertainment Tonight* and try to pick you out of the crowds of all the screaming photographers."

"I don't scream," Jimi says.

Sienna gives Troy a light punch in the shoulder. "See? I knew she wasn't a screamer."

"I never said she was," Troy says. He looks at his sister. "I wasn't sure if you just stood there or shouted out encouragement."

Jimi stares at her brother. She pictures him tuning in to the entertainment shows every night like clockwork, looking for a glimpse of her.

"Tell us everything."

Sienna's grin is sudden and almost catching, and the wine they're drinking is good. But Jimi is hesitant. Suspicious. This is what she's wished for, actually: an intimate conversation about her life in Los Angeles, hidden away from the rest of the world, feeling comfortable enough and tipsy enough to speak candidly. Everyone at tonight's dinner party had asked for gossip on their favorite actors, but they'd made her feel dirty. Ushering her aside where no one would see them.

"Really?" Jimi says.

"Absolutely," Sienna says. "Yes. We won't judge."

Troy and Jimi give her a look.

"Okay," she says. "We'll *try* not to judge."

Jimi looks at Troy again. He's trying not to smile. Trying to look disapproving and stern. But he's had too much to drink and it's obvious he's been waiting for an opportunity like this one. Just like Jimi has been.

So she tells them about her first stakeout with Russ. And the time a television actress called her a bitch, screaming it out loudly, calling attention to Jimi and her camera. And the time she agreed to sleep with a bouncer for a tip on a ubiquitous socialite, then backed out when she got it. The time she was buying a newspaper on Rodeo Drive when she spotted a rock star's black Suburban. Not even the tinted windows could hide him inside because Jimi recognized the license plate number. She'd pursued him for over twenty minutes before she lost him. And then he pulled up beside her, window rolled down, video camera in hand. He was taping her. *Taping Jimi.* Instinctively, she rolled up her windows and took off. The rock star raced after her. It was like playing tag, only in really expensive cars on the streets of Los Angeles. The rock star eventually caught up with her, got out of his car with a baseball bat and bashed in her windows. And the time she hid under a Dumpster behind a plastic surgeon's office to get a picture of an actress who'd just had her lips done. Jimi was going for a shot of the bandages, but they outwitted her by exiting through the front entrance.

She doesn't admit to the adrenaline rush she gets now, talking about it, while Sienna leans forward, laughing and poking Troy, both in danger of tipping over Jimi's wineglass.

"You actually hid under a Dumpster?" Troy says.

Jimi leans back and rests her feet in her chair. She stares at her brother, remembering the stench of the garbage. As bad as the smell was, she misses that time under the Dumpster. She nods and he shakes his head.

"I don't get it," he says.

What Troy pretends not to get is the allure. Why celebrity matters. But, really, he knows there's no feeling like the feeling one has in a fine restaurant: five waiters hovering around the table to cater to one's desire, the sommelier making a brief appearance to compliment the wine choice, feeling the buzz of the rich food, the expensive spirits, the complimentary champagne. She knows Troy understands because she's heard him rave about "good service." Not just good service, but the best service, reserved for the rich and famous. *She* understands because Russ would sometimes take his photographers out for fancy dinners, away from L.A., where no celebrity would spot them. They laughed at the irony of hiding in order to have a peaceful meal in an elegant restaurant. It went unspoken that they understood why people flock to Hollywood, give up their virginity for a chance at a small role in a film and change everything about their bodies, their teeth and their hair. Troy knows, too, but he pretends he doesn't.

Jimi shrugs. "I don't ask that you understand what I do. I ask that you respect my right to do it."

Troy sits back in his chair. "I'm sorry. I can't."

The doorbell rings. Sienna walks off to answer it. Troy and Jimi stare at each other. She leans forward, prepared to tell him about her last roll of film and the six hundred grand it made her, but Sienna comes back into the dining room before she can begin. With a man. Jimi looks up and freezes.

Caleb's standing by the kitchen. "I'm sorry I'm late," he's saying, looking at his watch. "It's after nine. I should have called to reschedule."

"It's not too late for us," Sienna tells him. "Dale said you don't remember us."

Caleb laughs. "When I saw the house, I remembered you." He looks at Jimi, does a double take. The shock on his face turns to confusion, then relief. The relief makes her nervous. She hasn't yet decided how to handle this.

"Troy," Sienna says, "you remember Mr. Atwood from last year?"

Troy nods, stands up to shake Caleb's hand.

"Call me Caleb," Caleb tells them. He looks at Jimi again and she realizes he's waiting for her to make the decision. Do they know each other or not?

"Jimi," Sienna continues, "this is our contractor, Caleb Atwood. Caleb, this is my sister-in-law, Jimi Anne Hamilton."

Jimi holds out her hand. Caleb stares at it. Something passes over his face and she can see him shut down completely. It only takes a second to make a bad decision and she knows she's made one. His eyes turn cold. Sienna and Troy don't notice. Sienna's pulling a chair out for him and Troy's checking if there's a clean glass on the table. Caleb shakes Jimi's hand, barely touching it.

Jimi sits down, trying hard not to stare at him. She replays her own words from a few minutes ago: *I don't ask that you respect what I do. I ask that you respect my right to do it.* Yet, she doesn't want Troy and Sienna to know she's been messing around with a local. And looking at him now, with his long scar and defiant tattoo, she knows most people would question her sanity. He's attractive, but it's a raw and crude kind of beauty. Not at all mainstream. And it certainly isn't enough to justify going home with him, fucking him, still wanting him. She knows so little about him. And he's so outside of her world. Not because he's white. She's experienced blue eyes before, or in his case, brown. He's outside of her world because, to put it simply, he's *country.*

He declines a glass of wine, but accepts a glass of water. He pulls a notebook from his back pocket and smiles at Troy and Sienna. He ignores Jimi. After five minutes, Jimi excuses herself and he finally looks at her, but there's nothing in his look. It's as if she isn't even there.

She stands in the hallway, where they can't see her. She doesn't care about the improvements, but she listens. Fifteen minutes later he excuses himself to use the bathroom, telling Sienna that he remembers where it is. Jimi watches him pass the bathroom and look up the flight of stairs. *Looking for her.* When he sees her standing in the hall, he pauses, then walks over. He leans against the wall, stares at her. She fidgets under his gaze.

"Don't ever run away from me," he says, his voice soft and his eyes cold.

"I'm sorry."

His eyes don't move from her face. "I called you. Lucy said you checked out Sunday morning."

"She didn't lie to you."

He presses the palms of his hands to his face, then removes them. His eyes are red, angry. But when he notices her swelled bottom lip, he touches it with the tips of his fingers. Her first instinct is to pull away, but his fingers aren't rough. His touch is so light she barely feels it. He smells like tobacco, clove and bourbon.

"Fucking Morgan," he whispers.

He turns away and goes back to the dining room to finish his meeting with Troy and Sienna. Jimi escapes outside, gets into Sienna's car, rolls down the windows and lights a cigarette. For the next half hour she smokes, listens to crickets, enjoys the evening country air and feels terrible.

When the front door opens, she tosses her cigarette out the window and sits completely still. She watches Caleb leave. Her breath catches as he pauses in the front yard to put his cap on and looks directly at her. She wills him to walk over and talk to her. But he walks over to his truck, starts his engine and drives past her, flashing his headlights over the Outback's windshield to let her know that he knows she's there.

When he's gone, she lights another cigarette and smokes a little longer. Sienna opens the passenger door and gets into the car. Jimi doesn't look at her as she reaches for the cigarette.

"I thought you quit," Jimi says.

Sienna closes her eyes as she takes a drag and cherishes it. She hands the cigarette back to Jimi and they sit in silence. "Don't tell Troy."

"Did he get the job?" Jimi asks after a while.

"Oh, yeah," Sienna says. "We adore him. He built our deck and he basically designed our entire kitchen."

Jimi's impressed. Their kitchen is pretty thrilling. She makes a mental note to pay closer attention to the deck. "You adore him?"

"Nice guy. You wouldn't know it from the look of him, but you can't always judge a book by its cover."

"So, he'll be back tomorrow?" she asks, keeping her voice casual.

"Monday."

"Monday," Jimi repeats quietly.

"I'm drunk," Sienna says. She opens the car door, but she doesn't get out. "Don't be hard on Troy."

Jimi takes a last drag on her cigarette and opens her side of the door. They get out of the car at the same time and look at each other.

"I wasn't," Jimi says.

"He thinks you can do better and he's absolutely right. You're too good for hiding under Dumpsters and racing through the streets of L.A. after Botoxed actresses."

"You said you wouldn't judge."

"I said I'd try. And, I'm sorry, I tried but now I'm judging. You and me? We're simply not the kind of women who do these things."

Jimi stares at Sienna's beautiful face in the moonlight, her unblemished brown skin and her relaxed hair pulled tightly back into a bun. Her dark eyes aren't even bloodshot after a full evening of consuming alcohol. She says she's drunk, but she stands there like a woman ready to take on the world. As usual, she's perfect. That works for her. Sienna isn't the kind of woman who does "these things," but Jimi is. Jimi's *done* them. And she loved every minute of it. Jimi's also the kind of woman who'd borrow Sienna's car to go have a one-night stand with a Frenchman's Bend local.

"Let's go to bed," says Sienna.

They walk back to the house together, but Jimi feels completely alone.

# Whiskey Road

# Sixteen

After all of her bullshit about him not being a stranger, last night she'd treated him like one. He should have seen this coming. When he called the inn Wednesday morning, Lucy told him Jimi had checked out over the weekend. He couldn't believe it. He was with her Tuesday night. Where was she staying if she wasn't staying at the inn? And then he remembered the first time they met. She'd asked how far Willow Run was from the Bend and he'd had a feeling she was on her way there. Or trying to avoid it. But he didn't put it all together.

He should have. Because how many black families has he worked with? Three, tops. All young couples, now that he thinks about it. Unmemorable to him, like all the other transplants he works with. He hadn't thought to connect Jimi to any of them simply because they're black.

He's avoiding Fifth Amendment tonight, even though it's Friday. He doesn't want to be anywhere she can find him. If she shows up at the bar, his absence will send a clear message that Caleb Atwood isn't playing games. Not that he thinks she'll show up. The look on her face last night said it all. She wasn't happy to see him, had probably planned never to see him again.

The checkout girl at Davidson's Food Market smiles at him. They've had an innocent flirtation with each other for the past year, but he's never even looked at her name tag. He glances at it now. Jane. She's pretty. He's always been aware of that, but indifferent. If he asks her to meet him after her shift to share the six-pack he's currently buying, she'll probably say yes. But he's not in the mood for Jane. He wants Jimi. *And that's just rich.*

"Have a good night," Jane tells him as she hands over his change. Her fingers graze his palm deliberately. He takes his six-pack and leaves, glad the week is finally over.

Morgan's Dodge isn't parked in front of the house, which means Caleb has the place to himself. Good. He likes to wallow in his misery without company. The porch steps creak. They could stand to be replaced. But why bother? No one comes up here. He doesn't want company. And how ironic would it be if he finally got around to renovating shit after his wife left him? Used to want to do it to bring her back. Now he doesn't want her back. Just wants to finally close that chapter of his life and move on.

He still lives like she's going to walk through the door any minute though. He puts the seat down. He washes the dishes at night and takes the garbage out before he goes to sleep—she hated waking up to a messy kitchen. He mostly smokes on the porch.

*Old habits die hard,* he thinks.

He puts the beer in the refrigerator. He's in the shower by ten, outside smoking twenty minutes later. He's never minded smoking on the porch. It doesn't feel like a chore to him. There's always a breeze up here. Tonight the air is thick and the breeze is a whisper, but it still feels good to be outside.

As he smokes, he listens to deer moving through the surrounding woods. He likes the sound of their gentle footsteps.

There's something both comforting and chilling about them. When he was a child, his aunt warned of leopards and cougars waiting to pounce so he wouldn't creep out at night when she wasn't paying attention. He was ten before he realized leopards and cougars couldn't be found here. He closes his eyes while he listens. The footsteps get louder, daring him to be spooked.

When he opens his eyes Jimi's standing in front of him and she gives him a start. She's the last person in the world he expected to see. His chest tightens. He's torn between liking the surprise and hating it. They stare at each other for a long time.

"Hi," she says.

The heat from his cigarette reminds him he's holding one. He takes a slow drag, blows the smoke in her direction.

"It's late," he says.

"No, it isn't."

He's been thinking too much about going to work in Willow Run on Monday morning. Unsure if he could ignore her; sure as hell he couldn't spend the day pretending to be a stranger. He's been thinking too much about seeing her face, wanting to know if she'd be able to look him in the eye. He waits for her to look up again, so he can have an answer.

"I was in the neighborhood," she says, looking behind him, at anything but his face. The pink lock of hair glints in the moonlight. After a minute she sighs. "Say something."

"I don't really know what to say."

She steps closer and finally looks directly in his eyes. "I wish I'd handled things differently last night."

He holds her gaze, trying not to show his ambivalence about her presence. He doesn't want her to be here. He doesn't want her to go.

She continues, "I wish I hadn't pretended you were a stranger."

"So you're here to, what, apologize?"

"Yes."

He chuckles and she looks annoyed.

"You don't think that's funny?"

"No," she says.

"Why'd you pretend not to know me?" he asks.

He watches her bite the corner of her lip. It takes her too long to answer. He starts to go inside the house to get the keys for his truck so he can drive her wherever she needs to go, but he turns back. "If it had been the other way around, and you saw me with my family, and I pretended not to know you, would you be pissed off?"

"That isn't fair," she says evenly. "I met your brother in the middle of the night. And Kennedy appeared at the window of your pickup while I was sitting in it. You didn't have to choose."

"Would you be pissed?"

"*Yes.*" She sounds frustrated. "But—"

"You think I would have chosen to pretend I didn't know you? *Hadn't fucked you?*"

"*I don't know,*" she says, sounding equally incensed.

"I'll drive you back," he says, losing steam, feeling dejected. The truth is he doesn't know how he would have handled a choice like the one she had. He pauses. "Wait a minute. How'd you get up here?"

"I left Troy's pickup on the road so you wouldn't hear me coming," she admits. "I didn't want you to be prepared."

He almost smiles. "You walked Whiskey Road in the dark?"

"Yes."

He's impressed. Whiskey Road is steep and narrow and his house sits at the top of the hill. It isn't the most welcoming path at night. Nearly impenetrable darkness could lead a person over the edge, into a ravine. No one would know until morning. Maybe not even then. And with a bad ankle, it couldn't have been easy. He pulls a lawn chair close to the porch steps and motions for her to come up.

She thinks about it, and after a moment she comes up and sits on the chair. He sits on the other one, near the front door, leaning forward, elbows resting on his knees. He keeps his head bowed so she can't see his face.

"It was a one-night stand," she says.

His laugh is short.

"And it would have been very inconvenient to explain to Troy how we knew each other at that moment," she continues, losing her temper. Caleb looks at her and she meets his eyes. Fierce and angry. "He thinks I was in Frenchman's Bend one night and I didn't want to be cross-examined about my reasons for being here for three days. So I took the easy route. I'm sorry. I didn't do it to hurt you."

"That's all?" he pushes. "Inconvenience?" He understands her dilemma right now. How do you tell your lover that he isn't good enough to be introduced to your family because he's a contractor, a townie, white? "Why didn't you tell me you were staying in Willow Run when I took you back to the inn Tuesday night? Why didn't you call me? I gave you my number."

She takes a breath, pushes her hands through her hair. "We declared nothing," she says. "I didn't owe you an explanation."

"No. But I thought you'd want to give me one."

"Not after meeting Morgan. He gave 'no strings' new meaning."

Caleb slouches back in his chair, embarrassed by the memory of his brother's actions. "Yeah, of course he did."

"I wasn't planning to see you again," she says. "Not because I didn't *want* to see you."

He looks at her. These last words make him feel stupidly hopeful. "I'm not Morgan," he says.

"I know. But that doesn't mean Troy would approve of you. You could lose the job with them."

He doesn't care about the job. But he needs it. Dale would be upset if he lost it. He finishes his beer and stands up. "Why? Because I'm white?"

"Because you have tattoos. And scars. He wouldn't care about the color of your skin."

He knows that can't be true. Everyone cares a little bit about skin color.

"Seriously," she says, "it would be about the scars and tattoos."

"I meant it when I said I want to get to know you," he tells her. "I won't back down. But I can't change the tattoos or the scars."

"I think they're beautiful," she says quietly.

He isn't sure he heard her correctly. "You what?"

"I wish I could take your picture."

He swallows, surprised, and then he smiles. "Why can't you?"

"My camera equipment was stolen with my bike."

"I'm sorry."

She looks away. "I won't tell Troy I'm sleeping with you. Not yet."

Caleb pauses. *Not yet* implies there's a future. She hadn't said *slept,* she'd said *sleeping.* He'd thought, merely ten minutes ago, he'd never be able to touch her again.

"You won't have to," he says.

She looks out at the yard. He waits.

"Maybe I should go move Troy's pickup off the road," she says.

# Seventeen

He holds the front door open for her. She steps inside and he follows. He left the air on low. The drone of the air conditioner is the only sound between them. He feels slightly self-conscious. In a way, this is almost like a first visit. The last time she was here, he hadn't bothered to turn on the lights. With her now, he sees the house the way a stranger would.

There should be a coffee table there, separating the television and the brown sofa. There's the antique trunk, purchased somewhere in Ithaca, instead. The grandfather clock in the corner is beautiful and grand, but dusty. He rarely looks at it now that it no longer works. There's a rowing machine in another corner, and a shopping bag overflowing with stuff, he isn't sure what. The square tan rug in the middle of the room needs to be cleaned. An end table is covered with mail he hasn't opened.

"It looks different," she says. "Now that I can see it. I like it."

He doesn't want to waste any more time looking at the house. He motions for her to follow him down the hall. She doesn't move.

"Can we ride Whiskey Road?" she asks.

"Right now? At night?"

"Why do you think I'm dressed this way?"

He hadn't been paying attention to her clothes. She's wearing her black leather pants, a white T-shirt and black riding boots. He loves the way the silver bracelets she's wearing look against her brown skin, loves the way the leather hugs her hips. *Loves that she's the first woman to ask him if they can ride Whiskey Road.* No woman he's ever been with has asked to ride down Whiskey Road. It's bound to be the best motorcycle ride of her life.

"Don't tell me you're afraid to ride that road in the dark," she says.

He scoffs. "I live at the top of this road. You think I haven't done it in the dark before?"

"I don't know. Have you?"

"Yeah. Thousands of times."

Years ago, before he was married, before he owned Bend Contractors with Dale, when the house, the cottage, and the land still belonged partly to Morgan, the place was a haven for him and his friends. They'd meet at the top of Whiskey Road every evening to drink bourbon, smoke weed and ride their motorcycles down the sharp curves in search of a new kind of daring. Once, Morgan flew off his bike and broke his arm in three places. Caleb and Kennedy took a few falls that required stitches. Didn't matter. Once they were healed, they were on their bikes again. At midnight, they'd go down at top speed, taking the pitch-black road recklessly, almost as if they were hoping one of them would ride off the edge. All of that ended after Morgan left for Texas and Sally moved in. It's been too many years since someone invited him to do it again.

The Harley is parked in back of the house. Jimi looks around, but in the dark nothing else is visible.

"Can I ride her?" she asks.

"No, I think I better do it. I've been on Whiskey Road a thousand times, which is a thousand times more than you."

Jimi sits on the bike. "Get on," she says.

He's never been the passenger, so it feels strange when he wraps his arms around her waist. She asks if he's ready before she takes off. And then they're riding past his house and onto Whiskey Road, instantly racing down the dangerous path at a speed not even Caleb would attempt. When they approach a steep turn that both descends and jackknifes, Jimi instinctively downshifts before Caleb warns her, and cuts a perfect turn that takes his breath away.

At the bottom, Caleb sits for a few minutes, gripping her tightly, glad it's too dark for her to see his face. He hadn't realized he was scared. He relaxes and they take their helmets off at the same time. She turns around, asks if he's okay.

"What made you slow down at the turn?"

Jimi stares at him, waits for him to get off the bike. Then she tells him about the split oak fifty yards before the turn. She'd noticed it when she walked from the car. Again, Caleb's impressed. He didn't think she could do it. Even Dale, after he'd been riding for two years and after driving his car to Caleb's house every day, refused to take his bike down Whiskey Road at night. He'd always opted to watch.

"Thanks for letting me ride," she says.

"I should be thanking you," he tells her. "It was the best fucking ride of my life."

She laughs, her head falling back in a way he's never witnessed. It's beautiful, that laugh. It makes him want to kiss her.

"Troy and Sienna aren't wondering where you are?" he asks.

"Troy and Sienna are in Connecticut until Sunday," says Jimi. "A wedding. So, I'm house-sitting."

"That's good news," he says and means it. "We don't have to rush."

She laughs again and he realizes he's in trouble. Because he wants to touch her, and there hasn't been a woman he's wanted to touch this badly since he first met Sally.

"What?" says Jimi.

"Let's go back."

She puts on her helmet and slides backward to make room for him. He gets on the bike and she wraps her arms around his waist and squeezes a signal for him to take off.

It's that time in the morning when the sky casts a bluish tint on the world around him and the heat isn't yet unbearable. He doesn't remember falling asleep.

When he sits up, he looks at Jimi lying next to him, looking serene. Last night, they'd taken things slower than they had the first time they slept together, but he still made sure the lights were out before he undressed. In the back of his mind was the knowledge that they weren't having a one-night stand. If his one visible scar would matter to her brother, he believes the rest of them would matter to her.

He dresses before she awakens. In the kitchen, he searches for something to feed her when she gets up.

"You're up early." She's standing in the kitchen archway, bedsheet draped around her naked body.

"It's been a while since I woke up with someone," he admits.

"Then we have something else in common."

"Yeah?"

"Yes."

He relaxes a little; he finds it odd that he was tense. He's had a lot of girls. For some reason he has to keep reminding himself of that. "This is different."

She smiles. "For me, too."

"Are you hungry?" he asks. "I don't have a lot of food in the house, but I can make eggs . . ."

"Coffee," she says. "Troy and Sienna don't drink it, so I haven't had any in a few days."

"I don't have coffee." He adds it to the mental list of things he'll have to buy so she'll come back, along with milk, bread and steak. "I can get some. I'll go to town. Fifteen minutes; there and back."

"No," she says, "don't leave me here alone."

Left unsaid is "with Morgan." Morgan will sleep until noon, but what if Caleb goes into town and Morgan picks today to wake up early? He nods, grabs a can of soda, keeps the refrigerator door open. He pops the tab and drinks.

"Cola for breakfast?" she says and he hears the implication in her voice. Drinking soda this early is unsophisticated.

Embarrassed, he puts the can back in the refrigerator.

"You're lucky," she says.

"Lucky?" He closes the refrigerator door.

"It's peaceful here."

"I guess," he says. "I don't appreciate it the way I should."

"It's hard to appreciate the place you grew up until you leave it."

"Is that how you feel about Brooklyn?"

"Sometimes," she says. "I'm sure if I'd stayed there I wouldn't have any romantic ideas about it. I was starting to hate it before I left."

"Good thing you left."

"I think I'll take a shower," she says. "Do you have a toothbrush I can borrow?"

Dale comes by while Jimi's still in the shower. It's seven thirty. He's carrying two cups of coffee from Leigh.

"Leigh wanted to come," Dale says when he steps up on the porch, "but she has a twelve-hour shift tomorrow and wants to sleep in. She told me to make sure you remembered dinner tonight. She figured I'd forget to remind you, so I'm reminding you first thing, before I even say hello."

"I'm reminded."

"Then, hi."

Caleb pulls over the two lawn chairs and sets them up on opposite sides of the front door. Tonight's dinner is in honor of Morgan's return and had actually slipped Caleb's mind. He couldn't decline when they called and told him about it, but he'd promptly forgotten about it. "Don't worry, we'll be there. What the hell are you doing here so early?"

"I went for a run. I figured you could use the company. And I thought you'd want to know Morgan came by to see me last night."

"You're kidding."

"Yeah, well, you warned me."

"What'd he say?"

"Not much. He asked for money, like you said he would. I asked what he needed it for and he wouldn't tell me." Dale shakes his head. "Has he been on you about it?"

"No. And I'm sorry he leaned on *you* for it. He'll probably hit up a few more people, and then come back to me."

"His wife's young," Dale says.

"Yeah."

"Quiet."

"Real quiet."

They look at each other, leaving unsaid what they really think about her.

"At least she's legal," says Dale, and then he grimaces. "That didn't sound right. Have you asked him about Sally?"

"We haven't really talked yet," Caleb says. "The first thing he asked for was money and I didn't know where to go from there, you know? I'll give them a few more days before I start asking more questions. I take it Leigh never heard from her."

"Not yet."

"You say that like you think she will."

"I do."

Dale drinks his coffee in silence, shifts in his chair and closes his eyes. Caleb puts his coffee on the floor and stares at the sky. Dale's the only man Caleb feels comfortable in silence with. He never feels like he has to fill up the time with inane conversation about the weather or a NASCAR race he's missed. Dale's been there for him through a lot of the rough bits. Sally. Morgan. Other things. And he was there for Dale when Leigh moved in with her mother in Moss Bluff for a while. They don't have to talk to know the other is there.

But some things have to be said out loud.

"So," Caleb begins, "that girl . . ."

The screen door opens and *that girl* Caleb was just going to tell Dale about is standing in the doorway staring at them. She's wearing a pair of Caleb's navy blue boxers, which ride low on her hips, and one of his undershirts, and her hair's still wet from her shower. He looks at Dale. Dale's eyes are open and his hand is shielding them so he has a better look at Jimi. He takes his hand away and his face is expressionless. If he's surprised to see her, he doesn't show it.

"Hello," she says.

"Hello," Dale says, standing. He shakes her hand. "I'm Dale."

"Jimi."

"Jimi? Unusual name for a girl."

"Not to me." She smiles, then looks at Caleb. "Do you have a blow-dryer?"

"There should be one in the closet with the towels," Caleb says. "I saved this for you." He reaches down for the mug of coffee Dale brought and hands it to her. "You'll have to microwave it." Dale stares at him as if he thinks the gesture means more than it does and Caleb frowns.

Jimi stares at the mug in her hand. "Thank you."

"It's from Dale's wife, Leigh," Caleb says.

"You look like someone got the best of you," Dale observes, sitting down again. He looks at Caleb, then motions to Jimi's ankle. The swelling has gone down considerably. She's hardly limping. "Leigh could take a look at you," Dale continues. "She's a nurse."

Jimi looks horrified by Dale's candor. She moves her bruised ankle behind her other leg. Caleb shifts. Uncomfortable. He isn't hiding anything, so why does he feel like he is?

"It was nice to meet you," Jimi says. "Tell your wife thanks for the coffee."

She goes back inside the house.

Caleb and Dale gaze at the front yard for a long time. So much for telling Dale about Jimi still being in town before he found out from someone else. The silence between them isn't awkward, but Caleb wouldn't mind at all if Dale left.

Dale drains his coffee.

"Well." Dale stands. "I guess I should get going."

Caleb stands as well. "Yeah."

They walk to his SUV parked behind Caleb's pickup.

"I appreciate the coffee," Caleb says.

"Anytime. You can keep the mug." Then Dale stops, stares at the ground, shakes his head and turns to look at Caleb. "The hell?"

"Yeah," Caleb says, rubbing his nose with his thumb.

Dale waits for him to explain. He doesn't.

"Okay," Dale says. "I'll state the obvious. She's the girl you had a drink with at Fifth Amendment."

"Yeah."

"She's still in the Bend."

"I was going to tell you just before she came out."

"Why is she here?"

Most of the time Caleb feels like he can tell Dale anything, but how can he explain what it was like to be with Jimi last night? Riding Whiskey Road. Making love to her. Waking up with her. When she showed up on his doorstep, he had no idea she would end up staying. But he had no intention of letting her go. He thought he'd never see her again. Not seeing her would be a loss. He's tired of losing.

"It's not obvious?" Caleb asks.

Dale stares at him for a long time. "So she's sticking around?"

"I don't know. I hope so."

"You hope so?" Dale looks shocked. "Well, you've been hiding her pretty good. Has she been staying here? With Morgan?"

"She was at the inn for a while."

"And now she's here?"

Caleb leans against the SUV. Maybe if he talks about it, he'll figure out why *she* is important. He meets girls all the time. Pretty. Sexy. Even unmarried. He likes them, sleeps with them, forgets them. He's never fascinated and he never allows them to stay. But this time it's different. He can't reconcile the hard-edged girl he's getting to know in the daylight with the gentle girl he had sex with last night. When he drifted off, knowing that he was falling asleep next to the wrong person, not his wife, he didn't care and he didn't want her to leave. It's been so long since a woman slept next to him the entire night. It didn't feel *right,* but it felt like something he wouldn't mind getting used to again.

"What?" Dale asks.

"Nothing." Caleb straightens. "Her."

"What about her?"

"I don't know," Caleb says. He wanted to say more than that.

"Is she living with you?"

Caleb decides not to mention Jimi is staying in Willow Run with her brother, one of their current clients. There's a difference between sleeping with a local and sleeping with a transplant. Transplants are their bread and butter.

"I have to go," Dale says. He pats Caleb on the back and opens the door to his SUV. He gets in, leans out of the window. "If you bring her tonight, would you call the guys first?"

"Kennedy already met her. And, of course, she's had the pleasure of meeting Morgan."

"Huh?" Dale says. "Why didn't Kennedy tell me?"

"It was my place to tell you."

Dale looks away for a minute, then back at Caleb. "I don't understand what you're doing. I mean, you don't need the grief right now. Or ever," he says without malice. "But you've always danced to a different beat. That's why I love you, man."

Caleb reaches into the window and grabs Dale's hand. Dale holds it for a second, then lets go and turns the key in the ignition. "I'll see you later," he says and honks as he pulls away.

The blow-dryer's going when Caleb enters the house, and then it stops. He hears her walk to his bedroom and shut the door. He makes a quick stop at the laundry room to retrieve her handkerchief from a basket of clothes he hasn't folded yet and returns to his bedroom. She's changing into the shirt she was wearing yesterday; he catches a glimpse of her stomach, navel and breast. Her hair has been blown razor-sharp straight. Only the lock of pink hair is still wet. She starts when she sees him.

"Sorry," he says, holding the handkerchief out to her. She smiles.

"I remember this." She stuffs it in a pocket of the leather pants she's dropped in a pile on the floor. "The first time we met."

"The second time," he corrects her.

"Right. You never talk about him. The guy who hit you."

"Ray? He's not worth talking about."

She stares at him for a little while, looks as if she wants to ask questions. Doesn't. She sits on the edge of the bed, lies back, eyes closed, resting. He looks at her lying there and feels the heat in his face like a furnace. He hates how much he likes her in his underwear.

"Does he come by often?" she asks.

"Dale? Yeah. Leigh sends him over with coffee a couple times a week to let me know I've been away too long."

She sits up in one fluid motion, folds her legs yoga-style. "That's nice."

"He's a good guy, yeah."

And then she stands up, stretches. Stomach showing. "Do you have cigarettes?" she asks.

He nods, takes a pack and a lighter from the top drawer of his dresser and gives them to her. She lights a cigarette. He doesn't tell her she can't smoke in the house. Morgan's been doing it since he got here.

"What did he think about finding me here?"

Caleb walks over to her, cups her face in his hands and caresses her cheeks. She leans into his touch and he kisses her, moving from her lips to her eyes, to the healing cut on her forehead. His kisses are light and almost urgent; his fingers push at her stomach, asking her to respond. She doesn't.

She pulls away and returns the cigarettes and lighter to the dresser. She leans against it. "Tell me something I don't already know about you," she says.

"All right," he says, slouching a little, trying to hide his discomfort. "What do you want to know? Anything?"

"Anything that's absolutely true."

He considers. He can't tell her about Sally yet, though that's the first thing that comes to mind. He avoids her eyes. "I was a bad kid. Me and Morgan and Kennedy. And our friend Joseph—you haven't met him. We didn't have *family;* not in the way most people think is normal. My mother . . . she passed when I was young and I never knew my father."

"I'm sorry," Jimi says softly.

"My mother's sister and her husband raised us, but they were old and reclusive. They couldn't do much with me, and definitely not with Morgan. People picked on us. It's easy to demonize kids without parents. There's no adult to look directly in the eye afterward. So we'd stay out, drinking, vandalizing things." He stops. She looks sad. "Don't pity me, okay?"

"I'm not." She shakes her head. "I wouldn't."

"Even though I'm older, different, when I'm in the Bend, *still,* it's like I'm that same boy. And, yeah, sometimes I still get into it with people, but not the way I used to. There's always a reason. It's not random. Not for fun. I hate that everyone still sees me for who I was, not who I am. Morgan doesn't help much." He shakes his head. "Nothing's changed. I'm invisible and glaringly here at the same time."

"Yes," says Jimi. "I know how that feels."

After a minute he says, "The way Jennifer treated you in Wheeler's?"

"Who?"

"The waitress in Darby."

Jimi nods. "Yes. Kind of. It's always different."

"I know," he says. "But not from my experience in Darby. I go there to get away from that feeling."

"It's funny how certain places can mean different things for different people, isn't it?"

He nods. "Tell me what happened in Pennsylvania," he says.

"I wouldn't know where to begin."

"At the beginning."

She pushes away from the dresser, taking a quick drag from her cigarette, and then she starts talking. She tells him about riding at night, way too fast despite the rain, skidding and spraining her ankle. Being sure she would have to sleep on the side of the road until morning. He understands accepting that ride; he would have.

"He was wearing a cross," she says. "On a chain around his neck. It made him seem trustworthy. A sign that he wouldn't harm me. The same reason you keep that cross on your rearview mirror is the same reason I trusted him. You make assumptions . . ."

He goes to her, touches her face. "Whatever happened to you out there—" Out there. It's important she knows it isn't the same as here. "It's all right."

She nods.

"I probably can't say anything that will make you forget how it felt to be hurt," he says against his better judgment, "but I'm here. That's all I can give. So take it, okay?"

She moves away from him abruptly, drops her cigarette in an ashtray on the nightstand by his bed and leans against the wall, watching him.

"Okay," she says after a minute.

This is all it takes for him to close the gap between them and start kissing her again. This time she responds and it feels like the first time he's ever touched her. He considers asking if they can go further, but doesn't because he knows it won't matter if she says no.

He pulls his shirt over his head and she steps back to look at him. He fights an urge to cover his body, forces himself to watch her eyes find his various scars. There are two on his abdomen: one from a bar fight and one from a car accident with Morgan when they were teenagers. She lingers on the scar on his right shoulder. It runs down the length of his entire arm, meeting his tattoo. It was a gift from Sally, who'd attacked him with a broken beer bottle the first time she found out he'd cheated on her.

"Do something," he implores.

Jimi reaches out to touch the scar from Sally. Her fingers are careful, tender, teasing. She doesn't ask how he got it and he relaxes as she explores the damaged parts of him. It's been a long time since someone bothered. Girls used to be his business. Now he doesn't even know what to do with his hands. So he lowers his eyes and feels her discover him, fascinated. The way the bruises on her face have managed to seduce and arouse him, she manages to find solace from his old wounds.

*See,* he wants to say, *we're both broken.*

When he finally looks at her, he notices her lips have formed a tiny triangle and he places a finger against it. He feels a light pressure, a kiss. His body reacts and within minutes he's holding her like he knows everything he needs to know about her and nothing else matters. This is all he can give, he thinks, but at least he can give something.

# Eighteen

They're lying in bed, listening to the rain pelting the roof of the house. Caleb says, "I don't want you to think I was raised poorly. I don't want you to look at me like I'm not worthy of you."

"Do you think I'd look at you that way?" Jimi asks.

He rolls onto his back, stares at the ceiling, says nothing. And Jimi decides she wants to give him another one of her secrets. So she tells him about the accident in Los Angeles, only leaving out that her pictures recently sold for three million dollars. Surely he'll know that someone who could chase a mother and her baby into traffic wouldn't judge someone like him.

He listens, but he doesn't say anything for a while. And then he turns back on his side to face her. "Why'd you decide to tell me?"

"So you'll know who you're dealing with."

"I already do."

"No." Jimi shakes her head. "In Pennsylvania . . ." Should she spill it? She watches his finger trace a circle around her left nipple and wonders about her reluctance to *share* with him. But most of all, she doesn't want him to have this angelic idea of her. "In Pennsylvania, I tracked them to a house about three miles from the road where they stole my motorcycle. I checked into a motel and waited until they went out the next evening. Nothing else mattered because I wanted my bike back. All I wanted was my bike. I searched the house and the garage. There were motorcycle parts everywhere, but my bike wasn't there. It was brand-new and beautiful. You wouldn't take it apart."

"You'd sell it," says Caleb.

Jimi nods. "My heart sunk."

She'd been tempted to trash the entire house once she realized the couple probably stole motorcycles for a living; sold the new ones and took apart the crappy ones for their engines or handlebars. But Russ had taught her how to sweep a hotel room one weekend in Las Vegas, how important it was to leave the place clean after she left, how to take something so the inhabitant of the room wouldn't know it was missing until long after he'd checked out. Jimi decided taking something this couple was sure to miss would be more satisfying than trashing a house that was already a mess.

"I took money I found in a garbage bag underneath the bathroom sink. Thousands of dollars. Probably cash from my bike and others. I left, but he tracked me to a motel on the border between New York and Pennsylvania. Don't ask how he found me. I don't know. I thought I had, at least, twenty-four hours before they realized the money was missing."

Caleb doesn't say anything. She wouldn't know what to say if the tables were reversed.

"There was a very long moment when I thought I was going to die in that motel room," she continues. "Everything else seemed really unimportant."

"He nearly killed you?" he asks.

"I nearly killed him back." She flinches a little, remembering how much her hands hurt. Her knuckles are healed now. Her wrists and fingers no longer throb. No one would ever know the difference. "When there's a gun to your head, your life is supposed to flash before your eyes and everything is supposed to become clear. For me, everything became muddled. What was I doing in Los Angeles for a year? Why was I rushing into oncoming traffic to get a picture? Causing accidents? What was I doing in Pennsylvania? Where was I going?"

"You were coming here," he tells her. "You made it here."

"I think about using the money to go somewhere else. I thought it would be satisfying to use *his* money to do something I wouldn't normally do."

"You still have the money?"

She nods. "I fought like hell for it."

"I remember," he says, "that first time I saw you in Darby. I knew you fought back. I looked at your hands and I could tell."

"But the money," she says, "isn't his. The victory I should feel over taking it is ruined by the reality that it's *my cash.* It's all I have of my motorcycle."

"*Use it,*" Caleb tells her. "For all of your pain and suffering and loss. Use it well."

A knock on the door startles them. Caleb opens it a crack and she hears Morgan ask whether they should drive two cars to Dale's house. She wonders how long he was standing outside the door, listening to them talk.

On the porch, as Jimi prepares to leave, Caleb grips her waist and pushes into her.

"Meet me tomorrow for lunch."

"I can't," she says and he kisses her.

"Please," he whispers into her mouth.

"I have to be there. Troy and Sienna will be back early and we're having people over for dinner."

"Don't . . . ," Caleb begins.

"Don't what?"

"Don't go back," he says. His hands encircle her waist and squeeze. "You think they'll figure out you're with me if you don't show up for dinner?"

"They would never guess—" She stops.

He lets her go. "They'd never guess you'd sleep with a guy like me?"

"I'm the kid sister. I'm not supposed to sleep with anyone."

He leans against the porch railing and watches her. He straightens at the sound of Morgan whistling in the living room.

"Lunch," he says after a minute.

"Maybe," Jimi relents.

He grins, triumphant, and she raises her eyebrow.

"I said maybe."

"Maybe's better than no," he says.

It's still raining. She kisses him good-bye and he tries to hold on to her, but she leaves him and walks into the downpour. She's soaked by the time she gets into Troy's truck. As she pulls out, she watches Caleb light a cigarette and take a seat on the porch steps while he smokes it. Behind him, the front door opens and Morgan comes out. He waves at Jimi with a smile that doesn't quite reach his eyes.

# Nineteen

Heading back to Whiskey Road after Dale's welcome-home dinner for Morgan, Caleb is plagued by distractions. He has difficulty concentrating on the road, so he stops the truck and asks Morgan to finish driving. Morgan says something to Tara about Caleb being unable to hold his liquor, and though Caleb had too much to drink today, he's feeling more disoriented and isolated than hammered.

Tonight, everyone except Kennedy treated him like an acquaintance. No one mentioned the new woman in his life, but they were thinking about her. He would have preferred if they'd asked him intrusive questions instead of treating him like he had suddenly become someone they barely knew. He rests his head on the back of his seat and feigns sleep so he won't have to talk to Tara or Morgan.

Morgan clears his throat. "So," he says.

Caleb opens his eyes.

"You don't want to work with me."

"Why do you say that?"

"You didn't seem happy about me asking Dale if I can work on the Willow Run job."

Caleb lolls his head to the side and stares out the window. A nice breeze is coming through. "I was surprised you wanted it."

"It didn't seem like Joseph or Kennedy wanted it."

Caleb sits up and looks over at Morgan. "You didn't give them a chance to tell us whether or not they wanted it. You jumped in when I told them I need a subcontractor. They didn't have a second to react."

"Kennedy would've told me to back off if he wanted the job. And Dale could've said no."

"Not after all the sobbing you did about needing money."

Morgan glances at Caleb, says nothing.

Morgan wants to work. He's decided *working* for the money he needs to get to Canada is the best way to get it. And Caleb isn't buying his sudden change of heart. When he vetoed the idea of Morgan coming back to work for Bend Contractors, Dale disagreed with him.

"I can do this job with my eyes closed," says Morgan, and then he sucks his teeth and lurches forward. He takes the turn onto Whiskey Road like a maniac. Tara grips the dashboard. "You think I lost my touch because I was in prison?"

"No," Caleb sighs, "you got the job. I'm not complaining."

Morgan looks at him a little longer than a man driving up a narrow, winding road should. "I need the money."

"I thought you needed it immediately."

Morgan makes the turn into the yard. "I did."

When he stops the truck, they sit for a minute. Tara, stuck in the middle, seems anxious to get out.

"I could have some company in the near future," Morgan says.

Caleb closes his eyes, wishing he were anywhere but in this truck with his brother. Preferably in another country. With Jimi. It had crossed his mind earlier, for the briefest of moments, to ask her for the money she told him about. It wasn't a full-fledged thought, but more like a notion. A fleeting one.

"Why'd you tell them where I live?" he asks.

"I didn't. They already knew."

"How?"

"They knew." Morgan opens the door and gets out. Tara follows behind him. He closes the door and leans into the window. "I know I've done some fucked-up things in the past and you don't have any reason to believe me now, but I've changed. I have a wife to consider. I need your support. I never thought my baby brother would turn his back on me."

"And if these guys show up?"

"I'll handle it," Morgan says with confidence. "And then we'll get out of your hair so you can go on living your life or whatever. I just wanted to warn you."

"Thanks for the warning."

Despite what he says, Morgan hasn't changed. And Caleb believes he never will.

Caleb avoids doing things with women, like eating, that might be construed as "dates." But when you like a girl, you can't stop liking her just because you're trying to maintain your reputation. He likes this girl. He wants to eat with her.

He takes her to lunch at Dusty's on Sunday. They catch the church crowd, which isn't too big because most Benders eat Sunday dinner early, at home. She ignores the few people who watch them and wins over their waitress with smiles and kindness and a big tip she insists on leaving. She helps him forget last night's dinner at Dale and Leigh's, and the drive home with Morgan and Tara.

On his mind, instead, is how much he doesn't want her to return to Willow Run for her brother's dinner party. Or he wants to be invited. He still has trouble picturing her hanging out with rich people with her pink hair and her leather and her fucked-up ankle. And now they've had sex. More than once. They're officially together. He wants to know what *they'll* be like with other people as a couple. How other people will be with them. But she doesn't invite him to Willow Run and deep down he knows he can't turn up to a client's party uninvited with that client's sister.

They walk to his pickup in silence. Caleb opens the passenger door for her and she gets in. He walks around the truck and slides in beside her. He puts the key in the ignition.

"Thanks for lunch," she says.

He wants to bring up his feelings about his friends, how he thinks the rift between them would still exist even if Jimi left tomorrow and he never saw her again. Because there was a moment when he felt *foreign* around them and he never thought he could feel that way with his friends. It damaged something he doesn't think can ever be fixed. And he doesn't know—*he does not know*—if it's because Connie said this thing Caleb always knew was wrong, or if he thinks it's wrong now that he's with Jimi and sees things differently.

He pulls away from the curb, silent, and Jimi reaches out to touch the air freshener hanging from the rearview mirror.

"You took down the cross," she says.

He nods. He'd taken it down last night, when he got back from dinner, and replaced it with an air freshener he found in one of the kitchen drawers.

"I don't want you to ever feel uneasy when you're with me," he says.

The one thing Caleb always counts on when he's doing a job is privacy. That's why he prefers weekenders. Weekenders try to see as little of him as possible because they're only around for two and a half days and they don't want to spend that time talking to a contractor. Unless there's a problem. Even then they prefer to use e-mails and faxes to complain or correct something.

Full-timers and transplants who stick around all summer are different. They're always at home and they hover around, offering help or conversation. Some of them try too hard to be his friend by inviting him to stay for a drink after he's finished work, never taking into consideration that he's tired and has a life of his own that he considers more interesting than theirs.

So Caleb isn't the happiest man in the world when he and Morgan arrive at the Hamiltons' house around noon and the first words out of Troy Hamilton's mouth are, "What do we have to do today?"

*We.* As if they all got together and decided to convert the cottage into a guesthouse as a group. No contracts. No credit cards handed over. Transplants like to pretend money hasn't passed between them.

"We're going to take some measurements," Morgan answers, overly cheerful.

Troy looks at Morgan curiously as he ushers them inside the house.

"Mr. Hamilton," Caleb says, "this is my brother, Morgan. He's going to be working with me on this job."

"Troy," Troy says, holding his hand out to Morgan. "Brothers? It must be nice to work with family."

"It's wonderful to work with family," says Morgan enthusiastically. "We have our disagreements . . . You know how it is."

"Actually, I do," Troy tells him. "I have a sister. I'm not sure we'd survive working together."

Morgan laughs and Caleb gives him a look.

Over breakfast, Morgan had shocked him by asking when he was going to get around to talking about Jimi's relationship to the Hamiltons. Said he'd overheard Caleb tell her that he'd see her at her brother's house, and wondered why Caleb would let her do that—treat him like the hired help. Good enough to fuck, but nothing else.

The implication had struck a chord with Caleb. Especially after yesterday. Jimi had come home with him after lunch at Dusty's. They had sex, and then they showered together. She laughed at his stupid jokes, listened. He played some of his music and she didn't ask why a white guy from Frenchman's Bend likes blues the way most people ask when they hear it playing in his pickup. They sat on the porch and Caleb talked a little bit about work and his daily routine. He was pleased when all she seemed to be was curious. Again, he didn't want her to leave, asking what would happen if she didn't go back to Willow Run and missed Troy and Sienna's dinner party. She hadn't answered.

But he didn't let on to Morgan this morning how much Morgan's comment bothered him. He'd been too preoccupied with making sure Morgan wouldn't let on that he knew Jimi from the Bend.

"Can I offer you something?" Troy continues. "Granola, muffins, green tea, juice . . . ?"

Both Morgan and Caleb decline so they can take a more thorough look at the cottage and shed than Caleb did last week, check the structures, take measurements and make sure it's worthwhile for Troy and Sienna to go through with both projects.

"Once we establish that," says Caleb, "we can discuss whether or not you have any design ideas and what kind of money you want to spend."

Troy nods, seemingly satisfied with Caleb's explanation of the day's workload. He checks his watch. "We're going to have lunch in an hour. Would you join us?"

Caleb shakes his head no, but Morgan says "Sure" with a big grin. They leave through the sliding glass doors in the dining room and before Caleb can ask why he accepted Troy's invitation to have lunch with them, Morgan admires the deck, knowing immediately it's his brother's work.

"Thanks," Caleb says, a little surprised Morgan noticed.

At the bottom of the deck's steps, Jimi's sitting on the ground smoking a cigarette. Caleb hesitates. Morgan bumps into him. Jimi looks up and smiles, but the smile fades when she notices his brother.

"Hi there," Morgan says, pushing past Caleb to walk down the steps. Jimi stands and tosses her cigarette as Morgan checks her out in an exaggerated manner. She's wearing boxer shorts and a sleeveless undershirt again. Her hair is pulled into a ponytail, including the lock of pink hair. Caleb starts down the stairs after his brother and stops in front of her. Their eyes search each other's faces. He shoves Morgan lightly and points at the cottage. Morgan grins and walks away.

"What's he doing here?" Jimi asks.

"He managed to get his old job back."

"Did you tell him not to—"

"He knows." He leans in to kiss her and she allows it.

Morgan starts to whistle. Jimi eyes him warily.

"This should be fun," she says.

"I'll keep a tight leash on him."

"I guess I'd better let you get started," she says.

Caleb kisses her again, and then he watches her as she walks around to the front of the house, glad they've reconciled because he's sure he would have had trouble pretending not to know her if they hadn't.

In a moment of generosity, Morgan decides to stay outside while Caleb goes in to talk to Troy and Sienna over lunch. The three of them are sitting at the dining room table, reading various newspapers. Jimi's still in her boxers and undershirt, eating a sandwich.

"Hello," Sienna says and they all look up. "Sit down. Are you hungry?"

Caleb checks out the array of fresh meats on a carving board, the bread and condiments. He wouldn't mind a sandwich. "It looks great," he says as he sits across from Jimi.

"Eat as much as you like," Troy tells him. "Where's your brother?"

"He's finishing up."

"Then we'll bring him a sandwich when we're done," Sienna offers.

Transplants often try to treat him like he's part of the family, or a very close friend. Usually, they try too hard and come off strained and insincere, making him uneasy and embarrassed for them. But he doesn't think they'd understand if he explained he prefers to eat lunch alone, in his truck.

But this time Jimi's sitting here, her eyes on him, and he doesn't want to go away. He feels a sharp, inappropriate throbbing in his groin. He shifts in his chair, clears his throat, reaches for the bottle of sparkling water in the middle of the table and pours some into the glass in front of him.

"The cottage's structure is fine," he says, "and it should be a fairly straightforward job."

"Good."

"The shed, on the other hand, isn't something I'd pursue if I were you. I'd tear it down and build a new one. Considering the amount of money it would cost you to stabilize the foundation, you might as well spend an extra thousand dollars or so and build something new. Then you can have your vaulted ceiling without tearing down Sheetrock and so on." He glances at Jimi. She's watching him, smiling. He smiles back, feeling good he's impressing her.

"Maybe we'll reconsider the shed in a few months," says Sienna.

"I'll leave that up to you," he says. "We can always discuss ideas and pricing in the coming weeks to make the decision easier for you."

A kettle in the kitchen starts to whistle.

"Jimi, would you get that?" Sienna asks.

Caleb watches Jimi slide smoothly out of her seat and go into the kitchen, forgetting where he is for a moment. When he turns away, Troy's staring at him. At first there's a sparkle of humor and condescension in Troy's face, but it disappears quickly and Troy looks stoic, cold, prepared. Because Caleb's own eyes are unfriendly and hard. Without meaning to be. He's glad, however, that the look in his eyes has triggered something defensive in Troy. The man isn't afraid of him. Caleb looks away first.

"So the shed is a dead topic for now," Caleb confirms, focusing on Sienna.

"I think it should be," Troy says.

"Then we can move forward and order the supplies we'll need for the guesthouse," Caleb says.

Jimi returns. "Water's boiled."

Troy says, "Why don't you get dressed."

Jimi sits down again, settles her feet in her chair and rests her chin on her knees. Then she realizes Troy is staring at her. She lifts her head. "You mean me?" she asks.

"You're the only one walking around in your underwear," Troy says.

Jimi glances at Sienna, then Caleb. Caleb blushes. He should look away, but can't. He's fascinated by how attractive they all are. Pretty people from the city. Briefly, he wishes she considered him good enough so they wouldn't have to pretend. Just as quickly he regrets thinking that, wishing he'd sent Dale to handle this project in his place. He looks down at his lap.

"I always walk around in my underwear," Jimi says.

"Yeah, and now we have company," Troy counters.

Jimi stares at her brother, and then she picks up her mug and plate and leaves.

Fifteen minutes later, Troy and Sienna have reached an impasse and decide to play around with a few of Caleb's sketches, then fax their ideas to the office in the morning. Caleb slips through the sliding glass doors to find Morgan. He isn't in the backyard. He isn't in the truck. Caleb returns to the house and finds Morgan slipping out of a room just behind the staircase.

"What the hell are you doing?" Caleb asks.

"Using the bathroom." Morgan's eyes are cold. "Nice private one in the den." He points to the room he just walked out of.

"Next time ask where the public one is," says Caleb.

"Oh. Hello." Sienna is heading up the stairs to the second floor. "I thought you left."

There's no indication from Sienna's voice that she thinks they were doing something wrong, but Caleb's sure they were, even though he has no clue what it is. Her trust in them makes him feel terrible.

"We got sidetracked," Morgan tells her. "You have a lovely home."

"Thank you." Sienna's smile is so bright, so warming. "A lot of the credit goes to Caleb."

"My brother's real talented," Morgan says.

Sienna nods in agreement. "Should I call you tomorrow?"

Caleb meets her eyes finally. "Why don't you fax me your ideas first. I'll take a look, and then I'll call you."

"Perfect," she says. "I'm looking forward to working with you both."

Morgan beams up at her. "We won't disappoint you."

It's been three days since he showed up at Troy and Sienna's house with Morgan. Jimi isn't wild about the arrangement. Caleb knows she has a point, but her feelings still bother him. He's reminded that Jimi is no Leigh. She doesn't truly understand why it takes some people a little longer to get their shit together. She can acknowledge and regret her mistakes, but her mistakes are a product of bad choices, not from being a victim of circumstance. She has the luxury of Troy and Sienna and their summerhouse and returning to a life in the city. He hates to see her that way, like she's just any other city girl he meets, so he tells himself he's being irrational. She has no reason to give Morgan a second chance. Even he wonders if Morgan deserves any more chances from him.

But Morgan has been surprisingly *good.* He runs every errand Caleb and Dale ask him to without so much as a frown. He's even taken a job doing deliveries for the Home Depot in Moss Bluff during his spare time. Tara's working part time as a cashier. Caleb truly believes they're trying.

On Thursday, Caleb spends most of the day in the office, trying to locate a divorce lawyer in Moss Bluff or Willow Run. There's a law office on Main Street, but he's married to the Bend's dentist. Word would get out that Caleb's filing for a divorce before he even reaches Sally. He calls two lawyers in Moss Bluff, but they're both on vacation for the next two weeks. The third number, to a lawyer in Willow Run, is busy. He also calls the Home Depot to order Troy and Sienna's supplies, instead of Percy's Hardware in Darby. As a rule, he only uses the Home Depot for smaller, local jobs because it's cheaper. With transplants and weekenders he prefers to give the business to Percy. But this is Jimi's family; he's going to treat them the same way he'd treat a local.

He leaves the office at five and stops for Chinese takeout. He's just settled down at the kitchen table with a beer and a carton of dumplings when a blue pickup pulls up behind his truck. At first, he thinks it belongs to the "company" Morgan warned they might be having. Then he remembers Jimi's been driving Troy's pickup, and hating it, making Caleb grin whenever she complains. He leaves the beer and the food on the table and opens the front door to greet her.

She leans against the pickup, looking both sheepish and beautiful. He falls in love with her at that moment, but he doesn't allow the thought to flower into a full-blown realization.

She says, "Been a while."

"Yeah, a full day." His grin broadens.

When she reaches the door he kisses her without hesitation, without discomfort. He feels as if she belongs *here.*

"What did you tell them?" he asks once they're inside.

"I'm at a movie," she says, looking around as if she's trying to decide where to sit. "I'll go back before they get up in the morning."

In his room they can't stop kissing. His hands move to her waist and he pulls her shirt up, lightly grazing her breasts. They separate for a second so he can take her top off, then start kissing again as if it's easier to breathe when they're connected. The feel of her nipples sends a pleasant sensation through him. He goes for her shorts, which easily slip to the floor once they're unbuttoned. She takes off his T-shirt and he leads her to the bed. He lies down first and she climbs on top of him. His hands move to the waistband of her boxers. She lifts herself a little so he can push them off. His heart's beating so hard against his chest he's sure she hears it. His hands remain on her hips while the tip of him grazes her.

"You're gonna break my fucking heart," he says. She moves forward to kiss him, but he stops her. Looks dead in her eyes. "You're gonna break my fucking heart?" he repeats.

"Wasn't planning to," she says.

He closes his eyes as she slides onto him. He wants to whisper something. Tell her she's killing him. But he knows she'll place a finger over his lips and tell him to be quiet. She rises slowly so he almost slips out of her. He grabs her to keep her in place and opens his eyes to see her smiling. She does it over and over until they reach a rhythm, slow and steady. And all he can think is that he doesn't want her to leave in the morning.

# Twenty

Jimi has become an expert at driving the narrow, rural roads of Frenchman's Bend and Willow Run in the dark. She drives fast, but not careless. She doesn't want to give Herman, the sheriff in Frenchman's Bend, an excuse to stop her.

She visits Caleb every night after Troy and Sienna, and Morgan and Tara, go to bed. They have sex, and they kiss, and they talk. But mostly they have sex. They know each other's bodies better than they know each other. They spend each day together pretending to be strangers; by the time they meet at night, all they want to do is touch. The beginning of a relationship is always like this, she thinks. There's sex all the time. It's an excuse to be close, to feel good.

It's been nearly four weeks since she met Caleb outside Wheeler's Coffee Shop in Darby. Things are almost serious. Troy and Sienna still don't know about them. And the only people in Caleb's life Jimi has met more than once are Morgan and Kennedy. This is more okay with her than it is with Caleb. He invites her to hang out with his friends, and she can tell he wants to be invited out with her family.

This morning she's awakened by the sound of someone moving around in the kitchen and realizes she's in bed alone.

She sits up. The clock on the dresser reads 5:00 AM. They've been doing this a lot, cutting it close—Troy and Sienna get up between seven and eight.

In the bathroom, she splashes her face with cold water several times and brushes her teeth with the toothbrush Caleb bought for her and keeps in his bedroom. When she comes out she smells coffee brewing. She can tell right away that it's generic because it has a cheap smell. She pushes the thought aside and thinks, instead, *He bought coffee for me.*

"Hey." He greets her with a kiss. He pours two cups, sets her cup on the table. He's wearing jeans; otherwise he's barefoot and shirtless. She stares at his back as he pulls a carton of milk from the refrigerator. This scar, the one that runs ragged so close to his spine, fascinates her. She hasn't asked about any of his scars because she wants him to want to tell her. This one, however, tempts her. She reaches out to touch it and he tenses.

"Your hands are cold," he says.

He's lying. Her hands are warm.

She takes her first sip of the coffee. It's strong. Stronger than she likes it. But it reminds her of home. This is the first time she's drinking morning coffee from an actual ceramic mug since she left California. An overwhelming feeling of gratitude overtakes her. She looks at him as she puts the coffee down. They smile at the same time.

"Coffee *and* a toothbrush," she says, trying to mask how she feels. "It's getting serious."

"It already is."

"It is, isn't it?"

He nods.

She smiles as she tries to sit on top of the counter. Caleb grips her waist and lifts her up. Her ankle is better, but she suspects it will never be the same. He places his hands firmly on her knees and she spreads her legs so he can move closer to her

"The first time I saw you in Fifth Amendment," she says, "you were with someone. A blonde."

He draws back a little. "You saw me inside the bar that night?"

"Was she your girlfriend?"

"Not a girlfriend," he says. "Just someone I see. She's . . . married."

"To Ray?"

He looks surprised. "How'd you know?"

"I could tell. That night, he was looking for her. Did you love her?"

"I liked having sex with her."

"Hmmm." She moves out of his reach, leans across the counter for her coffee. He stops her.

"I said *liked.* I haven't had sex with her since I met you."

This pleases her, but she says nothing.

"There was someone I loved," he continues. "Completely. But she couldn't love me the way I loved her."

"Why not?"

"I never asked her." He's quiet. He meets Jimi's eyes and she can see he's about to tell her something serious, something she may not want to know. He swallows, and then he looks away from her. "What happens when you leave?"

"I go back to Willow Run. Sleep. Watch television. Eat lunch with my brother."

"I don't mean today," he clarifies. "I mean later. When you go back to Brooklyn."

"Does it matter?"

"All of a sudden it does," he says.

"Why 'all of a sudden'?"

"Because it does."

"I can't say I know," she says. "Do you know?"

"I'll be here," he answers. "Where I always am. If you leave, the ball will be in your court."

He's right. When she leaves, *not if,* it will be unexpected and sudden. It'll be before Troy and Sienna wake up in the morning and try to talk her out of it. It'll be up to her to "keep in touch." She's never been one to successfully follow through on that particular promise.

"I'm not leaving tomorrow," she says.

"But you think about it."

"You know I think about it," she says. "I think about using the money in my bag and leaving Willow Run every day." But her feelings for Caleb stop her. She's afraid to admit aloud that she likes him, and wants to continue being around him for a while. She doesn't think he'll reject her, but admitting she cares will automatically make her vulnerable. She doesn't want to be vulnerable about him just yet. Maybe it's a mistake to continue visiting, pretending to have a right to keep coming here when she isn't ready to tell him how she feels.

"Are we going to see each other tonight?" he asks.

He never asks. They just do.

"I don't know," she answers.

Something in his eyes unsettles her. She isn't sure what it is.

"I want to show you something," he says after a minute, grabbing her by the waist again to help her down.

She follows him to the back of the house, through the laundry room, to the backyard. The door to Morgan's cottage is open and she can hear Tara singing. Her voice sounds lovely, giving Jimi reason to pause, but Caleb doesn't even glance in the cottage's direction. He passes it, and they reach a second cottage, concealed by trees and refuse. As they get closer, she sees the front side has been destroyed by fire. And then she realizes what he wants to show her.

He's turned the second cottage into a makeshift motorcycle garage. There are bike parts everywhere, and three unfinished bikes mounted on three separate steel worktables. It's a cross between cool and blasphemous. The cottages are quaint and pretty. It would break anyone's heart to rip the structures apart and turn them into this. But she gets it. Because the bikes are beautiful. More beautiful than a dainty cottage.

They step over the threshold. Even unfinished, each bike is exquisite. She rubs her hands over the iron and leather lovingly. She looks at him.

"They're beautiful," she says.

He pushes away from the wall.

"You only told me about a Harley," she says. "You didn't say anything about a collection."

He shrugs. "I don't talk about my bikes much. I never show them to anyone."

She examines a leather seat on one of the worktables more closely and thinks about her stolen BMW. "When are you going to finish one?" she asks.

"It's just a hobby."

She looks around the room again. "It's more than that," she says. "It should be."

Caleb looks into her eyes, holds them. Again, Jimi senses he wants to tell her something.

"Why did you want to show this to me?" she asks.

"I want to share it with you."

"So we have no more secrets?"

He looks down. She waits for an answer. When he looks at her again, he's smiling. "I'm thinking about selling the place."

"Really?" She looks around again, thinking it would be a shame to sell this place. "To travel?"

He nods. "You're going with me, remember?"

Jimi smiles and turns her attention back to one of the motorcycles. "Of course I remember."

One evening, ten days after Caleb and Morgan started working at the house, Jimi finds Morgan in the den. He's standing in the middle of the room, staring into space.

"Are you lost?" Jimi asks him.

Morgan starts, then looks at her. His face is blank; his eyes are empty as usual. "The bathroom," he says.

Jimi narrows her eyes at him. "There's a bathroom in here," she says, "but why don't you use the one in the hallway? It's bigger."

His jaw twitches. "I like privacy. Excuse me."

He walks past her, out of the room. She takes a cursory look around just as Sienna calls her to dinner.

"I think our contractor's in love with you," Sienna blurts over dinner.

Troy stops chewing. He looks alarmed. "What? Who?"

Jimi looks back down at the paper she was reading.

"The contractor is in love with your sister."

The silence goes on too long so Jimi looks up to see her brother staring at her. "Jimi?" he asks.

"What? I didn't do anything."

Troy looks at his wife. "What makes you think such a thing? Did he say something to you?"

Sienna looks amused. "No. I can tell by the way he looks at her. And he's here every day except Sunday."

"Where else would he be?" Troy asks.

"Oh, you know what I mean," says Sienna, laughing at Troy's reaction. "He owns the company. He doesn't have to come every day. But he does. Don't lose sleep over it, honey. He's just the contractor."

Jimi looks at her brother as he tries to laugh off the idea of the contractor falling in love with his little sister. She sighs. Because he isn't just the contractor. They've had sex again. Recently. Yesterday. Last night.

"Well he certainly has that devout-Christian, Satan-worshipper look down," Sienna says jovially.

"More like tattooed, scarred, scary person," says Troy.

Jimi bites her lip. She should say something. *Defend him.* But when she realizes Troy and Sienna are looking at her, she clams up.

"We were just kidding about the Satan-worshipper, scary-person stuff," Sienna says, looking embarrassed.

"*I* wasn't," Troy says. "He has a scar the size of—"

"You look upset," Sienna says to Jimi. "We didn't mean anything by it."

"Why would I be upset?" asks Jimi as she looks back down at the paper.

She searches the den. Finding Morgan here left her with a feeling that something wasn't quite right. She remembered that he may have heard her discussing the money she took in Pennsylvania with Caleb. She'd wondered how long he'd been standing outside the bedroom door, listening.

It's hardly a surprise, then, that the duffel bag is missing. She checks every closet in the house to make sure Troy hasn't moved it.

It's gone.

She calls Caleb, tells him she has to talk to Morgan. But

Morgan isn't home and Caleb doesn't know where he is. He knows something's wrong; he says he can hear it in her voice. She doesn't want to tell him about the missing bag over the phone so he asks her to meet him at Fifth Amendment because Kennedy's meeting him there.

She arrives first. Rose greets her with a wink and a smile. She starts to fix Jimi's ginger ale, but Jimi stops her. At the other end of the bar a blond woman is staring. Jimi stares back, smiles. She's distracted by Kennedy, who enters the bar before Caleb. A head nod is his hello. He takes the stool next to Jimi.

"Buy you a drink?" he asks.

"No, thanks."

He notices the blonde and his eyes are no longer passive, but hard. Jimi looks at her again and remembers. She's the blonde Caleb was with the first time Jimi came in here. Jimi stares straight ahead.

"You okay?" Kennedy asks.

"Not really," says Jimi.

"Maybe you should have this." He pushes his pint in front of her. She ignores it.

Caleb walks in a moment later. His eyes are focused on the blonde at the other end of the bar. He nods, but doesn't say anything to her. He sits on the opposite side of Jimi, looks at Kennedy and says, "Me and Jimi have to talk for a minute. I think we'll do it outside. You want to come with us, or you're okay to stay behind?"

Kennedy thinks about it for a minute. He looks around the bar again. "I better come with you," he says. "I'll stay a couple of paces behind."

Jimi's head is swirling. Is the blonde the married girlfriend Caleb was with before her? Why does Kennedy have to come with them instead of staying behind in the bar? She wants to focus on everyone else more than she wants to focus on her missing duffel bag. She wants the missing bag to be a mistake.

Outside, Caleb directs her around the corner so they can walk down a quiet block. Kennedy follows.

"Remember the money in the duffel bag I told you about a couple of weeks ago?" she asks.

"Yeah."

"It's missing," she says. "The duffel bag and the money. Gone. I'm pretty sure Morgan took it."

Caleb stops walking, stares.

"I found him in my room earlier," she explains, feeling uneasy. "I asked if he was lost and he said he was using the bathroom. But he was acting strangely, so my alarm bells went off and I checked my room this evening, right before I called you. I've checked the entire house."

"Why'd you automatically assume it was my brother?" Caleb asks.

"Why did I—? Are you kidding? You and your brother have been the only strangers in the house. I should have assumed it was *my* brother?"

Caleb just stares.

"Don't do this," Jimi warns.

"Don't do what?"

She looks at Kennedy. He's leaning against a wall, watching her intently. His eyes are hard like they were when he was looking at the blonde.

"Don't talk to me like your brother hasn't done anything to warrant suspicion."

Caleb is still quiet. His face is cold.

"*He's* the troubled kid, not me," Jimi reminds him. "*He* just spent two years in prison."

Her last comment ignites a fire in his eyes. "I didn't tell you that to have it thrown in my face."

Jimi backs down. "I'm sorry, but I think he was listening to us that day we talked about it in your room." She knows she's saying all the wrong things to him, but she can't believe he doubts her.

After a minute, Caleb says, "I'll ask him about it."

"Ask him? Why don't you search his stuff? He won't tell you he took it."

"How do you know what he'd tell me?" He starts to walk in the direction of the bar again.

"I understand that you don't want to admit he took the money," she says.

Caleb stops, gives her a hateful glance. "*Please.* Don't be condescending."

"Then, *please,* stop taking his side."

"I'm not taking his side. I'm . . . just let me figure it out."

He taps Kennedy on the shoulder and they walk away from Jimi together.

"Caleb," she says.

Both men turn back to look at her. Caleb no longer looks angry, but sad. "I'm gonna go home," he says. "I'll check his stuff in the morning, after he leaves for work."

Jimi nods because that's all she can do right now, but she's frustrated. It isn't the money. It's what the money stands for. *It's hers.* It's all she has left of her bike and no one has a right to take it. She thought Caleb would understand that.

# Twenty-one

He doesn't confront Morgan in the morning and he doesn't search through his stuff. He leaves early in order to avoid driving to the office with him.

On the way, he thinks about Jimi and how she made him feel like a loser last night. The way she looked at him. He'd felt like they've known each other for years and he'd done something utterly disappointing. Maybe he has. All he really knows for sure is that he's in a lose-lose situation. Defending his brother means he upsets Jimi, but siding with Jimi isn't an option until he has proof Morgan took her money.

There was a time in his life when there'd be no doubt Morgan was innocent, even if Caleb had witnessed the crime. That was when Caleb thought Morgan was cool, when they were younger. When Morgan would use him as an alibi when he did something stupid, and Caleb would have to pay the consequences in his place. Caleb doesn't want to be that kid again. He doesn't want to lose Jimi because of Morgan's stupidity. He's attached to her.

What *that* means, exactly, he isn't sure. He just knows he likes being close to her. He admires her resilience. He likes that she rode his Harley down Whiskey Road in the dark. He likes that she only wears his boxers to bed, and sleeps on her stomach, giving him a wonderful view of her back when he wakes up at three in the morning. Likes the tattoo of her motorcycle, small yet intricate, just above the crack of her ass. Likes that she never sleeps through the night, wakes him up while trying to be silent as she goes off to the porch to smoke a cigarette. Reminding him that she's there. Reminding him he wants her every minute and that he misses her when she's back in Willow Run.

How could Morgan have taken her money? When would he have had time to do it? He remembers finding his brother in the den the first day they showed up at Troy and Sienna's house. He hadn't known, at the time, the den was Jimi's bedroom. He thinks of Morgan's sudden desire to work with him. On *this* job. With Jimi's money, he can run off with Tara before anyone catches up with him.

Caleb pulls out his cellular phone, pushes the speed dial button for the Hamiltons' number, then turns the phone off. He can't admit it to her. He can find the money, put it back where Morgan found it and pretend nothing happened.

And there he goes again. Discreetly fixing Morgan's problems instead of facing them. He tosses his phone on the dashboard and shakes his head. He doesn't know what the hell he's doing.

He finds a space on Wynthrop Street. A block ahead, he spots Emma walking toward him. He stops. What the hell is Emma doing in the Bend this early? He braces himself for a tirade as she gets closer.

"Been a while," she says when she reaches him.

"How are you?" One look at her and he can see she looks good. "What are you doing in the Bend this early?"

"Dropping off a delivery on Maple." She touches his face

and Caleb meets her eyes. She says, "You deserve someone like you."

"Like me?"

"Oh, come on." She laughs. "I saw her. Last night. For a brief moment before you snatched her out of Rose's place. She's young, pretty, probably reckless. *Like you.*" She kisses him before he can stop her. The kiss is soft, but she lingers. When she pulls away, she's still smiling. "I wanted you for myself." Her voice is sad, not malicious. "I really did."

She walks away, sashaying her hips with exaggeration. Caleb watches for a while, and smiles when she turns a corner and waves without looking back. Ray's 4x4 is parked across the street. Caleb looks at him. He can't read the expression on Ray's face. *Well,* he thinks, *it doesn't matter.* It's over with Emma.

Dale's sitting at his desk when Caleb walks in.

"I didn't expect to see you here," Caleb says.

Dale stands up, walks around his desk and sits on it. "I was hoping you'd stop here before you went to Willow Run. I figured I'd try to catch you."

"Yeah?" Caleb frowns. "Why?"

"How are things going?"

"With what?"

"Everything."

Caleb shrugs. "Things have a way of getting in the way of each other. I guess that's the best way to put it."

"How are things going with the girl?"

"That's what this is about? She's fine."

"Are you serious about this girl?" Dale asks. "I mean, are you going to marry her? Are you going to set up house and have kids? Because if not, man, let her go. Don't string her along."

Caleb stares at his friend in disbelief. *Let her go for her own good. Don't string her along.* It's all meant to imply *Don't hurt her.* Well, that's bullshit. Dale doesn't care whether Caleb hurts Jimi or not. He just wants her away from Caleb.

"Stay out of it," Caleb tells him. "I mean it." His voice is even, but under the surface there's real anger. He doesn't want another marriage. Hell, he hasn't even ended the first one. Jimi was supposed to be a diversion. He wasn't supposed to like her. He knows that. He's *aware.* But this is his business. *Jimi and Caleb's business.* No one else's.

Dale just sits on his desk, waiting. There's something else. Caleb can sense it.

"What?" Caleb says.

Dale meets Caleb's eyes. "Sally answered Leigh's e-mail."

# Twenty-two

Caleb doesn't show up for work. Jimi knows it's because he doesn't want to see her after she accused Morgan of stealing her money last night. *Coward,* she thinks. He should have come to work.

Around noon she steps out on the deck to find Kennedy sitting on the flatbed of a truck, eating a sandwich. His hair is loose today, fluttering through the air, shielding his eyes as he and Jimi stare at each other. And then he puts his sandwich down, combs his hands through his hair and pulls it back into a ponytail. He hops off the truck and they meet halfway, in the middle of the yard. He tells her Caleb isn't coming. Something about handling an emergency for a client in Moss Bluff, then picking up supplies at the Home Depot.

"An emergency?" she says, knowing it's a lie.

Kennedy glances at the cottage, then turns his attention back to Jimi. He says, "I'm not saying Morgan didn't take your stuff, but what makes you think he did?"

Jimi gives him a look that makes it clear she doesn't want to talk about it with him. He holds her eyes for what seems like an eternity.

"He doesn't feel good about what happened," he says, retreating. "He's going to call you and ask you to meet him at Fifth Amendment. Go to him."

Caleb's sitting at the bar. He stands up when he sees her and offers his stool. She sits. Rose doesn't pour her a drink.

"I didn't think you'd show," he admits.

"I said I'd be here."

He shrugs, glancing around the bar to take in the other patrons watching them. And then his eyes settle on her again. He pulls over another stool, so close to her their legs are touching.

"Last night," he says, then shakes his head. "Every time I think I'm taking a step forward, something pushes me back. Like Morgan. I didn't speak to him. I didn't go through his stuff because he was still sleeping when I left this morning. But I'm sure I'll find your money."

Jimi takes a breath. "Why are you sure today?"

"Because it makes sense. Yesterday I didn't want it to be true."

"And today you want it to be?"

"Today I can't get you out of my mind. I don't want us to stop being friends because of him."

"We're more than friends," she says. "That's why we're both here now, isn't it?"

He nods and she feels one of his hands in her lap, searching for one of hers. She moves it so that it's within his reach. He grasps it, squeezes and then he lets it go. A second later he leaves to use the bathroom.

Rose looks at Jimi sternly. "Your boyfriend's been putting them away," she says. "I'm cutting him off."

"He's not my boyfriend," Jimi corrects.

Rose gives her a look that says she isn't fooling anyone except herself. "I'm still cutting him off."

Of course Jimi won't allow Caleb to get behind the wheel

now that she knows he's been drinking heavily, but she doesn't like the way Rose is speaking to her. Like Caleb is Jimi's responsibility. It makes her nervous. Because she knows he is.

She watches him return to the bar. He pulls his Chicago Bears cap from his back pocket and pushes it down low on his head so she can't see his eyes. He hasn't shaved. The hair on his face is dark. Auburn. He's wobbling a little. *This is mine,* she thinks. *So what am I going to do about it?*

"Let's get out of here," he says, placing a twenty on the bar.

Rose holds out a bottle of spring water to Jimi. "Make him drink that on the way home," she advises.

As soon as they walk out of the bar, Caleb shoves Jimi against the wall and kisses her aggressively. His hands slide to her waist and grip her tightly. "Follow me home," he says pushing away from her. He starts to leave, but stops when he realizes she isn't following him.

"Caleb," she says, "let me have your keys."

Caleb stares at her. "What?"

"Give me your keys," she repeats slowly.

He starts to walk again. She follows. When they reach his truck, he leans against the passenger door. She moves closer to him, deciding she has no choice but to take the keys from him when he isn't looking. "Why were you drinking so hard?"

"Get used to it."

Jimi rolls her eyes. "Here." She holds out the water. "Drink this."

He doesn't take the water, doesn't even glance at it.

"I started a bike for you," he says.

She searches his face for a hint that he's joking. She loved the unfinished motorcycles he'd shown her. She wanted one. But she reels in her excitement at learning he's actually building her one from scratch. She knows she can't say yes.

"I can't take it," she says.

He blinks, straightens, and all of a sudden looks very sober. "Why not? Because taking something from a townie like me might give me the wrong impression?"

"I didn't say that."

"I'm only good enough to fuck?"

"What?"

"You heard me."

"No. I didn't."

He's quiet, staring.

"Okay, I heard you. You're wrong."

"Then tell him."

"Tell him what? Who?"

"Troy," Caleb says. "Tell him you're 'into me.' Tell him you sleep with me. Tell him I want to give you another bike. Invite me over for dinner on Saturday. Let me kiss you in front of them."

*"Fine."* She sounds exasperated. "Show up to work tomorrow. I'll tell him everything. I'll sit outside and ogle you while you work if that's what you want. Wear something tight."

He pushes away from the truck, handing her a thick ring of keys. "You wanna drive me home? Knock yourself out."

Jimi takes his keys. "We'll take my car. This way I can drive myself back to Troy's afterward."

She walks away. Anywhere else, he would be embarrassing her. She's ashamed that she isn't embarrassed now because they're in Frenchman's Bend. *This is where he's from. They are like this. This is what I got myself into.* She almost apologizes to him for thinking it before remembering he can't read her thoughts. She turns around. He's finally following her, keeping a safe distance. She opens the passenger door first and he drops into it. They drive up Whiskey Road.

Halfway home he says, "I want you to tell them about us tomorrow."

"I will," says Jimi, gritting her teeth.

She stops a short distance from the house. Caleb doesn't move. Jimi gets out of the car, walks around it and opens the passenger door for him. He looks into her eyes, thanks her and steps out slowly. She trails behind him. She's thinking seriously about going inside with him. As soon as he falls asleep, she could search the house for her bag. But the front door opens and Morgan walks out with a carton of orange juice, wearing nothing but a pair of baggy jeans.

"Where's your truck?" he asks Caleb.

"He had a little too much to drink," Jimi explains. "It's on Main Street."

Tara sticks her head out.

"Is that Caleb?" she wants to know.

"Well, who else would it be, baby?" Morgan says to her.

"Emma's on the phone," Tara says. "She says it's urgent. Hi, Jimi."

Morgan smiles at Jimi. Jimi looks at Caleb. Is Emma the married girlfriend? The blonde from Fifth Amendment Bar? Caleb doesn't say. He trudges up the porch steps, stops at the door and looks at her.

"You aren't coming in?" he asks.

"Not tonight," Jimi says.

Caleb stares at her and Morgan says, "Go on. Don't keep a *lady* waiting."

Caleb heads into the house and Jimi and Morgan stare at each other. She thinks about asking him if he took her duffel bag yesterday. It's on the tip of her tongue. But her own advice to Caleb comes back to her. Don't ask. *Search.* She starts to walk away.

"His wife won't like that," Morgan says.

Jimi isn't sure she's heard him correctly. She stops walking. "What?"

Morgan takes a swig from the orange juice container. "His wife. She won't like it when she finds out ladies are calling him at the house." He holds out the juice to her. "You want a taste?"

Jimi stares at him blankly.

"He didn't tell you?"

Jimi shakes her head. She wants a better comeback, but she has none. "Why should I believe you?" she says.

"You don't have to." Morgan's grinning. "Ask him."

Somehow she knows Morgan isn't lying. What had she just been thinking? That Caleb belonged to her. That he is her responsibility. *What the hell is she doing here?*

She returns to the car. In her rearview mirror she can see Morgan standing in the middle of the yard watching her until the lights from the car no longer illuminate him and he is swallowed by darkness.

She goes to bed trying hard not to think about it, but fails. She's never slept with a married man. She has plenty of unexplored kinks, but that just isn't one of them. Sleeping with another woman's husband is a betrayal. And what infuriates her is his self-righteous attitude about her decision to keep their relationship from Troy. Maybe he forgot he was married when he was spouting his *tell him about us tomorrow* bullshit. What a half-wit she would have looked like if she'd actually done it.

But that isn't what's keeping her up. How could she have been such a bad judge of character? How could she not have known he's married? Where has his wife been hiding?

She *thought* she was getting to know him. She didn't think he was a guy who could sleep with her and never mention there's a wife out there somewhere, unaware her husband is having sex with someone else. How horrible she feels. How *had.*

# Twenty-three

Jimi avoids Caleb for over a week. No small task since he starts work at the house around nine thirty in the morning and doesn't leave until after four. And since Willow Run and its surrounding towns aren't the most exciting places in the world, Jimi finds herself at a loss for things to do that will allow her to avoid running into him.

She has spent some time at the Willow Run Library, wondering what to do about Morgan and her money. Now that she's avoiding Caleb she doesn't know how she'll find a way to search his house. She's walked the malls in Moss Bluff and watched locals swim in Willow Run Pond two days in a row. On the second day, some of them invited her to join them, but she had no swimsuit.

By Friday, she's grateful it's Caleb's day off. She wants to sleep late and wander around the house in her shorts.

When she steps out of the shower in the morning she hears voices in the kitchen and freezes. Caleb and Kennedy. The talking stops when she comes out of the bathroom. She returns to the den quickly and shuts the door. Five minutes later Caleb knocks and says her name. She doesn't answer. At noon Sienna invites her to have lunch with them. She declines. Around twelve thirty, someone knocks on her door again. She mutes the television. She can't concentrate. She wishes she could ignore how much she wants to talk to him.

Finally, she hears a truck drive away from the house at two thirty and she escapes the den to find something to eat. She makes a sandwich, carries it to the deck and sees him. He stops loading his truck when she opens the screen door. Feeling awkward, she returns to the kitchen. Fifteen minutes later she's still listening for his truck to pull away. It doesn't. She can't stand it anymore. She goes outside to check what he's doing.

He's wrapping a large cable around his shoulder. He glances at her as he trudges back to his truck.

"How's it going?" she asks casually.

He dumps the cable in the back of the pickup and wipes his hands on his already filthy jeans. He's breathing hard, sweating. His face is smudged with dirt. He looks exhausted and harassed.

"I thought you were avoiding me," he says, looking past her, at the house.

"I was. I thought you were off today."

"I was. I was also tired of not seeing you so I came in without telling Troy and Sienna."

"Sneaky," says Jimi.

"I knocked on your door. Twice."

"I wasn't ready to answer."

He nods and finally looks directly at her. "What'd my brother say to you that night?"

"You have a wife. You have a girlfriend."

"So you believed him and didn't bother to ask me if it was true?"

"Do you have a wife?"

He swallows. "I do."

She laughs, but not like she thinks it's funny.

He opens the door of his truck. "Get in," he says. "I want to talk."

Jimi stares at the interior of his pickup truck. She longs to slide inside it and sit next to him for a while. She lowers her eyes, lest he see something in them to give her feelings away. She didn't realize how hurt she was until now.

"He should have told you my wife left me," Caleb says, his voice so close to her ear she jumps. "Get in the truck and we'll talk."

She doesn't move, doesn't answer.

He sighs. "She doesn't live here anymore. We don't love each other. In fact, she hates me so much, she can't even stand to talk to me on the phone."

"Not exactly a great endorsement for future boyfriend material," Jimi mutters.

He laughs softly and she braces herself when he moves closer. "If I'd thought I had a shot at being your boyfriend, I would have worded it differently." And then his eyes focus on something behind her. She turns around in time to see Sienna coming toward them.

"Hello," Sienna says. "I thought you left."

"Not yet, ma'am," Caleb says, all business.

Sienna glances at Jimi. "Would you like to stay for dinner?" she asks Caleb. "It'd be nice to get to know you better."

"I'd need a shower and a new set of clothes before I could sit at anyone's dinner table tonight," Caleb says.

"We aren't picky," says Sienna.

A look passes over Caleb's face that isn't kind. If Sienna notices, she doesn't react to it.

"I don't usually eat dinner in my work clothes," Caleb tells her.

"Next time," Sienna says without realizing her faux pas.

"Maybe," he says.

"Jimi, would you help me in the kitchen?" Sienna asks.

"In a minute."

Sienna walks away, glancing back at them twice before going back inside the house.

Jimi turns back to him. "I don't get involved with married men," she says.

"I'm separated. And, hell, I'm not the kind of guy who'd try to start something serious with someone while I'm still in a relationship with someone else."

"How do I know that?"

"You don't?" The hurt on his face is palpable. "Okay," he says off her silence. "I have to go."

Jimi flushes in frustration. "The first time I met you, you said you didn't have a reason to lie to me."

"I haven't lied to you," he says.

"*I* had to apologize to *you,* and defend my decision to keep you from Troy. And all that time you were keeping your wife from me!"

"Sally left me," he says. "She isn't coming back. I haven't seen her in months. I wasn't hiding her from you the way you're hiding me from your family. You want an apology? Okay. I'm sorry I didn't tell you about her. I don't like to talk about her. And I didn't plan on it ever coming up with you. Not because I wanted to keep it from you. Because I didn't think . . . I didn't lie to you about her. I didn't tell you, but I didn't lie."

He opens the door to his truck and waits. After a minute, Jimi gets in and slides over to the passenger side. He looks at the house, and then he sits behind the steering wheel, closing the door to shut them in together.

"My wife was in an accident with her boyfriend a while back. He was okay, but she had a concussion and a broken collarbone. When I got to the hospital, he was there. He didn't have a chance to say anything to me before I was on him. I hit him hard. Nearly killed him. I woke up the next morning in jail."

"I'm sorry," Jimi says.

"Look at me."

Jimi looks at him. His eyes on her face are unrelenting.

"I was drunk the night you brought me home because Sally said yes to a divorce. I was celebrating the end of that part of my life, but at the same time I was sad about you. I knew you were angry with me about Morgan. I didn't know if you were coming by the bar, and then you came and I was drunk. I wanted to tell you everything, but I thought you hated me. I was thinking, I'm finally getting my divorce and it doesn't matter because I lost you." He picks up a pack of cigarettes from the dashboard and taps one out on his leg. "I'm sorry I kept her from you."

"I don't hate you," she says carefully. "I was surprised. I hate surprises."

"So do I."

"You nearly killed her boyfriend?"

"He lived."

She nods, sad. "It confuses me when people aren't disturbed by violence. When it's a natural reaction to conflict."

"I'm not that guy anymore."

"Why do you think you're different now?" she asks. "No longer violent."

"Because it scared me. I never want to lose control again."

She believes him.

"The last bike I finished was for Sally. They were riding it when they crashed. I guess that's why I don't finish them anymore. I've lost my joy in it."

Jimi rests her hand on his leg, genuinely sorry for him. He stares at it there, and then settles into the seat and rests one of his hands on top of hers. "I think it would be worth it to finish one," she says.

"Yeah? I think I'd finish one and give it to you. And then I think you'd take it and leave. Though I hope you'd take it and stay."

"Caleb," she says, then pauses. It takes her a minute. During her week away from him she'd thought about it a lot. Leaving Willow Run. Now that he has a wife, what other reason does she have for staying here the entire summer? To come up with a plan for her future? Soon there will be over a half million dollars in her bank account. Troy won't need to worry about her future.

"That night, before you found out about Sally, we acknowledged that we're more than friends, didn't we?" he says.

"The operative words being 'before I found out about Sally.' "

"So your feelings just disappear?"

"No, they don't just disappear. They don't even change. But things are different. You lied to me at the same time you were making me feel like shit for lying to you."

"Give me another chance," he says.

"Let me think about it."

He moves his hands from hers. They sit a minute longer.

He says, "I'll see you, then."

Her first instinct is to say something that will stop him from leaving, but what would that accomplish? She thinks they're breaking up now, not that they'd ever been officially *together.* He starts the truck.

"See you," she says. She opens the door and hops down. She

waits while he drives away. She can see him watching her through his rearview mirror.

When she reenters the house, Troy and Sienna stop speaking. They're in the kitchen. Sienna's washing lettuce for a salad and Troy's chopping vegetables. Jimi sits at the table.

"Need any help?" she asks.

Sienna looks up with an expression of mock surprise, as if she had no idea Jimi was sitting there. Jimi smiles.

"No, thanks," Sienna says.

Jimi nods, remains seated. She gives them a few minutes to either continue the conversation they ended when they heard her come in or flat out ask her what she was doing in Caleb's pickup truck for twenty minutes. She's sure they were watching from the window.

"You were out there for a while," Troy finally says.

"A little while."

"Are you doing freelance work for *American Contractor* magazine or something?" he asks.

"*American Contractor* magazine?"

Troy sets his knife down and gazes at her. "You seem to have taken an interest in our contractor. And he seems to share the interest."

"I wouldn't call it an *interest*," Jimi says.

Sienna dumps another batch of washed lettuce into a bowl and dries her hands. "What would you call it?" she asks pleasantly, but Jimi can hear the concern in her voice.

"I wouldn't call it anything."

Troy says, "I didn't think he was your type."

"I don't have a type," Jimi informs them. "And it was just a fling."

Troy and Sienna exchange glances.

"Does that mean . . ." Troy begins, but doesn't finish.

"That we've had sex? Yes."

"Is this because I said I thought he had a crush on you?" Sienna asks.

"Oh, Sienna," says Jimi, "*no.* It happened before that."

"It did?" Sienna is surprised. She shares another look with Troy.

"He's a nice enough guy," Troy says, sounding skeptical, "but what would motivate you to have a 'fling' with someone who epitomizes the stereotypical backwoods American?"

"What motivated you to move to a part of the world that epitomizes the stereotypical backwoods town in America?"

"We haven't moved here," Troy says. "It's a summerhouse."

"And it's quiet," Sienna adds. "You may think we're crazy, but we're productive."

"I wanted this when I first left Brooklyn," says Jimi. "A house and a little land someplace small and remote. I totally understand the appeal of living in the country. But why would you buy a summerhouse in a rural community when all you do is try to stay separate and above it all?"

"So we should go out and have a fling with our backwoods contractor?" Troy asks.

"He isn't 'backwoods.' He's working-class."

Troy sits at the table. "Have you met his family?"

"Oh, *please,* Troy."

"Have you?"

Jimi thinks of Morgan and hesitates. It would be like handing over the ammunition. "He doesn't have family anymore. I met a couple of his friends. But it's not like that. It was a one-night stand that happened more than once."

"Do those actually exist?" Troy looks at Sienna for confirmation.

Jimi stands up. "Forget it. *He* probably has."

"So it isn't serious?" Troy asks.

Jimi can't bring herself to say the word *no,* so she shakes her head.

"It looked serious," says Sienna.

"Believe me," Jimi lies, "it's not serious at all."

The next evening, a pickup pulls up in front of the house. Sienna, Troy and Jimi are preparing dinner when they hear it. Sienna wonders aloud who it could be, since they aren't expecting company. But Jimi recognizes John Lee Hooker's voice when the truck door opens. She goes outside, glad he's here. She's been thinking about him all day. About their conversation. She was going to borrow Sienna's car after dinner and drive to Frenchman's Bend to tell him it shouldn't be over, this thing between them. She isn't ready for it to be.

She watches him unload a motorcycle from the back of his truck. She stares in shock. It's his Harley.

"Don't thank me," he says brusquely, not looking at her. He glances over at the front door where Troy and Sienna are standing and nods at them. "It's to show you how I feel. You either take her and leave or take her and stay."

She touches the bike. It's beautiful. She feels a heavy, painful pressure behind her eyes. "Don't you need her?"

"I'm not going anywhere."

"I never said I'm going somewhere." She looks at Troy and Sienna and wills them to go inside, but they're rooted in their places by both curiosity and concern. When she turns back around, Caleb's already getting into his truck. He puts his cap on, pushing it down low and tight on his head.

"I've asked Joseph and Kennedy to take over the job," he says in a soft voice. "They'll explain it to Troy and Sienna when they come Monday." He swallows, finally meets her eyes. "I haven't found the money."

"Wait," Jimi says, but he turns up the volume on his radio. He waves once, honks and drives off.

Wisely, her brother and sister-in-law don't say anything. They move out of her way when she goes back into the house. She's sure Troy wants to bring up yesterday's conversation when she'd said, *Believe me, it's not serious at all.* She can hear the question forming in his brain: would a man who isn't serious about you give you his motorcycle? A person doesn't need to know bikes to know the significance of Caleb's gesture.

Sienna follows Jimi to the den and leans against the doorjamb as Jimi changes into jeans and a fresh T-shirt.

"I thought you might need these." Sienna tosses her the keys to the Outback.

Jimi catches them. How'd Sienna know she wouldn't want to ride the Harley when she goes to see him?

"Thanks," she says.

Sienna nods. "Why don't you go talk to your brother before you leave?"

Jimi hesitates, then nods.

She brings the stick and follows the unmistakable scent of cigarette smoke wafting from behind the cottage. Troy's sitting on the ground, staring at it. Caleb has gutted it, leaving the foundation intact. Troy doesn't look at Jimi when she stops next to him. He doesn't drop the cigarette.

"I thought he'd never be able to save this," Troy says. "He's talented."

They admire the old foundation and the care Caleb took not to damage it. Troy stands up, wipes off his pants.

"I didn't mean any of that shit I said about him being backwoods," he says. "I should know better."

"I won't mention it to him," Jimi says.

They walk in silence. Troy stops when they reach the edge of the road.

"Are you in love with this guy?" he asks.

"I like him."

"Can you honestly see yourself living here? Or are you planning to have a long-distance romance?"

"I thought I'd see how it plays out while I'm here with you," she says, then shakes her head. "I have this expectation of what a small town holds for me, and the townspeople have an expectation of what I am. And no matter what I do, I can't get past it."

"You still think, despite your contractor, small-town folks are insular and weird?"

"He's *your* contractor, and no. Some of them, here, have been kind to me. Let the others show me a reason not to distrust them and I *will* believe them. I've always only needed proof."

"But I do okay here," says Troy. "I mean, I'm not blind. I'm aware of what some locals may think of me. I'm not here for them. I'm not going to let a couple of people stand in my way. Why should I surrender the beautiful places to people who don't want me around? We can live anywhere. *Should* live anywhere we like. I limit my interactions with people who don't want me around. I think that's the best way to deal with their expectations."

Jimi understands a little better now. Troy and Sienna can be here, content, because they're above it all. They didn't choose this small town because they understand small-town living. *They don't live with these people*—these locals. They live on the edge, away from them. It's better than trying to be like them. Trying to be like them is disingenuous.

"I want you to have a good life," Troy says. "You deserve a good life."

Jimi thinks of the money Russ will deposit in her bank account and the future she can have with it. "I have a good life," she says. "It's just not your idea of what a good life is."

He looks doubtful as they continue to walk, finding themselves in front of the deck a few minutes later.

"I love you," she tells him.

Troy looks surprised by her declaration.

"I love you, too," Troy says.

Jimi kisses his cheek. "I will be okay. You shouldn't worry about me the way that you do. And as for Caleb? I can take care of myself. He *is* a good person, despite his scars and tattoos. I'm safe with him."

Troy nods as if he's giving her his blessing, releasing her.

"I need to talk to him for a minute," Jimi says, "and then I'll be back and everything will be good."

# Twenty-four

How are those pancakes?" Jennifer asks.

Caleb looks at his brother, eating a full breakfast at 8:00 PM. Caleb's drinking his fourth Budweiser. He isn't hungry.

"Darlin'," says Morgan to Jennifer, "these are the best pancakes I've had in two years."

Jennifer beams.

Caleb hasn't come into Wheeler's for a long time, and Jennifer has been hovering around them, curious about Caleb's disappearance and Morgan's return. So far, they've dodged all of her questions thanks to Morgan's shameless flirting.

"Are you married?" Morgan asks now.

"I am."

"Aww, shit," says Morgan, "I'm always too late."

Jennifer laughs. "It's good to see you two together again. It sure has been a long time."

"It sure has been." Morgan's smile is phony and sweet.

"Yeah," Caleb says, staring at his brother, thinking.

He has a memory. Of two boys. Two boys playing catch in a neighbor's backyard. As the younger boy is about to throw the ball, the older boy, his brother, picks up a large rock and throws it through the windshield of the neighbor's car. They stare at each other in silence until a man, their neighbor, comes out of the house to check what just happened. He looks at the boys. The younger boy is holding the ball.

Caleb remembers how the man came at him. Terrified, he'd remained rooted in place as the man grabbed his collar, lifted him off the ground, pulled his hand back and smacked him. Caleb cried and Morgan watched, his eyes cold.

Caleb was ten years old; Morgan was fourteen.

Later, Caleb was tucked underneath the covers, his aunt believing he threw a baseball into Mr. Bailey's windshield by accident. Caleb hadn't denied it. Morgan hadn't confessed. And then Morgan slipped into the dark bedroom and sat on the edge of Caleb's bed as Caleb pretended to be asleep.

"A man can't escape his destiny," Morgan said softly.

Caleb opened his eyes. He didn't understand what his brother meant. He wasn't a man. He didn't know what destiny was.

"Someday you'll know what I'm talking about," said Morgan before he left.

"You all need anything else?" Jennifer asks Morgan as she glances at a couple of kids sitting at a booth near a window, huddled close together, playing with each other's fingers.

"No, babe," Morgan says. "Not right now."

Caleb looks out the front window just as a motorcycle pulls up in front of Wheeler's. He watches, automatically reminded of the day Jimi arrived in a car, helmet and duffel bag in her hands.

This biker is a girl. Caleb knows her. He's done some work on her Harley. He's slept with her twice. She walks into the coffee shop, sexy as all hell in tight black jeans and a bright-yellow halter. No leather jacket to protect her bare arms. Her eyes dance around the room and settle on him. She nods.

"Know her?" asks Morgan.

"A little," Caleb answers.

She orders something to go and makes eye contact with Morgan.

Both times they'd had sex Sally was still around, not yet cheating on him and threatening to leave. This girl had always made it a point to bring her Harley to Whiskey Road when Sally was at the hospital. Back then, Caleb couldn't resist her.

"Now *that's* a woman," says Morgan.

Caleb looks at Morgan sharply. "What the fuck does that mean?"

Morgan looks innocent. "Nothing. You're paranoid, man."

She pays Jennifer for her food and exits the shop without giving Caleb and Morgan a second glance.

"Speaking of bikes," Morgan says, watching the girl get onto her motorcycle, start it and ride off. He looks at Caleb. "And women. I saw you take the Harley this morning. You gave it to her."

"I gave it to her," Caleb confirms.

"Why?"

"I wanted to."

"You love this girl?"

"Who said anything about love?"

"You give a girl a motorcycle . . ."

"It means I gave a girl a motorcycle."

Morgan's laugh is more like a bark. "Giving a girl a bike has a larger implication than just bringing her home for a fuck."

Heat creeps up Caleb's throat into his face and Morgan grins at his anger. He takes a cigarette from his back pocket and starts to stick it in his mouth.

"No smoking in here," Jennifer calls out.

Morgan pauses, cigarette poised in midair, waiting for the punch line.

"I'm serious," Jennifer says, no longer feeling friendly or flirtatious.

"Lady," Morgan says, leering at her from under slit eyelids, "I just spent two years in a prison in Texas. I paid my dues. I think I've earned the right to smoke anywhere."

Jennifer is unsympathetic. Her glare is withering. "Ask me if I give a damn," she says.

Morgan grins and continues to hold Jennifer's gaze. He sticks the cigarette in his mouth, but he doesn't take out a lighter. He motions for her to go about her business. She doesn't. She just stands where she is, watching him. Caleb watches the exchange with mild annoyance. He could be anywhere, but he's here. He's always here. Part of him is glad Jimi's leaving. She deserves better than this.

"Are you afraid of something?" Morgan asks. The cigarette is still hanging from his lips, but his attention is no longer on the waitress. "Afraid she'll turn out like Sally?"

Caleb drinks more of his beer. "You know why I asked you here."

Morgan ignores the question and makes a gesture to Jennifer for the check. He looks directly in Caleb's eyes.

"You took that money," Caleb says.

Morgan takes the cigarette from his mouth and starts to play with it. His eyes never move from Caleb's face.

"I don't know how you found it," Caleb continues, "how you got it out of there or where it is, but I know you have it."

Morgan sucks his teeth. "Guys like me get blamed for everything."

"Because guys like you are always guilty."

Morgan laughs and Caleb wants to punch him.

"What were you thinking?" Caleb asks.

Morgan leans across the table. "I walk into the house one day and I hear her in your room, pouring her little heart out to you, telling you she has ten grand in a bag that she doesn't want to spend. What the fuck do you think I was thinking?"

Caleb presses the heels of his hands into his eyes. The words spilling out of Morgan's mouth sound absurd, almost embarrassing. And Caleb thinks, *This is it.* He's finished. He's tired of the Bend. That's what Sally used to say before she left. She was tired of Caleb and tired of the Bend. Caleb would always say that he was tired of the Bend, too, but he'd never leave her. Sally thought that was funny. Caleb never left the Bend, according to her, because he was afraid to leave. He was a big man in a small town who knew all too well that he'd become a small man in a big world. She had been wrong. He hadn't left because of the business, the house, *her.*

Caleb comes to the same conclusion he came to yesterday, and the day before, and all the days he's spent searching for the money. He has to find it and he has to give it back to Jimi. Because it belongs to her. It doesn't matter whether she wants to use it, burn it or keep it as a souvenir. He's not going to reward her decision to confide in him by taking Morgan's side again.

"I need you to tell me something," Caleb says and Morgan blinks slowly, as if he's bored with the conversation. "Did you hurt those girls in Texas?"

"Oh, come on, man . . ."

"*Did you do it?* No bullshit."

Morgan stares at Caleb for a long time. "No."

Caleb sits back, swallows. "Then why are these guys looking for you? Why are you running?"

For a split second, Morgan's eyes are murderous, and then blank. "Fuck you, little brother," he says and slides out of the booth. He drops a five-dollar bill on the table. "I need to pick Tara up at work," he says. "I'll see you at the house."

Caleb, unable to look up from the table, listens to his brother walk out of the coffee shop. An urge to go after him bubbles up; an urge to shake him and ask him when he's going to change, stop lying, stop running, stop pushing everyone around him into danger.

But Morgan will never change. And Caleb will always be here, wondering. A man can't escape his destiny.

# Twenty-five

He isn't home. She tries Fifth Amendment, Dusty's and his office without luck. Then she remembers the first time she met him was in Darby, and that he once told her he likes to go there on occasion to get away from Frenchman's Bend.

Wheeler's Coffee Shop isn't hard to spot once she's in Darby. She recognizes Caleb's old Ford as soon as she drives into the lot. She thinks she would recognize the burgundy pickup truck anywhere, even in this darkness, but to be sure she shines her headlights on the license plate briefly—she'd memorized the numbers the first day they met. Her relief over finding him, however, is overwhelmed by uneasiness. The last time she was here she was vulnerable and lost. Darby at night is even less welcoming than it is during the day.

She pulls into the space next to Caleb's pickup. When she gets out of Sienna's car, she notices that same waitress from her first day here, standing behind the counter, talking to a customer. She'd disliked that woman intensely. She was mean. Not the kind of person you want to face after a couple of rough days. That day, Caleb had been a godsend.

"Are you looking for my brother?"

Jimi starts at the sound of Morgan's voice next to her. She

hadn't heard him walk across the gravel parking lot to reach her. Quiet as a mouse. Or a predator. His stealth makes her want to shudder.

"Yes," she says.

He moves a little closer. She tenses and he stops. In the light from Wheeler's windows she can see his eyes harden. His tongue darts out to moisten his lips.

"He's busy right now," he says. "You want me to give him a message?"

"I'd rather give it to him."

Morgan takes a long drag from his cigarette, reminding her of Caleb. It's easy to forget the men are related. With Caleb, she never feels as if there's a time bomb waiting to be set off inside his brain at any minute. Morgan, on the other hand, seems capable of anything. "You don't care that he's married?"

"They're getting a divorce," she reminds him.

"Oh, she'll be back," he assures her.

"Then, no," she says, "at this very moment I don't care."

Morgan looks amused as he gives her a once-over. There's something sinister in his expression. It could be indifference; it could be resentment or anger. He says, "Stay away from us for now. He'll call you when he's ready."

"I can't do that," she says.

Morgan smirks. "Good for you, darlin'."

"You have something that belongs to me," she says. "I'm going to get it back."

Sadness or exhaustion replaces the sinister look she'd noticed in his eyes just a moment ago. "I don't know what you're talking about," he says, "but I appreciate your spirit." He starts walking in the direction of the coffee shop. "Let me call him out for you, okay? He won't want to talk to you in there."

Jimi stares after Morgan, frustrated, and before he enters Wheeler's again, Caleb walks out and stops in front of her.

"Is everything okay?" he asks and she's touched that he's alarmed.

"I know you don't want me to thank you for the bike . . ."

He notices she's leaning on the Outback. "Where is it?"

"I need you to come back to Willow Run to pick it up," she says. "I can't take it."

"That's why you came to Darby? To tell me you won't take the Harley?" He frowns. "I don't want it back. It's yours. I don't ride her anymore. That time with you was the first time I took her out in ages. She just collects dust."

"I need you to have one of your own," she says, hoping she sounds as nonchalant as she's trying to be. He meets her gaze. "Because when I leave Willow Run, I need you to be able to—"

"Not here," he cuts her off. "Don't tell me something I want to hear . . ." He glances at the coffee shop. Some people are blatantly watching them, including the waitress she remembers. ". . . *Here.*"

"I need you to be able to find me," she finishes.

He stares at her for a long time. And then he moves to the front side of his truck so he's hidden from view of the coffee shop and its patrons. After a minute she follows him. And he's standing there, leaning on the hood, waiting for her. He takes out a cigarette, sticks it in his mouth, lights it and after an eternity he says, "So you're offering me another chance?"

"Yes."

He takes a drag from his cigarette, then tosses it. "I'm going to get your money back," he says. "Morgan's going to be leaving soon, and then things will be different."

He moves forward and kisses her. For a long time. And then he pulls back and stares at her intently. "I have to head home. I want to be there before Morgan gets back with Tara, okay? I'll call you."

She nods. Morgan drives by in his Dodge and honks. Caleb turns abruptly and gets into his truck. As he pulls out of his space, he leans out the window. "I'll call you," he promises.

On her way to Troy and Sienna's house, Jimi decides she doesn't want to wait for Caleb's phone call. They can sleep in; no need to rush back to Willow Run in the morning. They're no longer a secret.

She turns back. She drives to Whiskey Road and takes the narrow path up at high speed. There's a beat-up 4x4 parked in front of the house. She cuts her lights, gets out of Sienna's car. A man is sitting in the passenger seat of the 4x4, smoking. He tosses his cigarette through the open window, gets out of the truck and roots around for something on the truck's floor. Then he straightens and stretches, rolls his head around to get rid of the kinks in his neck.

She recognizes Ray. She watches him slip out of a denim jacket and dump it on the front seat before removing what she believes is a shotgun. She takes a breath. She hates guns. *Really despises them.* She tries to form some kind of plan to warn Caleb, but how do you form a plan against a shotgun? Especially when you're unarmed. It seems a very unfair disadvantage. You wouldn't engage someone in a sword fight if he has no sword.

And then Ray looks in her direction. She freezes. So does he. They stare at each other for a minute, neither sure what the other's going to do. Ray takes a step toward her. "Yeah?" he calls out. "What are you doing here?"

He doesn't know her. He wouldn't remember her from Fifth Amendment; he isn't one of Caleb's friends. She holds up her hands so he can see they're empty and she's harmless. He's frowning.

"Yeah?" he says again.

"Here to see Caleb," she tells him.

Ray glances at the house, then looks back at Jimi. "What business you got with him?"

"I'm his girlfriend."

There's a faint look of surprise, and then amusement on Ray's face. He motions for her to walk over to him with his shotgun. She steps back instinctively.

"C'mon," he says.

They walk to the house. Jimi walks slightly ahead of him, very aware of the gun resting lazily over his shoulder. She'd never given much thought to just how far away Whiskey Road is from civilization until right now. Who chooses to live so far from other people, supermarkets and cellular phone service? Not to mention the fucking cops? When she was on the road, riding, she thought she wanted this kind of isolation.

The part of her that still resides in L.A., the part looking out only for herself, is wondering why she doesn't just take her chances and run. But there's another side to her and that side knows she can't do that. That side of her is thinking about her right to choose what she *wants* to do no matter how dangerous that choice is. You don't care about somebody, then walk out of his life at the first sign of trouble. You just don't. No matter what. She wants to make sure he's safe.

It isn't a long walk.

The porch steps creak as they walk up them. The front door is unlocked. Caleb comes out of the kitchen with a can of beer when they enter. He stops in his tracks, looks from Jimi to Ray to Ray's shotgun.

"What the hell are you doing?" he asks Ray.

Behind them, Morgan walks into the living room. He pauses at the sight of Jimi, Ray and the gun. He looks to his brother, questioning. Outside, they hear a car pull up in front of the house. Morgan holds a hand up to Ray and goes to the window. Ray looks befuddled.

"*Fuck,*" says Morgan.

Caleb stiffens, his focus no longer on Ray but on his brother. Ray tries to get a look out the window from where he's standing.

Jimi looks at Caleb. "What's going on?"

"Wait in my bedroom and close the door," Caleb orders. "Ray, give me your gun."

"Hell no," says Ray matter-of-factly.

"Why? Who is it?" Jimi asks.

"*Go!*" Caleb shouts.

She goes, reluctantly, and positions herself at the open crack of the bedroom door to listen. There's a sudden scuffle, which makes it impossible for her to stay put. She heads down the hallway, almost running into a well-built blond man walking toward her. His eyes widen just a little at the sight of her.

"Who the hell are you?" he asks.

He's familiar. Not in the sense that she knows him. She knows his *type.* The same type who stole her BMW. Tracked her down in a motel on the border between Pennsylvania and New York, held a gun to her head. He's the reason she can't live in places like Frenchman's Bend, Darby, Willow Run.

"You hear me?" he says, stepping closer.

She opens her mouth to speak, but no sound comes out. She prepares to run, but her feet remain rooted to the ground. She has a second to decide what to do before he reaches her. She hits him with all the strength she can muster with so little time to prepare. The sound of bone cracking and blood gushing is deafening. The air around her goes still, the quiet gets quieter. Maybe she shouldn't have done that.

The man sways slightly, blinks, but doesn't go down. He touches his nose and pulls back bloody hands. Jimi meets his eyes. The first thing she sees is curiosity. Then shock, which quickly turns to rage. Before she can move, he grabs her, pushes her to her knees and punches her in the side of the face.

"*Fucking bitch,*" she hears him say before she drops.

The pain is crippling. She lies on the floor unable to see, hear or move for several minutes. He crouches next to her and she tries to work out how much pain she can endure before she actually passes out. He feels her up for weapons or identification. She has nothing.

"Who the hell are you?" he says and keeps groping. It's an incredible violation, but she needs some time to regroup and regain her composure before she stops him. He didn't break anything, but she's going to have one hell of a black eye again. Her jaw tingles. She opens her mouth. It hurts, but it's functional. Her face may never be the same after this. There's only so much trauma a body can withstand in such a short period.

The man moves away from her and she wriggles her fingers. They work. She opens her eyes. She hadn't realized she'd closed them. She stands, painstakingly slow, and the man laughs at her. She glances up at him. He's standing over her, waiting, grinning.

Men always underestimate her.

Before she's completely on her feet, she kicks him. The kick is a surprise, takes him down. He lands on his side and she cherishes the surprised look on his face. Just before she delivers another blow with her boot to his chin.

In the living room, another man is using his elbow to keep Caleb pinned to the floor on his stomach. Morgan's up against a wall, a third attacker holding him a couple inches off the floor by the throat. His eyes search and locate Ray, standing in the kitchen archway, confused.

"*Do something, man!*" Morgan screams.

Ray lowers the shotgun, resting it on his hip, and Jimi has the urge to turn away. But he fires it off before she has a chance to. The man holding Morgan to the wall releases his grip, lets out a howl and drops to the floor, unconscious. Ray hasn't killed him. He shot him in the leg, obliterated it. There's blood everywhere. Jimi feels bile rising.

Ray turns the gun on the man sitting atop Caleb. The man's hands are already raised. Caleb knocks him off and stands.

The man says to Morgan, "This ain't over."

Morgan says, "No, it ain't," and kicks him hard in the face.

The shotgun blast is still ringing in Jimi's ears. *Deafening.* But the total silence afterward is worse. She pushes her hands deep inside her back pockets to steady them.

Caleb's holding himself up with the wall, staring at her. "Are you okay?" he asks. His voice is hoarse. There's a nasty gash across his cheek; it's still bleeding.

And she hurts. Not as badly as she did when she escaped the motel in Pennsylvania, but hurt is hurt. "Fair," she admits. "You?"

"Just fair, too," he says.

They're messy with exhaustion and the stink of fighting and blood. Breathing hard, they all stare at the men on the floor. Jimi has a piercing headache. Morgan goes to the kitchen and comes back out with a bottle of Wild Turkey. He takes a gulp from it, passes it to Ray. He's staring at Jimi with something close to respect. She could be dead, she reminds herself. All of them could be dead. She doesn't want to have this in common with them, but she can't erase what just happened.

"You did good," Morgan says matter-of-factly.

Jimi stares at him as he holds the bottle of Wild Turkey out to her like an offering. A welcome to-the-club kind of gesture. It enrages her. He got them into this. All of them. Including *Ray,* who was there not as an ally less than ten minutes ago and now looks dazed, like he doesn't know what the hell he's doing in Caleb's living room, drinking his bourbon. She's wondering what the hell she's doing here, too.

"Please, Morgan," she says evenly, "shove that liquor bottle up your ass."

Morgan's face hardens.

"Morgan?"

Tara's walking down the hallway, stepping over the man Jimi knocked unconscious. She seems unfazed by the other men on the floor; both unconscious, one of them bleeding all over the place. Her eyes are red and her hair is mussed. She walks across the room to reach her husband.

"It's under control now, baby," Morgan tells her, wrapping his arm around her waist.

"It's always under control before it gets out of control," Jimi says.

Morgan meets her eyes. There's a warning there. But Jimi ignores it. She looks past him at Caleb.

"What happens now?" she asks.

"We tie them up." Morgan directs his answer at Caleb as he takes the bottle of Wild Turkey back from Ray and drinks. "Throw them in the back of the truck. Maybe Kennedy can help us with that. And drive the fuckers back to Texas." He looks at Ray. "You free for the next few days?"

"Why don't you call the police?" Jimi asks Caleb.

The question hangs there and Jimi stares at Caleb, willing him to know the right answer. He stares back, looks certain. And then Morgan puts a hand on Caleb's shoulder and says,

"Let's go, little brother, and take care of this. Can you give Kennedy a call?"

Caleb doesn't move. He looks at Morgan. "I'm going to call Herman before this bastard bleeds to death."

The silence in the room is dangerous. It lasts for a long time.

"I'm calling Herman," Caleb repeats.

"Heard you," says Morgan. He's looking at Jimi as if he wants to strangle her. Maybe he would if there were no witnesses. And she thinks there will always be someone like Morgan around in a place like Frenchman's Bend. That's not to say there aren't Morgans in the city. But in the city she can lose them, forget about them, pretend they don't exist. That's what she misses about city life. The freedom to ignore things. The *choices.*

But she isn't afraid of him. She's imagining him in a place that isn't Frenchman's Bend. Any city where hardworking people are too busy struggling with daily life to find someone like Morgan anything but absurd. The world is bigger than him. Bigger than the man who stole her motorcycle.

She looks at Caleb. He motions for her to follow him into the kitchen, where he lifts the phone's receiver and starts to dial a number. She stops him halfway through.

"You're sure?" she says. She doesn't want him to wake up some morning in the future and regret going against his brother's wishes.

He nods. "They were on my property. And Herman looks out for his own."

Jimi lets her hand fall away from him. There were moments on the road when she thought she understood why small towns in America made her uneasy. It was the absolute darkness once the sun set, and the absolute quiet and stillness in the middle of the night. But it's really the threat of small-town lawlessness that she finds unsettling. Country boys with shot guns and excellent right hooks. And sheriffs who look out for their own.

It hurts to know this.

When he's off the phone, Caleb wets a paper towel at the sink and starts to wipe Jimi's face. She appreciates it. This and the phone call to Herman make a difference.

"I'm sorry," he says.

"Who are they?" she asks.

He folds the paper towel over and wipes more blood from her lips. "The brothers of the girls Morgan went to jail for hurting."

"They tracked him."

"I suspect Morgan isn't so hard to track."

She agrees. She could see him being easy. "They could have killed us."

He stops wiping her lip. "That's what you think?"

"I think anything could have happened."

Caleb kisses her forehead. She closes her eyes, allows his lips to linger. "We wouldn't have let them," he says. He puts a finger under her chin and tips her head up. She looks at him. "This isn't what I am, usually," he says.

Ray hesitates in the archway, looking at Caleb. He still appears shell-shocked and Jimi almost feels bad for him. He'd turned up on Whiskey Road to take a shot at Caleb but almost got himself killed instead. Payback. Consequences. She wonders if he thinks about those things.

"Thanks, Ray," says Caleb.

Ray smiles weakly. "I gotta get back to Emma," he says. "She'll be trying to figure out where I am. I'm sorry I—"

"So am I," Caleb interrupts. "You okay getting back to Darby on your own?"

"Yeah." Ray waves and leaves and Jimi wonders about tomorrow; whether they'll be enemies again.

"I better get back to Willow Run before Herman gets here," she says.

Caleb pushes the lock of pink hair away from her eye and looks as if he wants to protest. He doesn't. He says, "It ends here. With this. Morgan has to run. He has to run for a long time. And I have to let him go. Please believe me."

When she was riding, she could imagine a perfect place. A place where she was anonymous, but she belonged. Life was boundless. People in passing cars smiled because they couldn't see her face underneath her helmet; the sky was extraordinary; trees were pretty. But whenever she arrived someplace—for a night, a few days, longer—all of it changed.

She doesn't know when she'll tell him that she's leaving. She'll begin by explaining how, all this time, she's been searching for a place to belong. Before she left Brooklyn, even before she left Los Angeles, she thought she'd find it in a small American town. But she realizes she escaped the one place she's always felt comfortable. The city. She can't live anywhere else.

But that isn't Caleb's fault.

"I believe you," she says.

# Twenty-six

When he walks inside Fifth Amendment, Rose pours him a shot of bourbon and sets it down near Jimi. She says, "When are you two going to learn how to play nice with each other?"

Caleb cuts her a look, but she ignores him.

Jimi doesn't look up when he reaches her, so he places her duffel bag on the bar next to the bourbon. It's been three days since they've seen each other. She doesn't look at the bag. She looks at him. And it strikes him how close she looks to the girl who turned up in Darby over a month ago—black eye, swollen lip, bruises. He also has another black eye and a swollen lip. White surgical tape covers the knife cut in his left cheek. When she returned to Willow Run that night, Troy was horrified by the sight of her. She'd called Caleb the next morning and told him to expect a call from her brother. Later, there was a message from Troy on the machine at the office, firing him.

She'd told Troy the truth about what had happened that night. Caleb's glad she did. No need to keep it from him. No need to try to hide what Morgan is. No need to try to reinvent himself anymore. He thinks he can be himself and still change things. And now he's here, with her duffel bag full of money and a hope that she hasn't changed her mind about him despite what he got her into. He reminds himself that she called him and asked him to meet her today. *She called him.*

"The money was under the passenger seat in my pickup," he tells her. "Herman found it when he searched my truck."

She looks at the bag. "Morgan has a sense of humor."

He sits next to her. "I always believed my brother hurt those girls in Texas," he admits. "Those boys had every right to seek vengeance. And we had every right to fight back."

Jimi lowers her eyes, and then she nods. "So Herman took care of things?"

"Looked into it. The guy Ray shot lost his leg, but Herman can't find the gun. We didn't tell him Ray had been there. So he'll hold the other two until the hospital clears his release."

"It's good to know a sheriff," she says, sounding neutral.

"I'm going to sell the place," he says. "Leave the Bend."

Jimi pulls back. "Really?"

Caleb nods. "Yeah. I'm ready. It's time to go and see what else is out there. Any suggestions where I should start?"

She stares at him. Long. "Brooklyn," she says after a moment.

He drinks his shot, pushes the duffel bag over to her. "Yeah?"

Jimi takes the bag, holds it close and meets Caleb's gaze. "Thank you," she says.

"No need to thank me. It's yours."

She nods and lowers the bag to the floor. Her smile is slow. "I highly recommend Brooklyn," she says. "And I just found out a nice commission I've been waiting for has cleared, so look me up. I'll take you out to dinner."

"I'll do that."

She motions to Rose and orders two bourbons.

Rose does a double take. "Not a ginger ale."

Jimi shakes her head.

Rose glances at Caleb. "I wondered what it would be," she says.

"What?" Jimi asks.

"Your drink. I wondered what you'd choose when you finally ordered one."

Caleb smiles. He'd wondered, too.

"Rose," Jimi says, "can I buy you a drink?"

Rose cocks her head to the side. "I'm not cheap," she says.

Jimi grins. "Go crazy."

Rose reaches below the bar and pulls up a dusty bottle of thirty-two-year-old single malt scotch.

"You weren't kidding," Caleb says.

Rose raises an eyebrow at him as she pours three generous shots. She lifts her glass and looks at Jimi. "Thank you."

"My pleasure," says Jimi.

Rose doesn't wait for them to drink. She downs her shot, eyes closed for a minute afterward, savoring it. Jimi looks at Caleb.

"To leaving," she says.

"And meeting again," adds Caleb.

"And meeting again," repeats Jimi.

They drink and when they're finished they say nothing, just let the scotch settle in them. He doesn't know what he expected, but he didn't expect her to appreciate it. He leans forward and kisses her black eye, kisses her other bruises. He lowers his head to her shoulder and breathes her in. She doesn't pull away, doesn't seem to care if people are watching.

When he looks at her again, her eyes are serious, but also confident. He stares at her, thinking, imagining. He's just a small-town boy who rarely leaves the Bend. And she's just a girl. But she holds so many possibilities.

9 780743 297622